Alex Br... ...ng author of twelve books including the hugely popular Carrington's series, *The Great Christmas Knit Off, The Great Village Show, The Secret of Orchard Cottage* and *A Postcard from Italy*. Her uplifting books are published worldwide and have been translated into twenty languages. She lives by the sea in South East England with her husband, daughter and two very glossy black Labradors.

www.alexbrownauthor.com

f facebook.com/alexandrabrownauthor
🐦 twitter.com/alexbrownbooks
📷 instagram.com/alexbrownbooks

Also by Alex Brown

Carrington's Department Store

Cupcakes At Carrington's

Me and Mr Carrington: A Short Story

Christmas At Carrington's

Ice Creams at Carrington's

Tindledale

The Great Christmas Knit Off

The Great Village Show

The Secret of Orchard Cottage

Not Just for Christmas: A Short Story

The Wish

The Great Summer Sewing Bee: A Short Story

Postcard

A Postcard from Italy

A Postcard from Paris

A COSY CHRISTMAS AT BRIDGET'S BICYCLE BAKERY

ALEX BROWN

One More Chapter
a division of HarperCollins*Publishers*
1 London Bridge Street
London SE1 9GF
www.harpercollins.co.uk
HarperCollins*Publishers*
1st Floor, Watermarque Building, Ringsend Road
Dublin 4, Ireland

1

This paperback edition 2021
First published in Great Britain in ebook format
by HarperCollins*Publishers* 2021
Copyright © Alex Brown 2021
Alex Brown asserts the moral right to be identified
as the author of this work
A catalogue record of this book is available from the British Library

ISBN: 978-0-00-846369-4

This novel is entirely a work of fiction. The names, characters and
incidents portrayed in it are the work of the author's imagination.
Any resemblance to actual persons, living or dead, events or localities
is entirely coincidental.

Printed and bound in the UK using 100% Renewable Electricity
by CPI Group (UK) Ltd

All You Knead Is Love and Baked Treats

For my best friend, Lynette, often in my thoughts.

Chapter One

Jingle bells. Jingle bells. Jingle all the way.

J   I turn the volume down on the radio that's playing festive favourites and grip the steering wheel of my cherry-red Mini Clubman, inwardly willing the temperamental old car not to conk out before I reach the crest of the steep cliff road winding down to the cosy seaside town of Mulberry-On-Sea. Or worse still, for the double doors at the back of the car to burst open and scatter the boot paraphernalia all over the road. It's happened before. A few years back when I was going up this very same steep road, my unzipped weekender bag fell out and tumbled away, flinging the contents into the hedgerows and front gardens flanking the road. I ended up having to retrieve my best, and most comfortable, bra from a sailboat moored up on a driveway after an extra keen seagull had swooped down in search of food, only to deposit the bra in the hull on realising that it wasn't actually edible. And now, with my children, fourteen-year-old twins, Oscar and Olly, and Freya who is six, two guinea pigs called Snuggle and Chewy (on account of his gingery Chewbacca style fur) and Henry, the family dog – a retriever with a wild, curly coat the colour of golden syrup – not to mention an enormous pile of luggage and my old bicycle strapped to the roof, the car is crawling under the strain.

'Any minute now,' I say as brightly as I can muster, in an attempt to keep all our spirits up.

It's been a long journey in the chilly winter weather, and it's starting to get dark now too. We are all tired and hungry and in desperate need of a hot drink, or a large mug of mulled wine in my case. There's a bottle of my homemade cranberry and orange spice-infused Christmas concoction in the back and I can't wait to arrive, get unpacked, and put my feet up in a bubble bath to unwind with a mug of warm wine and one of my baking books. I love looking at the tantalising images of festive orange and cinnamon swirls, or a batch of floury, soft baps enveloped in a comforting mist of steam straight from a hot oven, wondering if I can create the same look as they do in the pictures. Not that I'm a master baker, definitely not – very much an amateur baker – but I like to have a go. I even did a bread-making course many moons ago, and have the proper food hygiene and safety certificates too, to go with my dream of one day opening up my own little bakery business. I've always wanted to take my bread-making skills further, but never had the opportunity to pursue this in the past. Baking soothes my soul, which might sound a bit woo-woo but I absolutely do feel all Zen and serene inside after a good baking session. Plus, forty minutes or so of peace and tranquillity with a baking recipe book behind a locked bathroom door is often just the thing to perk me right up. Don't get me wrong, I love my children with every fibre of my being but it is fair to say that they can be very full-on and trying at times. I'm often exhausted and spend much of the rest of the time wondering if I'm even equipped to be a proper grown-up parent. Like lots of us, I mostly feel as though I'm making it all up as I go along. Either the twins are bickering or Freya is complaining about it not being fair when she has to go to bed earlier than her much older brothers, or some such other 'end of the world' problem is the order of the day. Yes, a lovely hot bath is often a welcome relief to recharge my batteries and get me ready to start all over again the following day. And being a single parent now means it's all down to me to keep the four of us, plus three pets, alive and thriving.

Tucking a chunk of curly chestnut hair back inside my knitted bobble hat, I glance in the rear-view mirror, my freckle-speckled rosy cheeks lifting into a big grin as I hope at least one of my three children will meet my eye and give me a reassuring thumbs up. But poor Freya is leaning forward with an earnest look on her face as she holds on with dear life to a length of bungee cord hoisted over her tiny shoulder, the other end attached to the inside of the car's back doors as a 'just-in-case' insurance measure to stop them bursting open again. And the twins, well... they are oblivious as usual, with the screens of their mobiles glowing mere millimetres from their fixated faces as their thumbs feverishly tap away. Only Henry seems excited, sitting up in the front passenger seat on account of his windy bottom banishing him from sharing the back seat. The twins refused to even get in the car unless Henry sat in the front, and so his tail is now sweeping the blanket-covered seat in feverish anticipation of all the cavorting in the sea and sand dunes he has to look forward to. It's extraordinary how, every time we reach this point in the journey, he always seems to know where we are heading and does his exuberantly panty dog-breath thing with his mouth wide open and his tongue lolling out to make the windscreen steam up. 'OK, handsome boy, nearly there,' I soothe, giving Henry's unruly mane a quick, affectionate ruffle before swiping at the glass with the back of my coat sleeve, keen to actually see the road ahead. Safety first and all that. Plus, I don't want to miss the moment I've been looking forward to ever since I came to the conclusion that moving back to Mulberry-On-Sea is the best possible option under the circumstances.

Any minute now and the powder-blue art deco building with arched windows and the golden, glittery Christmas window display that is Carrington's department store, is going to come into view. A landmark synonymous with arriving in the lovely little traditional seaside village with the peppermint-green railings leading down to the harbour and a glimpse of the sea beyond, it's the place where tourists take their pictures and the locals let out a sigh of contentment, happy to be home. And I can't wait, even though returning to Mulberry feels bittersweet. You see, I grew up here and first moved away in my early twenties, and it has been far too long since we have been back to visit as a family. We used to come here in the summer holidays and spend six long glorious weeks sunbathing and swimming in the surprisingly warm sparkling sea. But things are different now. Losing your home this close to Christmas time would do that, and so I packed up our whole world inside the car.

Apart from Ted, of course.

I think of the framed photos and his cartoon caricature sketches carefully stowed in the footwell of the passenger seat beside me, remembering lifting one of the lovely pictures from the mantelpiece to wrap in tissue paper for packing, running the tip of my index finger over the perfect beach scene it portrays: seagulls caw-cawing as they swoop and soar up high in a cloudless turquoise sky; the sun shimmering on the crystal-capped waves as they lull back and forth on the sandy shore; the grassy dunes rising in the background, nestling amidst the row of ramshackle old fishermen's huts; my late husband, Ted, as a child, making sandcastles and laughing into the camera as Jan and Ken, his proud mum and dad, captured the happy scene that now lives inside the silver photo frame. The other picture is a festive one taken of Ted as a young teenager with a red Santa hat on his head, grinning as he sits on a sledge in the snow-covered grassy slopes that lead down to the other end of the beach where a row of pastel-coloured beach huts hug the coastline. If it snows at Christmas time, it's a tradition for everyone in the little seaside town of Mulberry to go sledging on the slopes and I'm really hoping we might get to give it a go this year to help create some new happy memories.

It was just over a year ago that Ted died in the prime of his life at the age of thirty-seven, doing what he loved best: second only to drawing cartoon caricatures, he was playing football with his mates, when an unknown heart condition took him in an instant. 'Just like that,' as the late, great comedian Tommy Cooper used to say, according to my granddad who was a big Tommy Cooper fan. But on that fateful Sunday morning we had all thought Ted was messing around when it happened, staggering back and forth, with what looked like his daddy-dinosaur face on. The same goofy face he used to pull for the twins when they were little, and then for Freya, our 'surprise' baby girl – gasping and roaring, before clawing at his chest, making the children squeal and shriek in pleasure and faux fear at being caught and eaten up by the daddy dinosaur. And we had all been there that day, cheering Ted on as we did every Sunday morning before piling into the pub garden for a roast dinner and a good old family bicker about what film we would watch when they got back home. Whose turn was it to choose? And whose turn was it to hold the TV remote control and the enormous bowl of popcorn with mini marshmallows and Maltesers mixed in. None of the Carrington clan, as Dave, the pub landlord, called us, could ever remember any of these vitally important details for our afternoon of fun. I used to love those days all snuggled up on the sofa together, laughing and teasing one another. Only, there wasn't a film that day. Or a roast dinner, come to think of it. I've blanked out much of what went on. The section from when the referee realised what was really happening with Ted and blew the whistle, followed by an ambulance hurtling across the muddy field, has all turned into a hazy, muddled memory that hovers on the periphery of my consciousness, never quite coming back into sharp focus. But maybe it's better this way. Who wants to relive the moment their husband died over and over on a loop, like some kind of sadistic ritual? Not me, that's for sure. Instead, I try to remember the good times. The life I had with Ted before he died. And focus on trying to build a happy future for me and children.

Ted and I were young when we first met, still teenagers, in the sixth form at the local school, with part-time jobs in Carrington's department store in the centre of Mulberry, the place where we both grew up. Ted had arrived to work in the Christmas grotto, dressed as an elf, complete with tight green trousers that accentuated his solid-looking football-player thighs. I was working in Handbags and Accessories, having a laugh with my friends – the wickedly acerbic and completely camp Eddie, the funny and friendly Georgie, and her best friend, Sam, plus all the others that I knew from school. I lost touch with them all years ago after I moved away. I think Georgie spends some of the year in Italy these days and Sam runs the coffee and cake shop inside Carrington's. The last I heard of Eddie, he was having the time of his life as a TV celebrity living in LA, but I can still remember us all nudging each other and finding excuses to go and 'help out' in the grotto so we could get a look at the hot new boy, Ted Carrington, his dad a distant relative of one of the original Carrington family founders of the department store.

I did try to play it cool but I've never been very good at doing that and literally ended up on top of Ted soon after we first spoke. Not on purpose. No, definitely not. He asked me where the stockroom was so he could get more of the wrapped presents to top up the wooden toy box beside Santa's sleigh, and I had been so flustered that I tripped on the fairy-lights cable, bumped into Ted who put his arms out to break my fall, but skidded backwards on the fake snow strewn across the polished shop floor, and we both landed together in a clumsy heap. From then on, we were pretty much inseparable, laughing and flirting until the end of our shifts and I would have to go home and get back to my A levels revision. Not that I could fully focus on studying with thoughts of gorgeous Ted swirling around inside my head, and then inside my heart, with his cheeky, lopsided grin and twinkling blue eyes, and his wavy blonde hair that would flop into his eyes all the time and have to be pushed aside with his tanned forearm when he was busy turning the lever on the artificial snow machine.

I catch my breath, wondering for the umpteenth time if I'm doing the right thing in bringing us all here to Mulberry-On-Sea. It feels like the best thing for me, to be close to where I was happiest with Ted back in those early, carefree days of our relationship and then again on our family holidays there. It's always felt like a happy place and one that I'm hoping will make my family feel happy again. But the children's whole lives, friends and school, is all so far away now. Oscar didn't want to come and told me so, his teenage hormones fuelling his anger as he informed me how selfish I am to completely ruin his life. But after ignoring me for nearly a whole week, he realised too that there really isn't an alternative. Yes, our old home held all the precious, wonderful memories of Ted, but I struggled to manage financially after Ted died, eking out his modest life-insurance payment and then when the little local café I worked in closed down and I lost my job making afternoon cream teas, I fell behind with the rent. The landlord was very kind and understanding at first, but when his own circumstances changed and he had to sell the house, it meant that we had to move out as the new people were keen to 'be in before Christmas'. So rather than us all be homeless, I went for the only other option, after the council said they might be able to house us in a hostel (without Henry, Snuggle and Chewy though, who would all have to be rehomed somewhere else or given to an animal rescue shelter) but couldn't guarantee where the hostel would be, or for how long. The children had suffered enough after losing their dad, so there was no way I could even consider us being without our beloved family pets. Henry especially has been such a comfort; it's true what they say about pets just knowing how you feel, as Henry always rests his chin on my lap when I'm having a particularity tricky day and need a little bit of cheering up and tender loving care. No, we couldn't part with our gorgeous Henry, or Snuggle and Chewy, even if I do end up having to clean out their cage when Olly and Oscar promised me faithfully in the pet shop when they were pleading the case for me to buy two guinea pigs, that they would take care of all their needs. Of course, it never happened. But seeing the boys watching TV with a guinea pig each on their laps or nestled on a shoulder and the softening of their tense jawlines as they manage to unwind and release the daily stress of losing their dad… well, it's the very least they deserve to not be taken away from them too.

So I took up Ted's parents' very generous and kind offer of moving into their old holiday home. Jan and Ken have lived in Australia for over ten years now and have no intention of using the tiny two-bedroomed weather-boarded fisherman's beach house on the edge of the dunes and were very happy to be able to help us out. Although Ken made it very clear that the house needs some work and if I don't mind cleaning it up and giving it a lick of paint then I'll be doing them a favour too. And now that Ted's pension payments have started coming through and there isn't rent to pay each month, I should be able, with some careful budgeting, to keep the wolf from the door over the Christmas holidays and until I can find a new job. Even if the beach house is small and shabby and needs a bit of work, we'll make the best of it and, besides, it has to be better than being homeless or being parted from our beloved pets.

'Are we nearly there yet?' Oscar mumbles, managing momentarily to lift up his own eyelids and halt the perpetual motion of his thumbs, bringing me back to the moment.

'Almost,' I smile brightly at him in the rear-view mirror as the Mini splutters, makes a metal-on-metal grinding noise before eventually reaching the top of the cliff road. At last! I let out a small sigh of grateful relief. 'Why don't you give Freya a hand? She looks as if she could do with a break and you've been on that phone for the entire journey now,' I say, over my shoulder. Oscar reluctantly takes the length of bungee cord from Freya after muttering something about having to 'save the progress in my game' first. After giving her shoulders and hands a quick wriggle to release the tension of having held the blooming bungee cord for the lion's share of the journey, Freya presses her eager little face up to the window in anticipation of our arrival. Ever since her first trip to Mulberry as a toddler, she's always been keen to be the first one to spot all the lovely seaside sights.

I keep my foot over the brake, just in case, as the road

is icy and the last thing I want now is to lose control and end up skidding all the way into Mulberry. That has happened too. I was seventeen at the time and had just passed my driving test. I misjudged the descent, only to end up with the car swerving off the road and into Mrs Grace's front garden, with the tyres trampling all over her prized gladiolas. It was mortifying as, back then, Mrs Grace was the supervisor of the handbags and accessories department in Carrington's, and so after coming out of her house and checking that I was OK, she had been completely unimpressed on seeing the havoc I had caused. Mrs Grace went on and on about it every Saturday for months from then on, telling everyone, 'You should see the shocking state of my front garden after Bridget drove her car right through it.' Like I did it on purpose! Mrs Grace only let it go when I had saved up enough money to take a trip to the garden centre to buy the replacement gladiola plants. And then dug all the holes to put them in!

'Mummy, Mummy, look over there,' Freya squeals. 'I can see the lights! The shop ones and all the twinkly rainbow ones shimmering in the sea. They look pretty.'

And sure enough they do. Carrington's department store is coming into view on our left. The boats moored in the harbour with their swaying lantern lights on the horizon to the right. I inhale and swallow down the wave of sadness that comes over me on realising Ted is missing out on this moment, for he really loved coming back to Mulberry for the holidays. Any minute now and we would have both glanced at each other, Ted would have given my thigh a quick squeeze before returning his hand back to the steering wheel, and I would have leant over sideways and rested my head on his shoulder and whispered, 'We're home,' followed by a kiss on his stubbly chin and a burst of his warm, comforting scent of vanilla and spice. 'They sure do, darling,' I say to Freya, winking at her in the rear-view mirror. 'And we'll soon be in Granny and Granddad's holiday home, all tucked up warm. I'll make your favourite Lotus Biscoff hot chocolate when we get there. Would you like that?' I add, a smile in place to cover the mixture of emotions whizzing around inside me right now.

'No. Absolutely most definitely one hundred percent not.' Freya nods firmly, trying to keep a straight face.

'Oh, why is that then?' I ask, a little surprised that she is seemingly happy once again to participate in this old family game that Ted used to play with her. Freya used to love it, but that all changed when he died and no amount of coaxing since then has made any difference. Until now, it seems. I hold my breath as I wait and will Freya to deliver the punch line.

'Because I would LOVE it a trillion times over.' And Freya can't contain the giggles any longer as she bounces up and down in her seat, her fluffy blonde hair all static around her little red-cheeked face as she rubs her woolly mitten-clad hands over her head and up under her chin in glee. I feel as though my heart might burst with joy as I let out a massive big breath of sheer relief.

'Then it's a good job I put a giant bag of mini marshmallows and a jar of Biscoff spread inside my handbag then, isn't it!' I laugh. 'Now, sit back in your seat, sweetheart, and keep yourself safe.'

I reach the bottom of the winding cliff road and slow as the tarmac turns into cobbles with the white colonnaded walkway elevated at one side. Past the bandstand and the traffic lights which turn red just at the right time to give us a full view of the Carrington's Christmas window display.

'Mummy, Mummy! Look at all the elves. And the presents. They're almost up to the top of the window,' Freya says, unable to contain her excitement on seeing the magical scene set out in front of us in the enormous arched windows that are all frosted around the frames with sparkly fake snow. I smile to myself on remembering that first meeting with Ted, the pair of us rolling around in the fake snow. And to my surprise and dismay, for I haven't cried in such a long time on remembering the good times, my eyes pool with tears. Maybe it's the enormity of it all, losing our home that held so many memories, that's making the arrival here this time feel so different. Or maybe it's seeing Freya starting to bounce back after being subdued for such a long time. Or maybe it's the sense of relief, that just perhaps it is going to be OK after all. But whatever it is, I quickly brush at my eyes to restore my vision as I don't want the children to see my mixture of emotions and end up getting distressed. This is a special moment, marking a turning point for us, a fresh start, and I don't want anything to spoil it as I'm a great believer in starting as you mean to go on. 'And look at the merry-go-round,' Freya continues marvelling. 'And there's Santa on his sleigh. And—'

'Santa isn't rea—' Olly starts and so I jump in with, 'OK, Olly,' as I'm keen to preserve the magic of Christmas for my daughter for at least a few more years.

We carry on through the old cobbled square, where years ago there was an open-air market selling fresh fish and fruit and flowers, and on past the harbour. It's shaped like a horseshoe as if embracing the seawater that laps back and forth over the sand at low tide then turns into giant, frothy white-crested waves at high tide in a storm that thrashes back and forth against the harbour brick wall. The white lighthouse is majestic on the end of the stone pier, its golden light glowing in welcome. The harbour Christmas tree is constructed from wire mesh lobster pots and decorated with bright-orange buoys and flashing festive lights in crimson-red, holly-green and shimmery silver. I slow the car and we all sit in silence, just drinking in the view. Mulberry-On-Sea really is the most magical place to be. And what is that? I'm sure I can hear something drifting in the night air so I switch off the engine and wind down the window.

'Is that someone singing?' Olly whispers.

'I think it is.' I pop my head out of the window and can hear a deep male voice singing a rousing, emotive sea shanty, evocative with the clanging of the boats' halyards against their masts. I glance across the cobbles towards Our Lady Star of the Sea, the tiny old sailors' church built into the bottom of a cliff, with its whitewashed brick and arched porch and an anchor insignia carved into the stone above the open wooden door that reveals a light glowing from within. I wonder if it's possible the singing is coming from in there? It sounds so beautiful, melodic, melancholic and rich… and extremely emotional. It takes my breath away.

As the singing comes to an end, I wind the window back up and I drive on, past The Hook, Line & Sinker pub with its blue-and-white striped awning rolled back for the night, and then on to the promenade swathed in a myriad of twinkling gold lights looped like bunting between the old black-painted Victorian streetlights, each with three ornate globe-shaped bulbs; the lifeguard's cottage with the rescue boat on the jetty all ready to launch into the sea at a moment's notice; the little row of shops with a bookshop that doubles as a post office, a hairdresser's, an art gallery, a knick-knack store full of flip-flops, inflatables, snorkelling gear, sledges, floppy sunhats, and sun cream, a fish and chip shop and an ice cream kiosk; and eventually on to the winding unmade coastal road that runs the length of the beach, with marshy fields on one side and marram grass-topped dunes on the other, until it peters out all together and the tarmac turns into sand. That's where we will find our new home. The wave of relief that washes over me is palpable, even if it is pitch black by now and it has suddenly dawned on me that I haven't brought a proper torch. But the moon is full and ripe, the colour of butterscotch in the inky night sky, the sound of the waves welcoming as they sway back and forth, rhythmic and reassuring. The stars are twinkling and the boat lanterns winking in the distance of the harbour as if signalling our arrival and telling us it is all going to be all right. We will make the best of it. As we always have.

And so, bathed in a butterscotch glow, my three sleepy children, one dog, two guinea pigs, and I make our way across the sand to the little sunshine-yellow painted wooden beach house in the distance, enjoying the adventure of snuggling into our duvets as we wrap the padding around our shoulders, each of us clasping a collection of bags and boxes of belongings too. Henry is bounding around, biting the frost-topped sand in excitement, the wind from the sea muffling his barking.

Not that it matters if he is a bit noisy as we are the only ones here; the other little weatherboard holiday homes on this section of the beach are all empty and closed up for the winter.

I reach the rickety wooden steps leading up to the front door and after offloading my luggage I take a deep breath and turn towards the waves, the salty sea air making me feel vibrant and alive. Optimistic. For the first time in a very long time I can actually feel my heart lifting. It's a quiet fizz of excitement, but full of promise at the prospect of stepping into this new chapter in our lives. Wrapping my arms around myself, I tilt my head towards the sky and briefly nod at the stars as if to tell Ted we are here. The perfect place to spend Christmas as I try to put our family back together again. A new beginning. And Ted will always be with us – his ashes sprinkled around the old shipwreck that is only visible when the tide is far out – a fitting place for him to be, Ken, Jan, and I had felt. Somewhere he had been happiest – as a child making sandcastles in the summer, then later when we had run across the sand and sat in the shipwreck together as teenagers on balmy summer days. Or when we'd huddled together on crisp winter evenings with a beach barbecue to toast our marshmallows on. The place where we shared our first kiss. The place where Ted first said he loved me and I told him the same right back. The place where I told Ted

I was pregnant and then held my breath as I waited for his reaction in case it was too soon, as we were both still very young. But Ted had been over the moon, scooping me up into one of his trademark big bear hugs and twirling me around and around and around while we both laughed and cried happy tears until I had begged him to stop because I was feeling a bit queasy and didn't want to throw up all over the shoulder of his new denim jacket.

I smile to myself, certain I can see one of the stars twinkling extra brightly in this moment, as if to acknowledge my wish and convince me that, yes, Mulberry-On-Sea is the place we all need to be, surrounded by those happy memories of holidays and special times where nothing bad ever happens... or so it seems.

Chapter Two

'Mummy, don't forget Louis?' Freya exclaims, lifting the glass Kilner jar containing the sourdough starter that I've been cultivating for the last few months from the top of the wooden steps that lead up to the front door. My best friend, Lorna, gave me a small cup full of the fermenting yeast mixture and so far I've managed to grow the starter – aka Louis, as Freya has fondly named him – to a pretty impressive size. I've also managed to use a little bit of Louis to bake a few decent-looking sourdough loaves that have actually tasted pretty good too, when toasted and slathered in salted butter and my homemade strawberry jam or Cointreau chutney, with a chunk of tangy cheddar on the side. Absolutely delicious!

'Oh no, we definitely mustn't forget Louis. Thank

you, darling,' I beam, taking Louis from Freya and tucking the jar into the crook of my elbow as I fish around inside the pocket of my jeans with my spare hand to retrieve the door key. But it isn't there!

The four of us are grouped around the front door of the beach house. Henry is bouncing about on the sand nearby, happy to be free from the car at last, and Snuggle and Chewy are in a pet carrier with a blanket wrapped around it to keep them warm. Oscar is shining the torch on his phone towards the porch so I can see where the lock is on the front door. After handing Louis back to Freya, I try my other pocket, but no luck.

'Oscar can you shine the light over this way please?'

He does, and I have a good rummage through the contents of my handbag – two dog biscuits, a tangled hairbrush, the bag of marshmallows, a purse, book, lipstick, Lego figure, a multitude of sweet wrappers and all sorts of no-idea-why-I-have-it-in-my-bag type clutter, but still no key! My heart sinks. It is perishingly cold now and my fingertips are going numb. Freya is shivering and the boys are getting restless, elbowing each other in the side to see if they can make the other one fall over and faceplant the frosty sand. Even Henry has given up cavorting and is now sitting at my feet with his head cocked to one side as if wondering what on earth is going on? Fun time is over and he wants his dinner – 7pm on the dot. He always knows! And, sure enough, I push my sleeve back and glance at the digital watch screen where 19:00 is glowing in the dark.

'OK, kids, let's see if the key is in the car. Maybe it fell out of my pocket when I sat down,' I say, far more optimistically than I feel as I try to quash the swirly feeling of failure that is building inside me. So much for a fresh start and good new beginning. I can't even get us all inside our new home!

'Does this mean we *all* have to trudge *all* the way back to the car?' Oscar sighs, kicking the toe of his left trainer against the side of the wooden boards that once upon a time had formed a small jetty for the fisherman's boat to launch from, but which now serve as a pathway over the sand leading from the beach house all the way down to the sea.

'Yes it does,' I say, giving him an apologetic look. 'But it's hardly a long way, and besides, you've been sitting down for most of the day during the car journey so a bit of walking around will do you good.' I nod, as if to underline the sensible, no-nonsense mum vibe I'm desperately trying to channel.

'But it's bloody freezing,' Oscar continues, pulling the sides of his beanie hat further down over his ears in an attempt to keep warm.

'Well, I can't do anything about it,' I say, and then add, 'and please don't swear in front of Freya. She's only six. Come on, a brisk walk will warm us all up.' But it's no use. My cheerful chivvying and no-nonsense mum act aren't having the desired effect and they all stand and stare at me despondently. Henry too has his chocolate-drop puppy-dog eyes fixed firmly on me as if seemingly waiting for me to wave a magic wand. If only it were that simple. But then, as if by actual magic, Olly comes up with a suggestion.

'No need for us all to trudge back across the dunes. Why don't I go to the car and look for the key while you all wait here?' he offers.

'Oh, um,' I start, taken aback, but liking this rare and impromptu flash of maturity as I hand the car key to Olly. 'Well, that really would be a massive help – save us *all* having to trudge back to the car,' I say, giving my other son, Oscar, my special 'mum look'. The one that I caught myself doing in the mirror that time and was startled at how similar I looked to my own mum, Patty, short for Patricia.

A flamboyant woman who has never forgiven me for marrying Ted, 'that boy next door' as she called him, and not the prestigious pilot, shipping magnate, or property tycoon that prolific social-climber Patty always envisaged for her only daughter. We even fell out over it and didn't talk for a while as she was pretty mean to Ted, only reconciling after he died. Patty lives in Spain now, Marbella, on the Costa del Sol, where she reins over her chain of beauty bars bought for her by her third husband,

Derek, a property tycoon from Dublin! The irony isn't lost on me either, as Patty was very evasive when I reluctantly asked her if she might be kind enough to consider helping me out with a loan, just enough for a deposit on a new rental house, when it had first become apparent a few months back that we were going to lose our home. I hated asking for a handout, but in that moment I really hadn't seen any other option. Ted and I had never been much good at saving – not that we ever had any money left over at the end of each month in any case. So in the depths of despair and bracing myself for another 'Let's get you on the Sugar Daddies R Us dating website' chat, I had reluctantly turned to Patty after talking it through with Lorna, who would have loved to help me out if she could but had just spent the last of her savings on a new washing machine because her old one had conked out and couldn't be repaired. True to form, Patty had done her promo piece about the merits of Sugar Daddies R Us – it was where she'd met mega-minted Derek after all – before promising to 'give Derek a tap'. But a few days later had sent me a 'Sorry hun, no spare cash at the mo' text message with a sad face emoji and three kisses followed by another message offering me and the children free use of the apartment above Patty's 24hr Nail, Tanning & Karaoke salon on the main party strip in Benalmadena.

'Cool.' Olly shoves his hands into the pockets of his

padded jacket and goes to walk off across the sand back to where the car is parked on the other side of the dunes.

'Please put your torch on too, love.' I call after Olly, not wanting him disappearing into the dark. There are no street lights along this part of the beach and with the buffeting of the wind that has picked up now and the sound of the swirling waves, we'd never hear him if he got into trouble and called out for help or something. And then I suddenly wonder if it is actually safe for my fourteen-year-old son to head off into the night by himself? But before I can overthink and then doubt whatever decision I make, it's made for me, and Olly is sprinting off across the sand, the light from his phone torch bobbing about in the darkness.

After taking Louis from Freya and placing the jar back by the front door, I sit on the top step to wait for Olly, pulling Freya onto my lap for a cuddle to warm her up. Henry, instantly jealous as always and keen to get a look in, shoves his nose under my arm and makes Freya giggle by burrowing his head inside her duvet. Even Oscar knows a good thing when he sees it and slouches over to join us on the step, leaning into me until I am literally swathed in bodies huddling together to keep warm, all the while keeping a look out for the light that's reassuringly still bobbing around over by the sand dunes I can just about see in my periphery to the left.

Moments later, and Olly is coming back across the

beach, the narrow shaft of light from his phone shining brighter and brighter the closer he gets and I see that he has my cumbersome old bicycle beside him.

'Ooh, here he is! Come on, let's get inside,' I say, chivvying the three of them off me and standing up, desperate now to use the loo and get everyone inside in the warm and shelter from the wind. Henry bounces over towards Olly, greeting him as always with a big, waggy tail and a few quick circle spins as if Olly has been gone for an eternity and not mere minutes.

'Sorry, Mum. I couldn't find the key!' Olly gasps, dropping the bike sideways onto the sand and bending over with his hands on his knees to catch his breath from having trekked across the dunes in the biting wind.

'Oh, no!' I put my hand on Olly's back. 'But thanks for bringing the bike though. I completely forgot about it strapped up there on the roof of the car,' I say, wondering what to do now.

'No problem,' Olly grins, clearly pleased to have at least sorted out the bike, but is disheartened not to have found the door key as his grin fades. 'Yeah, I looked everywhere for it. Even under the floor mats in the car and in the boot in case the key fell out of your pocket when you were loading the car up this morning. I checked in the sand all around the car too.'

'Ah, well thanks, love, at least you tried,' I say brightly, pinning a smile on my face as my heart sinks and a tingle of unease joins the feeling of failure that has returned. What now? There isn't enough petrol in the car to get us all the way to Stoneley, the nearest big town where there's a garage open at this time of night – the local petrol station in Mulberry that doubles as a car repair garage was closed when we drove past, which is why I couldn't fill up. I'd figured there was enough petrol to get us to the beach house and then I'd sort it out in the morning when it was daylight.

'So what are we going to do now, then?' Oscar says, shoving his hands deeper into his jeans pockets as he kicks at a small pile of pebbles by the edge of the wooden boards.

'I could see if there's a window we might be able to lift open?' Olly offers, directing his phone torch towards the biggest window to the left of the door and then to a smaller one on the right. 'They're only wooden framed and remember when Dad managed to get one open years ago when Freya was a toddler and the door slammed shut in the wind and she got stuck inside the beach house all by herself.'

'Oh yes—' I start, but am interrupted by Oscar.

'Yeah, well you're not Dad.' Oscar scowls at Olly with a look of pure disdain in his eyes.

'And you're a total melt!' Olly retorts, flashing a look back at his twin brother.

'OK, boys, that's enough,' I say, cutting it off before it

escalates. 'Nobody is a melt, and I wish you wouldn't say that.' I look at Olly. 'We need to sort this out together.'

The last thing I want right now is for the pair of them to get into a verbal fight. Freya will get upset and then the whole 'happy to be here' vibe will definitely be spoilt. And I really want this move to work out for us all. A fresh start. That's what I'm hoping for. I look at the wooden-framed windows to see if it's feasible to try to prise one open, remembering when Ted had used a bank card to slide under the catch, and we joked about the ease with which he had 'broken in' almost like an experienced burglar. That's when Ted had confessed to 'having form'. As a schoolboy he had once broken into his dad's summer house using a similar trick with the card to help himself to three cans of lager for him and his mates. Of course, he had been caught and Ken had got his police officer best friend to 'have a word'. And I had teased him about it at any given opportunity.

'I wish Daddy was here,' sniffs Freya, crouching down and pressing her face into Henry's mane. The dog puts his paw up to Freya's shoulder as if to comfort her. And I can't help wishing Ted was here too. Most of the time, I can cope just fine, but every now and again, usually when I'm tired or there's a problem to sort out, there comes a moment when it suddenly feels so overwhelming to be without him. And this is one of those moments.

'Well, he isn't!' Oscar snaps and goes to walk off. It's Olly who grabs his brother's arm and pulls him back into the group.

'There's no need to be horrible to Freya. And you can't just storm off. We all know Dad isn't here anymore, and we all think it's shit that he isn't, but we have to get on with it. Come on, we can get a window open, I bet we can. We just need to try,' Olly tells Oscar, glancing at me. I give him a grateful smile, thinking how grown up he's becoming, before turning to Freya.

'Just give me a second, will you, boys?' and I bob down beside Freya and Henry. 'Darling, I wish Daddy was here too, but if you look out there towards the sea' – I point towards the waves that have lulled slightly as the tide has turned and is now trundling away – 'in the morning when the sun has come up, you'll be able to see the shipwreck...'

'Where we sprinkled Daddy?' Freya checks, her eyes widening.

'Yes, that's right,' Olly says, putting an arm around his little sister's shoulders and giving her a hug. A few seconds pass as Freya mulls it over.

'OK.' She eventually grins and shrugs, seemingly content with this news as she then moves onto a completely new topic and announces, 'I need a wee.' The boys and I laugh, all grateful for the mood uplift.

'Me too!' I grin at Freya. 'So in that case, we had

better get a window open and get ourselves inside the house as quickly as we can!' And I start walking towards the left of the beach house with Olly close behind me, clearly keen to see if he can follow in his dad's footsteps as he's already opening the Velcro fastener of his nylon wallet and pulling out a plastic card as he pushes back his blonde curls… just the way Ted used to.

'But I'm busting. I need to go now,' Freya says, hopping from one leg to the other.

'Go in the dunes then if you really can't wait,' Oscar suggests, pointing to the densest section of marram grass on top of the dunes that are almost as tall as the shingle-tiled roof of the beach house.

'I don't think that's a good idea,' I start, reckoning it's better for us all to stick together now and focus on getting inside the house as swiftly as possible.

'Me and Oscar used to go there all the time when we were here on holidays in the summer,' Olly points out.

'Did you?' I ask and stop walking, sure I used to make the children go back to the house.

'Yep. Dad said it was all right. Especially if we were building a massive sandcastle with him and didn't want to have to trek back to the house.' He looks at me and I tilt my head to one side, thinking this sounds exactly like Ted – he was always far more laidback with the children than I am. Whereas I worry about this kind of thing – or, more to the point, worry what other people might think –

whereas Ted wouldn't have been bothered in the slightest and would have just told the children to go behind the nearest and biggest grassy dune.

'Hmm, well, I'm guessing Dad only agreed because you were little and—'

'Well, Freya is little,' Oscar chips in. I turn to Freya.

'Can you try to wait, do you think?' I ask. 'It's too cold to be going in the dunes and we could have the window open very soon so you'll be able to use the bathroom in the beach house.'

Freya shakes her head.

'I really need to go right now,' she repeats, chewing her bottom lip.

'Well, here's a plan,' Olly suggests. 'Mum, why don't you two go while we try to get a window open?' he looks at me for approval.

'I'm not sure. It's very dark here for you two to be on your own,' I glance at Freya and then back to Olly and Oscar.

'We'll be fine,' Olly assures me.

'Are you absolutely sure?'

'Yes!' Both boys nod.

'There is such a thing as a torch on our phones.' Oscar pulls a face which Olly reciprocates.

'Hmm, well, OK then. But let's be very quick as we're all freezing.' I take Freya's hand. 'Please try not to break the glass. And no wandering off. You must stay together here at the house. We'll be back in a minute,' I tell them as I loop Henry's lead around a balustrade on the wooden deck that wraps around the front of the beach house.

'Mum, we'll be all right!' Olly looks at Oscar and shakes his head. 'We're not little kids, you know.'

'I know.' I smile. 'But it's still my job to look out for you both, isn't it?'

'Not to smother us though.' Olly rolls his eyes and pulls a cheeky face as he gives Henry's head a quick stroke.

'Yes, go on, you big smother mother!' Oscar jokes too, for a welcome change.

'Right, well in that case, come along, young lady.' After flicking on my torch phone, I take Freya's hand and we dart across the sand to find a discreet spot. Freya very quickly lifts her coat and whips down her leggings. I wait. And wait some more. Rubbing my hands together in an attempt to stop them from freezing completely, I will my daughter to hurry up, wondering if I should whizz back over here in a bit with a bucket of hot water once we've managed to get inside the house.

'Mummy, it's gone now. I don't need to go.' Freya pulls her leggings up and slips her hand back inside mine.

'Oh, are you sure?' I say, thinking *blooming typical* and inwardly cursing myself for not making doubly sure she actually really did need to go. Such a rookie parent mistake and one I thought I'd mastered years ago when the boys were little.

'Yes,' Freya nods, resolute. Now desperate to go myself and fearing an accident if we get back to the house and the boys haven't managed to get a window open, I push my phone under my arm so I can still see and make a snap decision to duck behind a sand dune too. With Freya standing with her back to me so I can keep an eye on her, I find a discreet spot and quickly push my jeans down, gasping at the sudden gust of icy cold wind that wraps around my bare legs. But just as I go to crouch and whip my knickers down, a very bright flashlight appears right behind me. I freeze, caught like a rabbit in a headlight, literally, with my knicker-clad bottom perched up in the air. There must be someone there! Right behind me. Major cringe! Freya whirls around with her head dipped and a hand on her forehead shielding her eyes from the dazzling light.

'Mummy, I can see your knickers! The Christmas ones with *Ho, ho, ho* written all over them,' she bellows, her high-pitched voice carrying in the wind so the whole of Mulberry might hear… or so it seems.

I'm absolutely mortified. And just as I'm desperately figuring out what to do for the best – jump up and sort out my jeans in one swift ninja-style movement or leap forward and pull my daughter into me before the mad, crazy beach monster or whoever it is behind me gets to us – an enormous grey shaggy-haired Irish wolfhound comes bounding across the dunes and bowls right into me. The next thing I know, I've toppled over sideways and can instantly feel a very hot dog tongue licking the side of my bare thigh as I try to get upright. This is an impossibility with my tight skinny-jeans wedged around my knees and the undulating sand dunes all soft and wobbly beneath my feet. Freya giggles as the dog wags its tail and then spins around in excitement thinking I'm a potential playmate stumbling about in the dunes purely for its pleasure.

'Ah, for feck's sake!' a deep, melodic male Irish voice sings out into the darkness, followed by, 'Sinead! Come on, girl. Sinead,' followed by a far more insistent and bellowing, 'SINEAAAAAD. For the love of god, will you cut that out! Stop licking the poor woman's leg. You'll have it worn down to the bone in no time with the speed you're going at!'

After grabbing at an extra thick wodge of grass and managing to scrabble to my feet in a ridiculously ungainly fashion, I swiftly yank my jeans back up. The very nanosecond my bottom is covered, I whip around to see who's there, willing my cheeks to stop flaming like a pair of plum tomatoes.

'Sorry about that. My dog is a proper eejit. Are you OK?' the voice yells to be heard over the wind and waves as Sinead, the dog, hurtles back towards her owner, I presume. I open my mouth to answer, but the man continues, 'I didn't mean to scare you and I'll not come any closer. Not that I was expecting to see anyone out here on the beach at this time of night...' This is followed by a muffled laugh, then, 'Sorry, but it's not every day you come across a pair of Christmas pants bouncing about in the dunes when you're walking the dog now, is it?' And he shakes his head like it's the funniest thing he's seen in absolutely ages.

'I suppose not,' I manage, swiping at a clod of icy sand still clinging to the side of my face.

'Are you sure you're OK?' he asks, sounding concerned.

'Yes, absolutely fine, thanks,' I say, dying a little inside as my voice jumps up a couple of octaves into embarrassing hysteria territory. And then for some mad reason I start nodding over and over and over like an absolute loon in danger of giving herself whiplash.

'What are you doing out here in the dark? Apart from the obvious.' He laughs a bit more, widening his eyes and motioning with his head towards my legs and then the sand. 'Have you lost your way?'

The person standing about two metres in front of me is a man in his thirties perhaps – it's hard to be sure exactly, as he's bundled up in a big padded jacket with a woolly scarf wound around the lower half of his face.

There's a brown leather dog lead hanging around his shoulders and a head torch strapped to his forehead, holding back a tangle of dark curls that accentuate a pair of twinkling amber eyes, dark lashes, and thick brows.

'Oh, um, no, we, er…' I manage, taking Freya's hand and pulling her in beside me before adjusting my own bobble hat that has gone skewwhiff so it's now perched like a little Christmas tree on the very top of my head, and my curly hair is flopped all over my face. 'We're fine, thank you. We were… um, just… taking a comfort break,' I cringe at how prim the words sound babbling out of my mouth as I swipe my hair back off my face and under my hat in an attempt to appear breezy and normal. A short silence follows as the man looks me up and down again, clearly trying to gauge if I'm completely bonkers or just a little bit daft. Because who in their right mind would be out here on the perishing cold beach, in the dark, taking a comfort break! Nobody sane, that's for sure. But before I can explain that we've just arrived and about the lost key and the beach house and everything else, Freya pipes up.

'Mummy, your knickers have got a big hole in them!'

Another silence follows.

'Oh,' I open my mouth to reply but I have no immediate clue as to what to say that sounds even remotely apt given the bizarre situation and a ludicrous Scooby Doo *ruh roh* noise comes tumbling out instead, followed by a feeble fake laugh. I want to shrivel up and die right here in the sand. And to make matters worse, Freya isn't letting it go.

'Mummy, did you hear me? Your knickers have got a bi—'

'Yes, yes I did hear you, darling. Come on now, we should get going.' I slip my hand around Freya's and mutter something about needing to get back asap, but my daughter keeps on.

'Mummy, what's a comfort break?'

The man bends down and gently puts his arm around Sinead's neck, giving her chest a fond stroke. Then he looks up at me with an amused look in his eyes, lifts one eyebrow, and tilts his head as if waiting for me to explain, his smouldering dark looks and Irish charm making me feel very uncomfortable indeed.

'Oh, it, er, just means… um…' I cough. 'Um, having a little rest in the sand,' I squeak. And the pair of plum-tomato cheeks make a monumental return as I scoop Freya up onto my hip, mutter a very hurried goodbye and attempt to run away, stumbling and staggering all over again in the deep sandy dunes with Freya bellowing that she's being suffocated every time we fall over and I land on top of her…

Chapter Three

The following morning I wake early as the gloriously crisp winter sun peeps around the edge of the faded nautical navy-and-white striped curtains, and Henry launches himself straight onto my chest after doing a running leap onto the bed and near crushing me in the process. I'm now downstairs in the open-plan kitchen and living area on my own as the children are all still asleep upstairs. Olly and Oscar are in bunk beds in the small bedroom at the back overlooking the dunes and I'm sharing the double bed with Freya in the bedroom at the front of the house with a lovely seaview window in the eaves that looks out across the beach.

'Here you go, boy.'

I give Henry's head a fond stroke before breaking off a corner of my buttered toast and handing it to him. I'm looking forward to sitting on the deck at the top of the wooden stairs by the front door to take a breath as I look out at the waves and contemplate the day ahead. Slipping my coat on over my cosy pink cotton rosebud-patterned pyjamas, I pick up my knitting and a mug of tea and make my way outside, pulling the door to behind me to keep the warmth from the old red Aga inside the house. Last night, I had been amazed that the Aga still actually worked, as it's a temperamental beast with multiple ovens and as old as the house which is itself at least a hundred years old, as Ted's dad reminded me in the phone call from Australia when he offered us use of the beach house. He had wanted to be doubly sure that the children and I would be OK in the little house on the sand, with limited amenities and throughout a cold British winter. Although, to be fair, it's been an unusually mild winter this year so I wasn't worried about that. We are hardy bunch, the children and I, and we can cope with cold weather in any case. But I thought Ken had been exaggerating when he'd also apologised profusely about the house having definitely seen better days and being in desperate need of modernisation, according to the estate agent that had taken a look over it when Ken and Jan had toyed with the idea of selling. But when Olly had managed to get a window open last night – very easily, as part of the rotten wooden frame had crumbled to dust when he slotted the credit card in behind the latch – and then climbed inside the house to let us all in, the first thing that struck me was that it was true. Ken hadn't been exaggerating.

The state of the house has deteriorated considerably since we were last here for a holiday and is definitely in need of some tender loving care – much more than a lick of paint. But I'm just grateful that we have a roof over our heads. Mind you, this might not be the case for very much longer as the plaster on the bedroom ceiling above the bed is cracked. I'm trying not to worry about it and I don't want to tell Ken and Jan as they don't have the funds for repairs, which is why they weren't in a position to do the house up to sell, so there is no point in worrying them too.

But what if the ceiling falls down in the middle of the night?

But I don't have the money to pay for roof repairs.

I try to push the thoughts from my head, determined to make the best of the situation. But the little cottage garden at the back is unkempt and overgrown, the bathroom tired and old fashioned with an ominous black damp patch creeping up from a skirting board, the red quarry tiles on the floor in the kitchen are cracked and lifted in places, and the walls have lumps of plaster missing so the rotten timber frame is exposed in places. But at least we found the key after all that palaver – it was in with the photos in the bag I put in the footwell of the car for safe-keeping. Despite all this, I still think the beach house has a gloriously rustic charm, and I was absolutely delighted on seeing the scrubbed pine table still here in the centre of the room with enough mismatched chairs for us all to sit around it. Plus the big old sofa that holds a lifetime of memories within its saggy, well-worn, but incredibly comfortable cushions. Yes, it feels homely and comfortable here, which is a welcome relief as I had to store our own big furniture items – beds, sofa, and wardrobes – in Lorna's garage because there isn't enough space for our furniture in the tiny beach house.

Placing my mug on the deck beside me, I pick up my knitting – a unicorn-coloured scarf to go in Freya's Christmas stocking – and smile to myself on remembering the last time we were here in the winter. It had been perishingly cold for the duration as we hadn't managed to get the Aga going. Ted had even called his mum in Australia to ask for her help in 'getting the knack of jiggling the switch the right way'. I stop knitting for a moment and then pick the mug back up and lift it out towards the shipwreck that is just becoming visible on the wet, sandy horizon as the tide retreats, and softly say a 'good morning' to Ted, smiling at how I had held my breath last night until the Aga started the first time I tried it. Ted would have laughed and then been mightily miffed that I had got the knack of it on my first go, when he couldn't.

I was so pleased. It had felt like a very happy and serendipitous moment indeed, not only in lifting my feelings of doubt about whether I'd made the right decision in bringing us all here, but it also means I can indulge my passion for baking. And there really is nothing better than an Aga with its multiple ovens permanently on and full of baking bread – not to mention the heartwarming, cosy aroma that will soon fill the beach house. In fact, as soon as the children are awake and have finished their breakfast, we're going to head to the shops in Mulberry to buy some eggs, milk and butter to go with the bags of flour and jar of mincemeat I brought with me to bake mince pies, bread and perhaps a small Christmas cake too. I've been stashing loose change and a pound here and there in a savings tin over the last few months so as to have enough to make Christmas as special for the children as it can be under the circumstances. Then, this afternoon, I'll get my crafting box out and we can create some Christmas decorations to hang up and make the house look festive. Oh yes, it is certainly beginning to feel a bit like Christmas now. I grin to myself and take a sip of the hot, sweet tea. Olly and Oscar will most likely protest at the prospect of getting involved in homemade stuff but Freya will love it and with no school now until January, I figure it will do the boys good to get off their phones, if only for a little while. Freya will be going to Mulberry Primary and the boys to the new secondary school, a bus ride away on the outskirts of a village called Tindledale. Both schools agreed that, given all that the children had been through this past year with their dad dying and them having to leave their home, it wasn't in their best interests to start a new school with only two weeks left until the end of term. Much better for them to be settled here in Mulberry and start afresh in the New Year after a lovely Christmas together, hopefully.

'Morning!' a cheery-faced woman wearing a bright-yellow mackintosh waves as she walks past on the beach, her wavy blonde hair piled up in a messy, windswept bun. A little brown-and-white terrier is scampering along behind her until he spots Henry sitting beside me on the deck and makes a beeline straight towards him. I smile and wave back at the woman.

'Oh, gosh, sorry, he's such an inquisitive little fella!' she says, smiling back. 'Skipper, come on, boy,' she calls out, and her dog instantly stops sniffing Henry and runs back to the woman's heel, clearly far better behaved than Sinead, the exuberant Irish wolfhound from last night. I cringe all over again on recalling the hideous moment in the dunes, just managing to keep my smile firmly in place as I call back to the woman who is now trying to clip Skipper's lead onto his collar.

'Morning! Skipper is fine if he wants to come and say hello,' I tell her. 'This is Henry and he's as soppy as they come, but very inquisitive too.'

'If you're sure you don't mind?' the woman checks, putting Skipper's lead back inside her pocket. 'Are you staying here for the Christmas holidays?' She indicates towards the beach house, seeming to think it's a holiday home like many of the other beach houses further along on the next section of the beach.

'Yes. Well, sort of… We arrived last night. But we're living here now for good, me and my little girl, and my teenage twin boys too,' I explain.

'In that case, welcome! I only moved here a year ago myself.' She smiles enthusiastically, the sea breeze making her hair float around her face.

'Thank you,' I say, taking a sip of the tea and cupping my hands around the mug to keep them warm.

'Are you on your own?' the woman asks, and then instantly slaps a gloved hand over her mouth. 'Sorry, that sounded so nosey. What I meant to say was, do you have a partner, a husband perhaps, joining you for Christmas?' She rolls her eyes and shakes her head as if admonishing her own audacity.

'Oh, um…' I hesitate, wondering if it's right to tell her, but quickly decide against it as I've made this mistake before, explaining about Ted to a mum in the playground when she asked about my husband. The woman had burst into tears before giving me a big hug which had upset Freya and it had made the whole moment embarrassing and painful and, well, just awkward. So I settle on, 'No, it will just be me and the children.'

'I see.' She smiles kindly. 'I'm Rita, by the way, the landlady at The Hook, Line & Sinker down there by the harbour. And I'm very obviously still learning to try to engage my brain before I speak. I really hope I didn't offend you.'

'Oh yes, I know the pub,' I grin. 'And really it's fine, no offence taken. I'm Bridget, and it's very nice to meet you.'

'Lovely to meet you too, Bridget,' Rita nods, then pauses, her forehead creasing as if deep in thought, recalling some forgotten fact. But then she lifts an index finger in the air and proclaims, 'Ho, ho, ho! Ah, so you must be the woman in the dunes! Of course, it all makes sense now.' And with her smile widening, she shakes her head some more as I gulp and catch my breath.

'Er, what do you mean, the woman in the dunes?' I ask, as casually as I can muster, but as soon as the words are out of my mouth I know exactly what Rita means. News travels faster than a fireball comet in the close-knit community of Mulberry-On-Sea and a newcomer scrabbling about in the dunes in the dark would definitely have been a talking point in the pub last night.

Oh God. I make a mental note to give The Hook, Line & Sinker a very wide berth for evermore.

'Jack, he's the barman in the pub... the one who spotted you,' she says, then pauses before adding, 'well, it was Sinead, really, who spotted you first, from what I gather, with her boundless energy and fickle nature, she'll turn her attentions to anyone, that dog.'

Rita shakes her head as if recalling the whole story, presumably having been given a blow-by-blow account with no detail overlooked it seems, by Jack, the barman! What's the betting too that he knows everyone in Mulberry so they will all know by now about my ho-ho-ho knickers with the big hole in them? My heart sinks. In fact, it properly plunges into the pit of my stomach as this isn't the new beginning I had in mind when coming here. I envisaged a cosy Christmas in the beach house with Ted's kind soul close by and perhaps exchanging warm pleasantries with the new people we meet in Mulberry. Not wondering if they're sniggering about the state of my lingerie situation. I make a mental note to never ever wear the ho-ho-ho knickers again. In fact, they're best off in the bin with their big hole that Freya pointed out.

'I see,' I dip my head to take another sip of tea before going to explain how it really was, but Rita is holding up a palm, poised to carry on.

'Honestly, love, don't worry yourself about it. We see

all sorts on the beaches and Jack's not the malicious type. He did think it was hilarious though as you ran away over towards your beach house.'

Oh god, so he saw me stumbling about in the dark too, all the way back home because my mobile battery had chosen to die at that exact moment so I couldn't put the torch on to light the way. I inhale through my nose and let out a long breath through smiling lips in an attempt to cover up the cringefest that's tumbling about inside me.

'Mind you, I think I'd want to make a swift exit too if I'd been caught short, as it were, in my jokey Christmas knickers.' And Rita roars again. I open my mouth to explain that I wasn't exactly 'caught short', not really, more of an opportunity in case I couldn't get in the house to use the actual bathroom, and that Jack didn't actually see anything, er… revealing! But then, hang on a minute, this is the seaside! People prance around in swimsuits and bikinis all day long in the summer months when the weather isn't baltic, so there really wasn't anything unusual to see in any case. Not really! But Rita waves and carries on talking again and I miss my moment to explain. 'Anyway, cheerio, I had better get going.' She lifts a hand to wave goodbye and goes to walk on, but then stops as if remembering something and says, 'Ooh, maybe see you online some time… if you like a bit of a sing-song? The local choir is always on the lookout for new voices.' Rita gives me a hopeful smile and I gulp because the last time I did any singing would have been circa 1996. A Spice Girls karaoke duet with Lorna in the local pub. And it was diabolical. 'No I flaming wouldn't!' a grumpy bloke had heckled from the crowd as we had revved up for the 'wannabe my lover' line!

'Oh, I er... I'm not really much of a singer.'

'Nor am I, love,' Rita laughs. 'It's just a bit of fun. We call ourselves the Mulberry-On-Sea Shanty Singers, but, to be fair, anything pretty much goes... It's very rousing and keeps the spirits up. Online every Wednesday at 8pm. Come the summer, choir practice is in the pub, or on the beach if it's a particularly lovely evening, but until then it's a virtual get-together as it makes it easier for the older members to join in. They don't much fancy coming out in the cold, especially when it's icy, as the steep hill roads can be very treacherous.'

'Ah, that must have been what we heard coming from the sailors' church last night,' I say, remembering the beautiful singing. 'It sounded incredible, very professional.'

'Yes, that'll be it. Vicar Joe is a proper singer. He used to be in a real band back in the day... before he found God. He went on *Top of the Pops* and everything. Our local celebrity. He runs the choir now,' Rita beams proudly. 'But don't let that intimidate you and put you off. Definitely not. We have all sorts of singers, some good and some blooming dreadful – we stand those ones at the back when we do our little choir concerts in public.' She chuckles some more. 'Anyway, pour yourself a glass of whatever you fancy, log on, and snuggle up with a blanket and prepare to feel thoroughly energised. Honestly, it works wonders for the mental health.' She pauses to tap the side of her head. 'Just pop by the pub sometime and I'll give you the info.'

She waves again and walks on, leaving me with a grin suspended on my face as I press my cold hands up to my cheeks to stop them from flaming all over again at the mention of the pub. Where Jack will be. Hmm, maybe I should give Mulberry a miss today, after all. Rita is kind to invite me to join the sea shanty choir but the pub is right in the centre of where the row of shops is by the harbour and so it will be near on impossible to avoid potentially running into Jack. I'm just not up to dealing with the awkwardness of it all right now. No, I have so many other things to fill my thoughts – there really is no space for a bubble of anxiety over something so silly. I want to concentrate on getting the house cleaned up and doing the Christmas crafting today and then I'll see about tackling a trip into Mulberry tomorrow when hopefully my being 'caught short in the sand with jokey Christmas knickers on display for all and sundry to see' story will be old news. And there's bound to be a festive film on today so we can drink hot chocolate and snuggle up by the log fire instead. Perfect. Bliss is staying at home and being wilfully avoidant. I nod to myself and sink the last of my tea in celebration of this decision.

Later, having made a mountain of colourful paper chains between us all – even Olly and Oscar joined in after complaining about it being a 'lame' thing to do for a good fifteen minutes or so – I stood on a chair and pinned the decorations to the four corners of the main living and kitchen area and then joined them into the middle where the light is, so we now have four lovely, colourful loops that remind me of my childhood Christmases when Patty would ask whichever boyfriend she had at the time to do the honours with the paper chains. Pleased with my efforts to make our new home feel Christmassy on a budget, I stand back by the door to get a good look.

'Brilliant! Well done, everyone.' I beam, hands on hips as I assess the room. I've put some of the extra paper chains down the sides of the mantelpiece and filled a big glass bowl with some too, to create a colourful red, gold, and green centrepiece for the table.

'Hang on,' Oscar says, lifting himself up from the sofa with a sulky look on his face. 'I made this too.' He holds out a star-shaped lantern fashioned from an old brown paper bag, shells, and driftwood.

'Ooh, that's lovely,' I tell him, taking the lantern, and it really is! Traditional and with a very *cottagecore* vibe indeed. I give his arm a quick rub in thanks, but he shrugs me off and shoves his hands into his pockets instead. 'Where shall we hang it?'

'I know!' Freya squeals excitedly, bouncing up and down on her knees from where she is sitting at the table with a glue stick in one hand and a piece of red card covered in silver glitter in the other. 'We can put it in the window… so Daddy can see it from his shipwreck!'

Olly and Oscar look at me as if waiting for a cue as to how they should respond. A short silence follows and I'm caught unawares again when my eyes suddenly spark with tears. I turn around on the pretext of finding the ball of string on the kitchen counter and use the moment to quickly wipe my eyes on the back of my sleeve before the children notice. Swiftly gathering myself, I then walk over to Freya, who has fallen silent now with a worried look etched on her little face so I give her taut shoulders a comforting squeeze.

'I think it's a fantastic idea, sweetheart. Daddy will absolutely love it!' I smile at Olly and Oscar who silently set about carrying a chair towards the window and taking the string to tie to the star lantern to attach it to the wood at the top of the window frame.

'Oh, hang on,' I says as I remember the little pack of gold fairy lights on a length of wire that are in the bottom of the crafting box and quickly go to retrieve them. Pressing the button on the battery pack, I'm delighted to see that the lights are still working and so carefully entwine them inside the lantern until each point of the star twinkles in a rhythmic sequence.

'Let's turn the house lights off and go outside so we can see what it looks like in the dark?' Oscar suggests, and so we do. He seems to have perked up a bit now; even the scowl has lifted from his lips.

We stand on the wooden path that leads down to the sea and look back at the house. It's four o'clock in the afternoon and already dark, and so we have a glorious view of the golden star shining out at us. Welcoming and warm, the little beach house looks like a happy, bright beacon, dazzling in the dunes by the light of the butterscotch moon.

'Mummy, it looks really pretty,' Freya says, clapping her hands together in glee. 'Like magic and twinkles.'

'It sure does, darling. Magic and twinkles,' I repeat, wrapping my arms around my daughter's back to give her a hug, drawing strength from her childish fortitude and simplistic outlook on life as we stand together for a moment looking at the house from our vantage point on the sand. As we start to wander back inside, it's Oscar who spots Henry hurtling around with a French stick hanging from the side of his mouth and making us all laugh as Oscar tries to catch him.

'Hey, Henry! Come here, boy. What have you got there?' Oscar yells, but Henry is having the time of his life trying to scoff the bread as fast as he can – no doubt thinking all his Christmases have come at once – as he bounces about, speeding back and forth across the sand, sending Freya into a fit of uncontrollable giggles as her two big brothers spread their arms and legs wide in an attempt to corner the very naughty dog. Eventually, Oscar manages to grab hold of Henry's collar while Olly whips the French stick away from Henry, letting him keep the hunk hanging from his mouth. 'Mum, look here, someone has left something on the deck!' Oscar calls out, pointing to it with his foot as he shoos Henry back inside the front door.

'Really? What do you mean?' I call back as I make my way back to the house too, with Freya next to me and Olly close behind with what's left of the French stick in his hand.

'Here! It looks like a present.' Oscar lifts a wooden beer crate up to show me. 'We must have missed it when we rushed out here a few minutes ago.'

'Oh, what a surprise. I wonder who would do such a lovely thing?' I crease my forehead and hold the door open so Oscar can carry the crate into the house and put it down on the table. We all peer inside to see that it is crammed full of goodies – a catering-size box of twenty-four eggs, six plump sausages, butter, jam, milk, tea bags, bread, crisps, cans of Coke, and a small jar of coffee. There is also a white envelope peeping out from behind a bottle of rosé. I open the envelope and read the words on the card inside.

Dear Bridget,

A little housewarming gift to welcome you and the children to Mulberry and to see you right for the next few days until you can get sorted with a big shop. Don't be a stranger and please do pop by the pub soon. Maybe I can tempt you with one of my roast dinners!

All the best and look forward to 'seeing' you at choir practice, with a bit of luck.

Rita (from the pub) x

I turn the card over and see a gorgeous picture of The Hook, Line & Sinker all swathed in pristine sparkly white snow with the stone harbour wall curving to the side and frothy waves behind; the red, blue, gold, and green lights from the boats create a picturesque frame around the central image.

'Well, isn't this the kindest thing,' I say, placing the card on the driftwood mantelpiece above the fireplace as the thoughtfulness of a complete stranger makes me well up all over again. They are definitely happy tears this time. With a sudden burst of bright optimism, I turn around to face Olly, Oscar, and Freya and clap my hands together, remembering the box with my baking staples inside – flour, sugar, cinnamon, dried fruit, ground ginger, and bicarbonate of soda – that I brought in from the car last night. And now that we have some fresh ingredients – eggs, butter, milk, and sausages – I'm going to thank Rita in the best way I know how.

'Who's up for some baking?'

Chapter Four

'F a la la la laaa, la la la laaaaaa!'

The glorious aroma of homemade sausage rolls mingled with the festive mixture of cinnamon and citrus fills the beach house as I bustle about in the kitchen. I'm in my element, checking timings and seeing if the mounds of dough I prepared several hours ago are now proven enough to be ready for knocking back and kneading some more. Louis, the starter, was perfectly prime to do his magic with a multitude of air bubbles popping up to the top, ready to make a lovely loaf or two... or, well, ten to be exact! Plus umpteen gingerbread biscuits and mince pies – I lost count at around the two dozen mark.

I got carried away, as always seems to be the case, and have ended up making far more than we can possibly eat. But tomorrow morning I'm going to drop off a fresh loaf, some gingerbread biscuits, mince pies, and a batch of sausage rolls as a thank-you gift for Rita (by the door of the pub so I won't run into Jack) and the rest of the bakes I can freeze to see us through the Christmas period and into the New Year when, hopefully, I'll find a new job and things will become a bit easier. I'm going to have to budget very carefully if the money in my savings tin is to stretch to buy a couple of presents for each of the children too – I can just imagine the twins' faces if they only have a homemade scarf and gloves set each this year! Plus, they are all going to need new school uniforms and shoes and trainers, and what happens if the crack in the plaster on the bedroom ceiling gets bigger? Or actually cracks right open and caves in on me and Freya while we're sleeping? A knot of overwhelming worry lodges in my throat and so I take a few deep breaths in an attempt to restore some sense of rationality. Maybe Freya and I should sleep on the sofa, just in case? But then I remember that the house is over a hundred years old and it hasn't fallen down yet, so clinging onto this far more sensible thought, I tell myself that it will be OK. It has to be. Besides, there isn't much more I can do this close to Christmas, other than stand in the market square and see if anyone would like to buy a fresh homemade sourdough loaf or a mince pie or two!

I stop bustling.

After tidying my hair back into a bun, I ponder on this idea some more, wondering if it could possibly work? A bubble of excitement replaces the knot of worry as a plan starts to percolate inside my head. Maybe I could give out some free samples to start with, just to see if the people of Mulberry like my bread and then take it from there. Nothing ventured nothing gained and all that. I take another big breath and catch my eye in the mirror above the fireplace, nod to myself, and go back to bustling about in the kitchen.

The fire is lit, using logs from a small pile the boys found outside in the back garden, giving the room a gorgeously cosy crackling atmosphere to go with the Christmas anthem favourites that are playing from the old pastel-pink Roberts radio on the window sill. After making a fresh sheet of flaky pastry, I use the meat from the sausages, together with some caramelised onions and then add my special ingredient mix of Tabasco and Worcester sauce with a handful of chopped dried cranberries. The twins declined to get involved in the baking, but Freya is happily icing some Christmas tree-shaped cinnamon biscuits that she helped to bake and I'm now contemplating whether to make some stollen bites too. I remember packing a packet of ready-to-roll marzipan into one of the boxes from our old kitchen cupboard. I glance at the clock on the kitchen wall, and, on seeing that it's almost eight o'clock, I decide to leave the stollen bites for another day as it's past Freya's bedtime.

'How are you getting on, sweetheart?' I ask her, taking a look at the tray of biscuits that are now coated in thick, gooey green and red swirls of icing with edible, sparkly silver baubles scattered all over them, plus the entire surface of the family-sized dining table. But Freya is beaming and seemingly in her element. Her concentration is very apparent in the tip of her little pink tongue poking out from the side of her mouth as she pours yet more sprinkles into her chubby hand to toss about all over the place.

'Oh, I think you probably have enough of those now. Let's put the sprinkle jar away after you've *carefully* added the ones already in your hand,' I say diplomatically.

Henry is sitting by the side of Freya's chair with an expectant look on his face, ever hopeful of more food falling into his panting wide-open mouth. Anyone would think he was starving and hadn't had his dinner only an hour ago; he clearly has an extremely short memory. 'And I think you've had enough too, you cheeky dog.' I laugh and after helping Freya to wash her hands, chivvy her upstairs to bed.

Having read to Freya and given her a cuddle, we lie together listening to the ebb and flow of the waves. Freya wonders if Santa will also see Daddy's star lantern (as she's taken to calling it now) twinkling in our window, and I try to ignore the ominous crack in the plaster above me. I think it looks bigger than it did before – or maybe my eyes are playing tricks on me... That must be it, surely. I hope so as there most definitely isn't enough in the savings tin to cover the cost of repairing it.

I go back to the kitchen, ready to tend to the dough. Olly and Oscar are flaked out on the sofa, fingers and thumbs skating over the keypads as they play games on their phones, and so I've poured myself a mugful of my warming mulled wine and got stuck into the moment I love most: the kneading and stretching. I slap a big dollop of supple, fresh dough on the floury table top and work it into a lovely, smooth, and very satisfying mound before folding it over and kneading some more. It heals my heart. And nowadays, staying up late and baking is my idea of a fantastic night in. Often, when I can't sleep, when the children are in bed, and when Ted's absence hits hardest, the baking soothes me. It's so relaxing and a wonderful way to while away the time, baking and creating and sifting and sorting through all my thoughts for the day. Rinsing my head – that's what my granny used to say, and it really does feel this way as I'm always refreshed and revived after a baking session. And today is no exception. I'm already feeling lighter and less worried about visiting the pub tomorrow to drop off Rita's thank-you gift. I've also come to the conclusion that… so what if I bump into Jack? I take another big swig of the mulled wine, my bravado building. My brief encounter (pun intended) was a genuine mishap. Anyone could have found themselves locked out and caught short. It really is no big deal. And besides, he shouldn't have been mooching about in the dunes at that time of night in the dark. Ha! Yes, I will tell him this if I do bump into him and he brings it up. And then to go and mention what he saw to everyone… Well, it's not exactly a very gentlemanly thing to do in any case. Yes, I'll tell him that too!

As I'm pondering all the possible scenarios, my mind wandering further and further until I've built the incident up into a full-blown novella – or melodrama, more like – inside my own head, my mobile rings. It's Lorna, so I quickly wipe the flour from my hands on my apron and swipe an index finger across the screen to take the call.

'Only me! How's it going, Bridge?' Ah, I smile on hearing the cheery, familiar tone of my best friend's voice as I wander over to the comfy armchair by the crackling fire. I can always rely on Lorna to brighten my day.

'Hiya. It's going OK, thanks,' I tell her, not wanting to start with the fiasco from last night.

Then, on realising that it's absolutely roasting here near the fire, and with the heat from the Aga at the other end of the living area too, I grab a cushion and my coat and bobble hat from the hook by the front door so I can take the call on the deck outside where there's a semblance of privacy and the refreshing, salty sea air to cool me down. I can't wait to hear all about Lorna's online date last week – a guy called Liam that she has only met a few times in real life as he lives at the other end of the country and is a doctor so works all kinds of unsociable shifts at the local hospital, but with whom she has now shared several candlelit cook-along dinner dates. Lorna is a big fan of long-distance dating, declaring it so much easier than all that palaver of finding a new outfit, getting her face on and curling her long hair extensions and then having to toddle out on public transport in the freezing cold. Plus, the money she used to spend on taking a taxi home at the end of the evening now pays for a very nice steak dinner with a bottle of her favourite prosecco too.

I plop the cushion on the wooden step and, after retrieving my mug of hot mulled wine from inside, I sit down and welcome Henry to snuggle in beside me, seeing as he's scooted out of the door too.

'So how are things with Liam? And what are you cooking this week?' I ask her, grateful for having the foresight to grab a blanket too as it's a touch chillier than I had anticipated out here and there's a plump slate-grey sky that looks perfectly ripe for snowfall.

'Ooh, it's going brilliantly. We watched that cosy,

Christmassy film *The Holiday* together last night – him on his iPad and me with his lovely face beside me on the screen of my laptop while I curled up on the sofa with a blanket and an orange truffle Baileys. So civilised. And warm! And effortless – I didn't even need to get ready as I've found the perfect 'au naturel' makeup filter so I looked all glowy and gorge on the screen. And it's Taco Tuesday this week so I have that to look forward to as well,' she says, pausing to draw breath.

'Ah, of course. I forgot about Taco Tuesday,' I laugh, recalling the last Taco Tuesday. 'Just make sure you don't blow the poor guy's head off this time, yes?'

'Hardly! And that was a genuine mistake. How was I to know it was just a teaspoon of chilli powder to go in the actual chilli mix and not a tablespoon? They should put the actual word in full and not an abbreviation: *tsp* could easily mean tablespoon and not teaspoon!' she declares, still clearly exasperated about getting it so very wrong. Liam had bitten into his taco and then suffered a choking fit resulting in him having to cut their dinner date Zoom call short while he rinsed his mouth out with milk. 'But yes. I will be careful this time.' And she laughs some more. 'Anyway, so tell me about this new man you met! The one you showed your knickers to, you saucy minx! You've only been there five minutes.'

'Pardon?' I splutter, startling Henry who sits bolt upright and proceeds to panic pant right into my face, his

hot breath whiffing of dog treats and curling into spirals of mist in the cold air. I pull him back in beside me and give him a reassuring cuddle so he settles once again with his head resting on my lap like a lovely hot-water bottle keeping me warm. 'How on earth do you know?' I ask, lowering my voice on remembering that Freya is asleep in the bedroom directly above my head and I don't want to wake her up.

'Ah, nothing gets past me!' Lorna laughs. 'Your gorgeous little girl told me this morning. I called and she answered your phone, and then said that you were busy downstairs, so of course we had a very lovely little chat.'

'Hmm, I bet you did!' I tut and shake my head. I might have known. Freya loves talking to her Aunty Lorna and will chat away to her about all kinds of nonsense and stay on the phone for hours at a time, if she could. 'And what else did my gorgeous and extremely chatty child tell you?'

'That you met a man and showed him your knickers, and something about the knickers having a big hole in them.' Lorna does her famous, filthy-sounding, throaty laugh.

'OK, it wasn't *that* funny!' I tell her, but can never resist when Lorna gets going and so I end up laughing too as I explain what really happened.

'So was he fit?'

'I didn't hang around to get a good look, to be perfectly honest,' I whisper.

'Why on earth not?' Lorna asks, baffled.

'Well, his face was covered in a scarf for starters. Not to mention it wasn't exactly the most appropriate moment to be checking out a guy. Besides, you've got Liam now so you don't need me to talent scout for you anymore,' I say, inwardly sighing with relief.

Lorna has been quite relentless over the years in her pursuit of the perfect partner, not wanting to end up on her own with a pile of cats to keep her company, as she has been known to bemoan.

'Don't be daft, darling. Liam is deffo in the keeper category. I meant for you, my love.' Lorna's voice softens and sounds hesitant as if she is feeling her way. Not that it's the first time she's broached the subject of me meeting someone else, but, well, I never really know what to say in response, and so I don't answer. But this doesn't stop her from grilling me for more clues. 'So you must have something else about him to share? Freya said he sounds like Derek. Is he Irish?'

'Yes. He is. His name is Jack, if you really must know, and he works in the pub,' I reluctantly share.

'Ooh, so you do know who he is then... OK, hang on a mo, I'll get my wine and then you can tell me more.' Lorna's voice is all perky and full of enthusiasm again. A short silence follows. 'Right, I'm back. So, come on, how old is he?' she quizzes.

'Oh, stop it!' I shake my head. 'I've told you all that I know.'

'Well, that sounds good. When you will see him again?' I swear I can hear Lorna holding her breath in anticipation of my answer, as if this is so much more than it really is when it is absolutely nothing at all.

'Never… with a bit of luck.' I take a sip of mulled wine, making a mental note not to let my phone out of my sight from now on as I know what Lorna is like. She'll never let this go – not if she thinks there's a chance of me meeting a man. She's as bad as my mum, always trying to pair me up with someone, but I don't want to be paired up with someone. Certainly not a complete stranger with a torch strapped to his head who clearly doesn't know the meaning of the word 'discretion'. I know Mum and Lorna mean well. They've both told me many times that they just want me to be happy and not spend the rest of my life on my own, and that Ted wouldn't want this for me either. But the truth of it is that I'm still in love with my husband and quite certain this will always be the case.

'OK, I can take a hint. I'll shut up about him now, but it would be nice to have someone to cuddle, yes?'

'I do have someone to cuddle. I'm sharing a bed with

Freya, remember? And Henry loves nothing more than jumping on me at every opportunity!' I can't resist.

'You know what I mean...' Lorna says gently.

'Sure. And in any case, I don't need a man to make me happy, to "complete me".' I do quote signs in my head as I say the words to my best friend, but then wonder if I've gone a bit too far as all the time I've known Lorna, she's always been keen to find the perfect guy. It has consumed her at times, as if she isn't enough on her own and nothing else really matters.

'Of course you don't! It's just nice. It makes life a bit sweeter when you have someone special to share it with. But then we're all different, and, let's face it, some people are a pain in the backside and don't enhance your life whatsoever. Being single, casual dating, one-night stands... it all has a lot going for it too! Whatever floats your boat, as my old nan used to say.' And we laugh.

'This is true,' I smile. I should have known my lovely friend wouldn't take offence. Lorna is a proper Pollyanna who always sees the positive and really does just want everyone, including herself, to be happy.

'So what's it like there in Mulberry in the middle of winter?' She laughs, changing the subject.

'It's cold. And very dark,' I tell her, 'but calm, you know? The wind has settled this evening and I'm sitting here on the deck looking out across the beach towards the waves that are quietly lapping back and forth and the air is comfortingly still. And the sky is studded with stars. And I can see the twinkling lights in the distance – on the boats in the harbour. It's picturesque, like living inside a beautiful painting,' I gush, getting carried away.

But as I glance around, I see my new surroundings as a newcomer might – through tourist eyes, if you like. And I realise just how glorious and special it really is. For a moment I can't even remember why Ted and I moved away all those years ago. We must have been mad. Or maybe we simply wanted a change. Perhaps that was it. We were young and naïve, and we thought the grass was greener everywhere else. There wasn't a lot to do in Mulberry, other than work the boats, and fishing had never really been Ted's thing. There was Carrington's department store of course, which was where lots of us locals worked, and there used to be a casino and a couple of exclusive restaurants to cater for the visiting glitterati when the cruise boats docked, but when cruising stopped being fashionable all of that faded away. So other than the tourist shops and the pub, chip shop, and ice cream parlours, or the hotel on the outskirts of Mulberry, there weren't so many opportunities. Plus, when you're young and have grown up in a small fishing village where everyone knows everyone and you're keen to spread your wings and venture further afield, then the lure of a big city is very appealing indeed.

'Oh, it sounds idyllic. And romantic. And what's the house like?' Lorna asks.

'Very small. And falling apart in places – to be honest it needs completely renovating, but it's a million times better than being homeless and I'm grateful for that. Plus it's wonderful being on the beach.'

'I'm so pleased for you, Bridge, and relieved that you and the kids have somewhere to live. I just wish it wasn't so far away,' she sighs.

'I know. You'll come and visit us soon though, won't you?'

'Try and stop me. I'll be there as fast as my size-four feet can carry me!'

'We're going to miss you this Christmas,' I say, feeling a wave of sadness for the Christmases we used to have before Ted died. Lorna always throws a big party a few days before the main event on Christmas Day for all our friends, and the children too who end up falling asleep, top-'n'-tailing in her superking-sized bed. But I'm determined to make Christmas as good as it can be for me and the children.

'And I'll miss you too,' Lorna says.

'Won't you be lonely?' I ask. Her mum and dad have booked themselves onto a Mediterranean cruise this Christmas and it's Liam's turn to work over the holidays, so he's going to stay at the hospital just in case the weather is extra cold and icy which could make it tricky for him to travel on the roads at short notice if there's an emergency. 'You could always come here. You're welcome any time – it's small and you'd have to sleep on the sofa, unless you want to put up with Freya wriggling around in the double bed all night long, but we'd make it fun,' I offer.

'It really suits me fine being here on my own. Don't get me wrong, I love our big, crazy Christmas parties together but I'm so over sitting in the overheated conservatory with Mum and Dad on Christmas Day and them going on and on about me settling down and giving them a gazillion grandchildren! You know what they're like. I love them dearly, but it'll be a whole lot easier chatting to them online and having a laugh in the family quiz instead, with my magnificent all-day cheeseboard right by my elbow and a large salted-caramel liqueur hot chocolate in my hand.'

'Well, if you put it like that!' I grin, picturing one of Lorna's legendary cheeseboards laden with every kind of cheese there is, plus grapes, sticky figs, olives, chutneys, crisps, peanuts, pitta bread, and crackers, not to mention the gin bar she'll have set up on her bar cart – a beautiful glass and rose-gold art deco affair that she found in a vintage shop many years ago. Ted and I helped her wheel it all the way home one Christmas Eve before cleaning it and stocking it with a selection of cheap wine and cans of beer and crisps; it was all we could afford at the time but it turned out to be one of the best Christmases ever.

Feeling a sudden pang of nostalgia for those happy days gone by, I take a sip of mulled wine and resolve to think of the present moment and the different type of Christmas I have to look forward to in this cosy little sunshine-yellow house on the beach with my three children. To be perfectly honest, last Christmas without Ted was bleak. Of course I put on a brave face to disguise the hollow feeling inside, mostly for Freya's sake. The twins pretty much retreated into their phones for comfort, but it's different for Freya as she lives more for the magic of the moment, even if Daddy was 'having his turkey dinner in the sky' as she declared last year before insisting we all lift our glasses of apple Shloer up in the air to toast him. It had been poignant. And sad. And I had cried in the bathroom later on with my hand clamped over my mouth so the children wouldn't hear my great gulping, snotty sobs. But I had also wiped away my tears and smiled and had a lovely little chat with Ted inside my head, just to let him know that I missed him, and loved him, and held him in my heart. And that I wished he had told me where the bloody Christmas tree was stored! It hadn't been in the loft, or behind my old bike in the shed, and so I'd had to drag a brand-new actual real bushy pine tree all the way home from the market down the road because Freya had begged me for it and it had been too big to fit inside the Mini. I was sure Ted would have laughed at that! And it made me feel happy to think of him and how he reacted to stuff. It keeps him alive – at least in my head… and my heart.

'I do! I most definitely do put it like that,' Lorna says, bringing me back to the moment. 'And you'll join in the online quiz, won't you? Please,' she pleads, 'I need you and the boys on my team for all the gaming questions that my nerdy brother-in-law is bound to include.'

'Yes,' I laugh, 'don't worry. I'll prise Olly and Oscar's phones from their hands and we'll be there at the kitchen table all squidged together around the laptop screen with a mountain of mince pies on the go,' I assure her.

'Excellent! We'll make it a very merry Christmas.'

'Yep, we will indeed. Oh, I'd better go. I can see Mum's name flashing on my phone,' I tell her, looking at the screen where the suntanned, smiling face of Patty is displayed. Dressed in a fuchsia-pink and white floral-patterned floor-length kaftan over a teeny tiny metallic-silver bikini, Patty is strutting up and down and fluffing her big hair by her floodlit outdoor swimming pool like she's Beyoncé or someone, about to go on stage. There's even a hazy plume of steam rising from the water in the pool amidst the leaves of the palm trees that are rustling in the background.

'The sexy Irish man! Who is he?' Patty announces as a conversation starter and my mouth jettisons open.

There's a beat of silence. My mind boggles as I take a big breath and reunite my jaw with the rest of my face.

'Er... um... what? Who are you talking about?' I splutter in a daze before mumbling, 'The barman?' My mind races all over again, wondering how on earth could she possibly know all the way from the Costa del Sol.

'A barman!' She's clearly aghast that he's not a pilot or whatever. 'Hmm... But how come I have to hear about your new man from my six-year-old granddaughter?' She bats her baby-doll lash extensions at me. Honestly, is there nothing that doesn't escape my mother and my best friend's notice? And most likely the whole of Mulberry, via the local barman, these days? And since when did my love life, or complete lack of it, become everyone else's business too? I left my phone unattended for twenty minutes maximum and now my mother is completely miffed at having missed out on all the salacious news as she envisages her daughter in a full-blown romance with a complete stranger. I sink the last of my mulled wine and prepare to put my mother straight, wondering how long it will be before Patty's hopes are dashed and she starts rhapsodising about the benefits of a premium subscription to Sugar Daddies R Us...

Chapter Five

I turn the key and try the car's ignition again. Still nothing.

Taking a deep breath, I murmur a little prayer, coaxing the Mini to liven up and actually flaming start its own engine. I've packed a loaf of potato and rosemary sourdough, six sausage rolls, some gingerbread biscuits, and a homemade Christmas card back into the wooden beer crate for Rita, plus there are half a dozen extra white sourdough loaves in the car too. Because when I went to store the surplus bread in the freezer, I completely forgot that there isn't actually a proper freezer at all! Well, there is an ice compartment with a little door at the top of the fridge, but it's not even big enough to fit one whole loaf of bread inside it, so I ended up cutting a loaf in two and cramming it sideways into the tiny space. I then stowed the other half, plus two other loaves I've kept from my big baking batch, in the bread bin, which will have to do us for now. And I'm going to see if any of my neighbours might like a nice homemade loaf. It will be a great way to share some samples and you never know, there might be a few people who would like to buy a loaf from me next time. It would be a shame to see the extra loaves go to waste but there is no way the children and I can possibly eat that much bread between us before it goes mouldy. Plus, the loaves are still lovely and warm as I ended up baking through the night. And to while away the time as I waited for the loaves to cook in the Aga, I decorated a pile of white paper carrier bags that I found inside my crafting box – presumably intended as goody bags, left over from one of the children's birthday parties – with a festive holly stencil to put the loaves, mince pies and gingerbread biscuits in. Nicer than handing over baked goods without any wrapping.

'What's wrong with the car, Mummy?' Freya asks, from the back seat.

'It's old and knackered, that's what!' Oscar huffs, 'and embarrassing too.' He glances sideways at me as if it's all my fault. Oscar won the toss of the coin with Olly to decide who got to sit in the front seat as Henry is staying at home alone. He was last seen snoring contentedly on his bed by the Aga, absolutely worn out and wet through after his hour-long run across the sand dunes and in the sea earlier this morning. I managed to coax the three of them into going for a walk with me after breakfast and so we wrapped up warm and filled a flask with cinnamon hot chocolate and then trekked a good few miles – hard work in the sand – before finding a sheltered spot in amongst the dunes where Freya and I could sit and enjoy mugs of the warming hot chocolate while the boys skimmed pebbles in the sea and Henry bounded around biting the frothy white tips of the waves and generally living his best beach life. It was a nice sight to see the boys off their phones for a change and spurring each other on to see who could skim the furthest and manage not to get caught by a particularly big wave. I think Oscar at one point even cracked a smile which was also nice to see.

I try the ignition a few more times.

'It's no use, Mum, I don't think it's going to start,' Olly says sympathetically.

'So how will we get to the harbour then?' Freya asks with a wobble in her voice.

'Well, sweetheart, we'll have to walk, I guess.' I glance in the rear-view mirror to see my daughter's head dip and her little shoulders droop in defeat. Like Henry, she is clearly exhausted too. Maybe the walk earlier was too much for her after the long car journey to get here. On top of all the packing and the change to her routine with the move and everything, it's no wonder. But how else am I going to get the thank-you gift to Rita and see if anyone would like to sample the surplus bread?

'I'm not walking all the way to the pub!' Oscar protests again. 'It will take ages and I've already done at least *twenty thousand* steps today.' He pushes the sleeve of his jacket up and dramatically checks his Fitbit just to be absolutely sure he's right to revel in his own indignation. I sigh inwardly, wishing I was prone in a bubble bath behind a locked door with a baking book in one hand and sticking two fingers up for zero fucks with the other. But I do care. Of course I do. But I also wish Oscar would stop moaning and think of the impact his carry-on is having on the rest of us. I can see Freya is fretting and Olly is closing his eyes and puffing out big gusts of air in exasperation.

'Oh, come on, Oscar, that's a bit of an exaggeration,' I try, but already know that I'm on to a losing battle with two of my three children already despondent at the prospect of another lengthy walk.

'And then we've got to schlep all the way back afterwards and that's hardly exciting. Didn't you say it would be an adventure coming here? That it would be *really* exciting?' He actually rolls his eyes in contempt at me. 'Why did we even come here if it's just going to be a

load of old walking about on the beach. It's boring A F.'
Oscar crosses his arms now and shakes his head, and, to
be honest, I can kind of see his point as the thought of
walking all the way to the pub and back doesn't excite
me either. But I think I have a rescue plan.

'I know! Why don't we walk and—'

'Oh, Mum, please, no!' Oscar groans, followed by an
enormous huff of despair. Then he clutches his head in
both hands as a grand finale.

'OK, I know we're all tired, but listen, just hear me
out.' I swivel in my seat to look at Freya and Olly in the
back and then to Oscar, making sure I have their
attention. 'Come on, it might work. Here's the plan: how
about we use my bike and take it in turns to ride it? We
can take the coastal road instead of trekking across the
sand, and then at least that way we won't all have to
walk all the way....'

I grin hopefully and lift my eyebrows... a little bit
manically, I realise on catching sight of my wide-eyed
face in the rear-view mirror with its overly arched
eyebrows and unruly curls springing out from
underneath my bobble hat. But I'm so blooming keen to
keep them all going because if I don't or can't... then
what will become of us all? At the end of the day, I have
to be the rudder of our little family ship and keep us all
afloat. They've already lost one parent, so if I give up,
where will that leave them? In the apartment above

Patty's 24hr Nail, Tanning & Karaoke salon on the main party strip in Benalmadena? Silence follows as they all look at me. After what feels like an eternity, Freya pipes up with a solemn, tentative look on her face.

'My feet can't reach the pedals on your bike!'

Silence follows.

My heart goes out to my daughter, who is now frowning, her bottom lip wobbling with the effort of keeping all her emotions from spilling over.

More silence follows as I gather myself and think of the right words to say.

'I know, love. And it's OK,' I quickly reassure Freya, reaching around the back of my seat to give her mitten-clad hand a pat. 'It was a silly idea. Tell you what, I'll try the car one more time and then if it doesn't work we'll call it quits and go back inside and we'll just have to… well…' I pause in an attempt to think of more right words to say to buoy the three of them back up. 'We'll just have to eat all the bread ourselves!' I settle on. 'Yes! That's what we'll do. We will live on sandwiches.' I nod resolutely. 'And toast… for the next fortnight! Slathered in your favourite strawberry jam. Or chocolate spread. With sprinkles too,' I promise, wishing with all my heart that Ted was here. If only to lighten the mood or to help get the car going or to take the box to Rita and share the bread out so the children didn't have to go too… and everything would have been fine. And I know it isn't a massive thing, but having a purpose today felt good; sharing out the samples was something to focus on. But now I just feel deflated. Jaded. And a bit wired from lack of sleep from having been up baking for most of the night. We all sit in silence for a few seconds more until, eventually, Freya pipes up again.

'Please can I have squirty cream on top of the chocolate spread and sprinkles on my toast?' I can't help smiling as I nod like an absolute loon in sheer relief. At least one of my children is still talking to me!

'You can have whatever you like, my love.'

I turn around towards the steering wheel and with a hopeful heart I try the engine. And keep trying. It makes a metallic churning noise, over and over and over until eventually Olly gets out of the back seat, closes the door behind him, and then opens my door.

'Mum, it's not going to start.' He puts his hand on my shoulder but I brush him off and keep trying again and again. Each time the futility of the situation increases but I can't seem to stop myself. It feels as if a mini tsunami has been bubbling inside me, as if the dam that's been keeping it at bay is about to burst wide open and there isn't anything I can do to stop it. The mounting surge of panic because I can't make this happen is overwhelming. I give the key another turn. Still nothing.

'MUM. Please,' Olly says, more insistent this time. 'It's not going to start.' He gently takes my arm and goes to help me from the car. And in this moment as I turn and look up at my son with his blonde curls and kind face, just like his dad's, I can't keep it together any longer and the smile slides from my face. God, I so wish Ted was here. Just for a moment. I'd give anything right now for it to happen.

I grip the steering wheel and dip my head to hide the hot, salty tears of frustration that spring from my eyes and plop into my lap. It's been just over a year since Ted died and this hasn't happened in absolutely ages. I wonder if it's the move. They do say it's one of the most stressful things to do, but I thought coming back here, with all the marvellous memories that Mulberry holds, would be a good thing for us all. For the children. But right now it feels like I've messed everything up.

Nobody says a word.

And now I can hear Freya crying too and it breaks another little piece of my heart. I scrub at my face with my coat sleeve, take a deep breath, and get out of the car, mustering up every iota of stamina within me to keep on keeping on as I fix a big smile firmly in place. Olly steps forward and gives me a hug before pulling the back door open to let Freya out of the car. Moments later, Oscar is by my side too with a worried look on his face – but at least he isn't scowling at me for a change. Silver linings and all that. We all hug it out.

'I'm so sorry,' I say, stepping back and rubbing

Freya's shoulder as she slips an arm around my waist and squeezes herself in tight to my hip. Olly and Oscar are standing opposite us now with their hands pushed deep into their coat pockets to keep warm. 'Come on, let's all go inside.' I go to walk towards the beach house, keeping my arm around Freya's shoulders.

'Mum, hang on.' It's Oscar who speaks this time. And with a tentative look on his face he steps forward and made a suggestion. 'You could go on your own! We know you really want to do this…' He lifts his eyebrows and shrugs as if feeling his way into this next stage of maturity.

'Oh no, I couldn't do that, love.' I shake my head. 'Absolutely not.'

'Why not? We can look after Freya. We'll just watch TV or something. A Christmassy film! And you'll only be an hour or so,' he says, sounding very pragmatic and not his usual surly self at all, and this momentarily discombobulates me. But then on second thoughts he is a teenager and isn't it their job to have mood swings mingled in with glimmers of the grown-up adult they are going to become? I make a mental note to try to remember this from now on.

'Yes, Oscar's right. Why don't you go on your own? You can cycle there and back, no problem.' Olly looks at his brother and for once the twins seem to be on the same page as they both nod in agreement before fixing their gaze on me. Even Freya leaves my side and goes to snuggle in between her two big brothers.

'Yeah, and you really want to share out the loaves and biscuits and stuff... spread some Christmas cheer! You've made gift bags and everything for them. It would be a shame to waste all that,' Oscar adds, lifting one persuasive eyebrow.

I look at my three children. The two boys who look like grown men, their height and build giving them the appearance of twenty-somethings; the pair of them even have the shadow of stubble on their chins and top lips. But they are only fourteen. And I've never left them all at home alone before. Partly because they were barely thirteen when Ted died, and partly because, well, it changed everything. Grief made the twins regress emotionally and for a long time they seemed somehow much more vulnerable than their friends, the other boys their age who weren't going through a grieving process.

'So what do you reckon, Mum?' Oscar picks Freya up and she flings her arms around his neck. I open my mouth and close it again as I study the three of them, pulling my top lip down over her teeth and biting into it as I try to decide. I'm not even sure what the law says about children being left at home alone, but have a vague notion of it depending on maturity... And the twins are mature; they can be trusted. Yes, Oscar is a bit moany and petulant sometimes, like most teenagers when the hormones take over, but he's being very sensible now, standing here caring for his little sister, and astute. And he's right; sharing the loaves and baked goods is important to me. A stepping stone almost. A purpose, to take me from being insular and spending another day consumed with thoughts of Ted and wanting to stay in the safe bubble of my little family, to perhaps… thinking about something else. Yes, it felt good to have a plan this morning. Of course, I don't want to risk offending anyone by offering them free bread in the street as if implying they are in need. Perhaps Vicar Joe in the sailors' church could help me find out which of the residents in the neighbouring cottages around the harbour would like to try some freshly home-baked bread and gingerbread biscuits.

'Mum, do you think you could decide, like, soon? Now, even? Because we're all freezing out here,' Olly says, rubbing his hands together and stamping his feet on the concrete of the parking bay.

'Yes! Sorry. OK. Right. I'll go on my own.' I nod, very decisively, before I change my mind. 'But only if you're all sure that you'll be all right?'

'Of course we will,' both boys chime in unison.

'And if we're not… say the house catches on fire or one of us falls down the stairs then we'll just phone the emergency services… and then Childline!' Oscar quips, tickling Freya to make her laugh.

'No!' I yell, flinging up a hand in panic, 'don't do that.' I have visions of social services turning up and taking the children away, but then what if something does actually happen? Ted may have been outside in a field when he died, but everyone knows that the majority of accidents occur in the home so now I'm not sure what to do. My world view feels distorted by what happened in the past… and I wish it wasn't all on me. And now I feel cross, angry even, with – dare I feel it or even admit it? – I feel angry with Ted for blooming dying and changing everything! Arghhhh! I close my eyes and inhale through my nose, willing myself to stop procrastinating. And, more importantly, to stop blaming my poor dead husband.

But then it's all decided for me.

'Right, it's settled then. Come on, guys.' Olly turns around and after chivvying his brother and sister to follow, the three of them start walking back to the beach house. I open my mouth to say something more, but what can I really say? It seems my children have taken control. And despite my reservations, a small smile of pride forms on my face as I tilt my head to one side, do a little nod, and mutter to myself, 'Fair enough'… then immediately dash after them.

'OK. But do not open the door to strangers and do not light the fire or go in the bedrooms in case you really do trip on the stairs on the way down and definitely do not let Freya have one of those Chupa Chups lollies she loves in case it comes off the stick and gets lodged in her throat. And on that point, do either of you boys know about the Heimlich manoeuvre? Basic first aid? Or what to do if someone gets burnt? Drop and roll. DROP AND ROLL! DROP AND ROLL!' I bellow after them like some kind of complete loon. I'm practically gasping with the exertion of wading through the sand and barking out all the safety measures and so I feel even more exhausted by the time I get back to the beach house.

After letting them all into the house and reiterating the lengthy list of rules again, I check that the boys have full batteries and sufficient credit on their phones which they are to use *immediately* to call me if they need absolutely anything at all. But they are not to go gaming on their phones for the whole duration I'm away and must keep a proper eye on Freya. I give each of them a hug and a big kiss, ignoring the boys who immediately pull faces and swipe their cheeks with the backs of their sleeves. I fill Henry's bowl with water just in case they forget to check it and Henry overheats and dies of dehydration or whatever. I look in on the guinea pigs too – water, bedding, food, check! And then, when I'm satisfied that I've managed to pre-empt and put a plan in place for every possible scenario or situation that could possibly pose a problem or cause harm to the three people I love with all my heart, I wheel my big old rickety bike out from the garden. I'm going to store all the bags of baked goods in the basket at the front, and strap Rita's thank-you gift box on the back with the bungee cord from the boot of the car, and then I will be on my way to spread a little Christmas cheer…

Chapter Six

Half an hour later, and I've arrived in the old market square by the harbour wall in the middle of Mulberry which is looking gloriously festive with all the twinkling lights looped between the lampposts and a giant Christmas tree in the centre decked in red and green tinsel. It would have taken far less time to get here if I hadn't had to stop to take a breather in the dunes at the side of the coastal road and then walk the last leg of the trip, pushing the bike alongside me with one hand, the other clenched around my mobile phone as I'd refereed a dispute at home over who was allowed to have the last extra-large sausage roll. In the end, I suggested they slice it into three equal parts which seemed to satisfy everyone and I was able to end the call and breathe a sigh of relief. I then continued wheeling my bakery load, knowing my children are all still alive and seemingly thriving, if their bickering is anything to go by. But I've quickly come to realise that cycling when you have a wicker basket full of bread by the handlebars and a wooden box on the back of a cumbersome and very heavy old bike is actually exceedingly hard work, especially when you've been up all night baking and it's a trillion years, at least, since you last did any form of proper exercise. I make a mental note to rectify this right away with a mixture of scheduled bike rides and beach walks from now on, vowing to become a vibrantly athletic outdoorsy and sunny beach-living kind of person by the time the weather warms up and the summer months come along.

I came back to Mulberry to put my family back together again and generally feel happier and hopeful, after all, and that includes my own wellbeing too. Maybe I could even grow my hair and let it get naturally bleached in the sun for a proper surfer-girl vibe like it used to be when I last lived here in Mulberry all those years ago. In the months after Ted died, my hair fell out in alarmingly big tufts – stress and grief the doctor said at the time – and it's only in the last few months or so that my hair has begun to feel stronger again. Much like myself to be fair. And being here in the market square, I already feel more invigorated and uplifted as I look around at the narrow cobbled alleyways that run in between the stone cottages where I once used to hang out on balmy warm evenings with my school friends.

I think of those days, carefree and continuously coated in sand on my bare legs, the taste of salt from the sea air on my lips as I enjoyed a two-scoop ice cream cone of cherry and bubble gum flavours with my friends Eddie, Georgie, and the gang, and then of course with Ted. I feel a tingle of optimism and for the first time in a very long time I feel like I can breathe. Properly breathe. I stand for a moment and look around at all the familiar sights, at the scene of my childhood and teenage years, and with every inhalation I draw in the memory of how it used to be. How I used to be... happy and hopeful, and not with a millstone of grief cloaked around me making everything feel harder. And it feels like a fresh start, a new beginning, and I really hope I'll be able to hold on to this feeling. Closing my eyes momentarily as if to bank the thoughts, I take a big breath and nod to myself, inwardly promising, 'onwards and upwards, happy and hopeful' over and over like a little mantra to keep me going as I carry on pushing my bike across the cobbled square.

Moments later, and breaking my reverie, an enormous seagull swoops down and goes to peck at a loaf that's peeping out from underneath the pink gingham tea towel I used to cover the basket. I stop pushing and wag a gloved hand in the air to shoo the seagull away.

'Bloody seagulls!' an old man in a thick overcoat and a navy fisherman's peaked cap bellows from over by the bus stop, remonstrating with his knarled wooden walking stick. 'They'll have the skin off your head too if you don't keep an eye on them.' And he lifts his cap to reveal a bald head with a large square plaster stuck on the top. 'Minding my own business I was when the biggest seagull you've ever seen swooped down and tried to swipe my hat right off my head,' he tuts. 'A harpoon! That would make them scarper but we're not allowed to cull them these days.' He shakes his head and pulls a face as if he thinks the whole world has gone completely bonkers. 'Who are you then?' he continues. 'Not seen you around here before on that big old bike of yours!' He points a bony finger in my direction.

'Oh, I'm Bridget.' I smile and walk towards him.

'How do you do!' He nods in greeting. 'They call me Mack… on account of all the mackerel I caught back in the day. When the bloody seagulls weren't trying to steal the catch from the ice box on my boat, that is!' he adds, before doing a big harrumph.

'Nice to meet you, Mack,' I say, thinking how nice it is

of him to chat to me, even if he does seem to be on a downer over the seagulls. But then I remember how much of a nuisance they can be – I lost a whole bag of deliciously salty chips one time when a seagull swooped down to steal one and ended up ripping the paper bag from my hands and scattering all the chips across the sand. Of course, all the other seagulls had then immediately swooped and demolished the chip feast in record time. And not forgetting the bra in the boat incident too! Plus, seagulls are very noisy when they gather on the roof tiles. I remember that too from my childhood – Patty bellowing about the blasted gulls and their incessant squawking when they woke her from her beauty sleep at six in the morning. But despite all that, for me, the sound of seagulls caw-cawing on a summer's day is always a lovely reminder of fun times and carefree days here on holiday so I guess I'm very happy to overlook their bad habits.

'Likewise. And why have you got all that bread?' Mack uses his walking stick to point towards my bike. 'Are you the one that keeps clearing all the shelves in the bakery section at the supermarket in Stoneley?' He eyes me suspiciously.

'Oh no, I—' I start, but he huffs and keeps on.

'I'm on my way there now… if the bus ever turns up. Been here half an hour already. And I waited over an hour yesterday – the bus got delayed on account of all the ice up there on the steep cliff road. Bloody perishing it was too. And a waste of bloody time as there was no bread left by the time I got there. Not that I'm complaining when there's them that have nothing at all, but it's the highlight of my day having a nice bacon sarnie for my tea.' He shakes his head.

'Ah, yes, I know what you mean. You can't beat a bacon sandwich,' I say cheerfully, but my heart goes out to the old man as he stands in the little wooden bus shelter with his empty nylon shopping bag. He's clearly cold with his purplish blue mottled cheeks and shoulders hunched over in an attempt to keep warm after waiting for so long. Reaching into the basket, I lift the tea towel away and pick up one of the carrier bags, figuring I've found my first person to offer a sample of the surplus bread to.

'Would you like to try one of these?' I wheel my bike over to the bench at the end of the bus shelter and after resting my bike against it, I pick up one of the bags and go to hand it to him.

'Oh no, I couldn't take it from you.' His bushy monobrow creases in concern at this unexpected turn of events. 'I didn't mean anything by it… you know, about you taking all the bread off the supermarket shelves.'

'Please, it's for you. And it hasn't come from the supermarket. I baked these loaves myself. Last night,' I tell Mack, seeing the mixture of hesitation and suspicious interest in his rheumy old brown eyes.

'Last night?' he lifts the monobrow and then falls silent for a few seconds as if mulling over what to make of this useful piece of information, before deducing, 'So you're a baker then? I know they make an early start in the middle of the night.' And motions with his head, this time towards the basket where the rest of the loaves are poking out from the tops of the bags. 'We used to have the baker's shop over there by the harbour wall, but that packed up when old Jilly retired.'

'Oh, no, I'm not a proper baker. Not really. But I'd like to be, as I love to bake,' I reply, remembering Jilly's bakery from my childhood, the delicious aroma of fresh baked bread wafting in the air as I used to run to catch the bus on my way to school every morning. 'And, well, I got a bit carried away and ended up overdoing it and now I have all these loaves and festive biscuits and mince pies so I've come to see if anyone would like to try them.' I point to the basket.

'Well, I never…' he declares in astonishment.

'You'd be doing me a favour.' I motion with my head towards the bag dangling from my woolly-gloved index finger. After hesitating some more he eventually takes the bag.

'But what about your husband? What does he say about you being up all hours? Mind you, I'm sure he's delighted to have lots of lovely fresh bread for his bacon sandwiches.' The old man's wiry shoulders bob up and down as he chuckles to himself. And just like that, my grin vanishes and I glance away as the bubble of optimism, the happy and hopeful feeling from a mere moment earlier, fades away.

A beat of silence passes between us until Mack asks, 'You OK, love?'

'Oh, yes, sorry, it's—'

'No need to apologise, dear. You've done nothing wrong... that I know of! Quite the opposite in fact. You've made my day... if you're sure I can have this bag of treats,' he eyes it keenly, still perched there on the bench.

'Yes, absolutely. I hope you like the bread... with your bacon. And there are some Christmas biscuits and a couple of mince pies in the bag too. They're very nice warmed up with a dollop of cream on top and a mug of tea too.' I grin, trying to perk back up and figuring he looks like a tea-drinking kind of man.

'That's a girl!' he smiles at me encouragingly. 'Can't beat a bacon sandwich. Or a mince pie with a good, strong cup of tea. Builders, with a tot of rum! None of this Darjeeling or Earl Grey for me. Tastes like perfume all that,' he shakes his head and frowns, clearly aghast at the mere thought of a fragrant tea. 'Anyway, shan't you hold up any longer. Your husband will be wondering where you've got to.'

I wave and go to walk on but then stop and turn back. After taking a breath I open my mouth and gently say, 'My husband died,' and as soon as the words leave my lips a pleasant feeling of relief radiates through me as if the pressure of keeping it inside has been released. It's very freeing. But the feeling is closely followed by a little surge of panic, because it's all well and good being honest and open and unburdening myself and all that, but what if Mack is taken aback by my bluntness or is shocked and I've upset him. People have varying responses to death, as I know very well, after my experience with the woman in the school playground that time. But it's all OK as Mack gives me a kind look, his weathered face seeming to soften as he responds.

'My wife died too.' And his hunched shoulders actually drop a good couple of inches as he straightens his back and appears to light up on telling me.

'Oh! I'm very sorry,' I reply, unsure of what else to say, but then quickly add, 'What was her name?'

'Dotty. Well, Dorothy really, but we all called her Dotty. She preferred that – no airs and graces, she used to say.' Mack's whole demeanour brightens and lightens as he speaks about his late wife. He straightens the collar of his coat and the peak of his cap and I catch a glimpse of a much younger, less dishevelled and more distinguished-looking man as he carries on talking. 'It was ten years ago now, in her sleep. Very peaceful it was and she had a good innings. It was just before her eighty-fourth birthday and we had sixty years together all told, so I'm not complaining.' He shakes his head, stoically. 'But you know, it feels like only yesterday that she was still with us. Right here in the bus shelter. Not far from where you're standing now, love. And she'd be gassing on about something and nothing and telling me off for not listening. She could talk the hind legs off a donkey for a good half hour without drawing breath, my Dotty. I'd never get a word in even if I had tried. And I don't mind telling you that it used to do my head in. But it's a funny old thing as it's what I miss the most about her these days… her going on and on and on about a load of old nonsense – the weather, the news, the price of fish, or some bargain or another she had her eye on in Carrington's. That's the local department store.'

'Oh yes, I know it. I used to work there years ago, as a Saturday girl!'

'Did you really?' he says, astonished. 'Well, I never… Our Dotty did too. Haberdashery. But she packed it in when we got married. That was the way of it back then. This would have been way before your time. Yes, she loved having a mooch around the store, stopping for a gasbag with her friends. Or she'd be updating me on the goings-on with the girls in her knitting group. I used to drive her over to Hettie's House of Haberdashery in Tindledale for a knit and a natter – this was before the old peepers got bad and I had to let the car go. Not safe for me to drive anymore, they said, with dodgy eyesight, and they'd be right as I flaming well reversed into my own garden wall the last time I drove the car. Bloody great big flint rock wall that's been there hundreds of years and I didn't even see it.' He pauses to shake his head in disbelief. 'But it'd be smashing to hear our Dotty gasbagging again. Life and soul of the party, she was, as they say...' And with a faraway look in his eyes Mack smiles and nods at me.

'Ah, I would have liked to have met Dotty. She sounds wonderful and like she was great company. But I really hope I haven't upset you,' I say quietly.

'Not at all!' he replies, and a wide smile spreads across his face. 'You know, you're the first person who didn't know our Dotty to have asked me what my late wife's name was, so you've made my day twice over now.'

'Well, in that case, I'm very glad I did ask as it's been lovely to hear about Dotty.'

'She would have liked you. Warm and friendly with no airs and graces, and tells it how it is... It's not easy to open up about the painful stuff, but you just did, so good on you, girl.' He tips his head as if to underline the words. 'So what was your husband called?'

'Oh, his name was Ted... Edward,' I correct, and nod right back, feeling comfortable for the first time to chat to someone who didn't know Ted without fear of having a wobble. It's as if I've joined some kind of club where Mack and I instinctively know the rules and so can relax and chat freely.

'And how did he die? He must have been a young'un... with a smashing wife like you, if you don't mind me saying so. It's not often you see a cheerful face these days, positively glowing you were when I first saw you pushing your bike across the cobbles. And not many youngsters want to talk to the old folks like me. And a baker too... Your husband was a very lucky fella!'

'Thank you,' I smile. 'It was very sudden. Ted had an undiagnosed heart condition. He was playing football one minute and then...' My voice tails off.

There's a moment of silence and then Mack declares, 'Well, that's a bloody shame! The poor bugger.' And for some unknown reason this tickles me and I can't help laughing.

'Oh dear, I really shouldn't...' I start trying to explain, but the look on Mack's face is an absolute picture. He seems completely aghast on Ted's behalf for pulling the short straw in the life and longevity stakes.

'Ah, you've nothing to be sorry for. It's better out than in! I reckon your Edward would sooner you be laughing about him popping off early, instead of moping about forever.' And this just makes me laugh even more.

'You know, I think you're right!' I want to chat more as I'm having such a good time with Mack, but then in the distance I see the bus chugging around the corner by the harbour wall. 'I've not laughed this hard in a very long time. It was very nice to talk to you, Mack.' I point to the bus in the distance.

'You too, dear, but I'm not traipsing all the way to the supermarket now – no need! I have bread and a couple of lovely-looking mince pies, thanks to you,' he says, peeping inside the bag, 'and I've had my daily chat. A proper good one too – it was nice to talk about Dotty and hear about your Edward. Keeps them alive, don't you think?'

'Yes,' I agree, 'it's been really nice to talk about him and to hear about Dotty and have a little laugh too.

'I try to make sure I speak to someone every day. That's why I go to the supermarket, you see,' Mack tells me as he waves the bus on. 'It can get very lonely being on your own. Not good for the old head, and a please and thank you at the till can make a world of difference.' He taps the peak of his cap and gives me a wry smile. 'Anyway, cheerio. It was very nice to have a proper chat with you, Bridget,' he says, lifting his walking stick. 'And I'll look out for you when I'm here at the bus stop next time.'

'When will that be? I could pop by and bring you another loaf if you like?' I quickly offer, figuring it could work very well with my plan to do more exercise with regular bike rides.

'Every day, dear.'

'Well, I enjoyed our chat too and if you ever don't fancy waiting around for the bus then I could drop a loaf off to you at home, if you like. Do you live nearby?' I ask. And it's true; I've thoroughly enjoyed chatting to Mack and the thought of having someone else to bake for feels wonderful.

'That would be marvellous! I'm in Seaview Cottages, the end one over there with the sky-blue front door and the Smuggler's Rest plaque next to the letterbox. If it's not too much trouble… I'll pay you of course. Don't expect something for nothing!' Mack says resolutely, and points again with his walking stick to a row of three brick-built cottages at the far end of the square near where the harbour wall peters out and becomes the long stone cobbled pier that leads out to sea with the lighthouse on the end.

'Oh yes, I know the Seaview Cottages,' I nod, pleased to have found my first customer. 'So I'll pop by in a few days' time to top you up with another loaf. It'll be my pleasure, Mack!'

'Then I'll look forward to it. I'll even put the kettle on and make a mug of tea to warm you up.'

And then we both go our separate ways. Mack with a spring in his step, I'm sure of it, as he's whistling and swinging his bag of treats, which in turn lifts my heart and makes me smile as I hop onto my bike and ride across the square towards The Hook, Line & Sinker to drop off Rita's gift box.

Chapter Seven

'Bridget! How nice to see you again.'

It's Rita, standing on the path leading up to the solid, old wood-panelled door of the pub with a shovel of grit in her hands. There's an iron anchor on a chain mounted on top of a big wooden flower trug, the other end crammed full of vibrant, crimson-coloured festive flowers. The pub sign that hangs from a rod attached to the white weather-boarded wall is swaying gently in the breeze and the blue-and-white striped awning is rolled out making the pub look lovely and cosy, especially with the orangey-golden glow of the flames in the inglenook fireplace that I can see through the mullioned windows.

'Take it you've come for the choir meeting details,' Rita beams, giving the shovel a hearty jiggle to sprinkle the grit along the path to prevent ice from forming and becoming a slip hazard.

'Oh, er...' I start, leaning my bike against a wooden barrel that's been repurposed as a table in the front beer garden on the beach; the top has a hole drilled in it for a parasol to provide shade in the summertime. And suddenly, a velvety, warm, glowy feeling floats through me on remembering when Ted and I would sit here in the beer garden on a summer's evening sharing a bag of crisps and a pint of refreshing Mulberry Brew, a locally produced cider that comes in lots of delicious flavours. Pear was my preference. Apple was Ted's, and so we used to take it turns to choose. This was when we were students at the sixth form college and working in Carrington's at the weekend, so we could probably have afforded a drink each to be fair, but it seemed nicer, more intimate – romantic even – to sit side by side and share as we gazed out to sea and watched the sun set over the waves. Together. Me feeling happy to sit and glow in contentment as Ted took his sips and then sketched cartoon caricatures – grumpy-looking seagulls strutting around or an exuberant dog running on the beach. Sometimes Ted would sketch me, with an exaggerated grin or doing kissy lips as I held onto the rim of my sunhat to stop it from blowing away.

I sigh inwardly, and like how the memory of those days feels different now, nice and warm, and not sad...

Chatting to Mack seems to have shifted my ever-changing grief onto a very welcome new setting. For now. It might be temporary, but I'll take it! I know what a fickle friend grief can be. One minute it's wrapped around you like a cloak, then it's by your side and other days it's walking far behind you keeping out of the way, only to be perched on your shoulder the very next day. But at least it's a start, and just what I hoped for in coming here.

'Fantastic!' Rita says, bringing me back to the moment. She puts down the shovel and fishes in her coat pocket. 'I knew you'd come around. You look like a sea shanty kind of woman.'

'Oh! Er, do I?' I ask, baffled and wondering how she's come to this conclusion, and also if I have the heart now to tell her again that singing really isn't my thing and that I haven't come here to sign up to sing sea shanties at all. But it's too late now as she looks so delighted to have recruited another singer for the choir and so I figure it really wouldn't hurt to give it a go. I might even enjoy it – a singalong while I'm waiting for Louis, the sourdough starter, to do his magic and make the dough rise and while the boys are gaming on their headphones and Freya is in bed... it could be just the thing. And it's not as if I have any kind of social life these days. But it could be a great way to meet more of the community here in Mulberry. Maybe I'll make some new friends, seeing as my old ones that were here have all moved away.

'Yes, hearty and rosy-cheeked… and you've got a very lovely smile,' Rita says kindly. 'Have you got your phone on you? I can text the details to you.' She taps on the screen of her mobile. 'Oh dear, the battery is flat. Not to worry, I'll go and find a piece of paper and fire up the laptop to get the info that way. Shan't be long.'

She bustles off inside the pub, so I start unstrapping the bungee cord to remove the wooden beer crate from the back of the bike and take another look around. It's funny how I never really noticed until now just how old this pub really is. There's even a boot scraper and a metal basket on the wall where I imagine hay used to be stored for the horses. In *Bridgerton*-times, perhaps. I can just see the Duke of Hastings riding his stallion across the undulating grass-topped cliffs overlooking Mulberry-On Sea, with the wind beneath his billowing jacket and a devilishly brooding twinkle in his deep chocolate-brown eyes. Or smugglers – there have always been rumours dating back to the seventeenth century, of contraband tea, tobacco, silk, lace, and spirits being brought ashore from fishing boats under the darkness of night and hidden in the caves that run underneath the coastal cliffs.

We did a school project about it, and our whole class of ten-year-olds went on a field trip and almost got stranded on the beach as the tide came in faster than our teacher anticipated when we were in the caves with our clipboards 'looking for clues' of smuggler activity. Many of the quirky white weatherboard houses around the harbour have secret trapdoors and storage chambers under the floorboards where precious goods were hidden, or even the smugglers themselves when the tax officers rode into town. I found it fascinating learning about the winding cobbled alleyways and streets that run along behind the seafront being awash with sailors and 'ladies of the night'. I can even remember my school friend, Eddie, cocking a cheeky eyebrow and pushing his hand up to ask our teacher to explain this further. She told him he had, 'done enough research for today, thank you very much!' followed by a hurried chivvying of us on to the site of the old Ship Inn that used to stand on the corner of Dolphin Street. It's been converted into luxury getaway apartments now. But centuries ago in those smuggling days, the landlord was suspected of being the gang ringleader and ended up brawling with a sailor when he was cheeky to his wife over a supply of the finest silk and lace.

It's funny how certain things from childhood stick in your mind. Interesting too, to grow up in a seaside town steeped in history. I used to feel a part of it, intrigued by the lives of all those people that had lived and loved in Mulberry-On-Sea all those years ago before me. And suddenly it feels exactly right to have returned. My love may have left, but the children will be happy here, I'm sure of it... and they will grow up knowing where their dad came from and, hopefully, forging their own connections with this wonderful little seaside town. I smile and drink in a big lungful of the wonderfully restorative, salty sea air as if to seal the deal.

As I turn to place the crate on the beer barrel table top, Sinead, the Irish wolfhound, suddenly comes hurtling from around the side of the pub. Oh no! I put the crate down and shove the bungee cord into my pocket and swiftly adopt a brace position, determined not to get bowled over this time and end up writhing around in the dunes again. But it's no use. Like an Olympic sprinter going for gold, Sinead has done a galloping bodyslam and is now standing on her hind legs with her front paws pressed squarely on my boobs, her tail wagging and her doggy breath near singeing the peach fluff right off the side of my face, it's that hot.

'Oh, good girl. Come on now, get down,' I say, too lamely, and so of course it makes absolutely no difference at all. In fact, Sinead thinks it's a cue to cavort some more and goes to slobber at my face. I turn my head sideways and just as I manage to lift her paws off me and gently go to ease her front legs away from me, she jumps down and grabs at the end of the bungee cord, that's hanging from my pocket, and hurtles back off across the pub garden, twice around the beer barrel table taking my coat pocket, that's got tangled up in the hook, along for the ride. And moments later, after losing my footing on an icy patch of wet marram grass, I'm bowled over. Again. Face-planting the sleet-sodden grassy mound of sand, prone, with Sinead dragging me around as I wrestle with my own coat pocket, desperately trying to unhook it so I can stand up and resume a modicum of normal behaviour before Rita returns and believes that everything Jack has been saying about seeing me in the sand that time is true. I'm a flaming liability. Because who in their right mind makes a habit of writhing around on a sandy beach all the time? Once is explainable, but twice is just daft! And highly embarrassing.

'Sinead. SINEAAAAAAD. For the love of God!'

Oh no! No. No. No. No. Noooo.

My heart plummets.

I know that accent.

And my cheeks scorch red hot. Flaming typical. How on earth am I going to front this out? So much for my plan to be bold with Jack and tell him it's no big deal and he shouldn't have been mooching about on the dunes in the dark, blah blah blah, like he was the last time this fiasco unfurled. Because here I am again. On the sand scrabbling about like some kind of fruitloop. For crying out loud! I stop struggling and let Sinead tear my coat pocket away, setting the hook of the bungee cord free so that I can scrabble up into a standing position. My legs are slip-sliding like Bambi on the slippery marram grass.

'You OK, Bridget?' his sing-song Irish accent bellows, and I'm one hundred percent sure there's a hint of relish mingled in there too. I wince at the familiarity. He knows my name... But of course he does; I told Rita, who must have told him, and I bet he's told everyone else with his big, gossipy blabbering mouth that I see is curled up into an enormous grin, as I tentatively take a look to see where his voice is coming from. Jack, dressed in a navy slim-fit shirt that accentuates his broad, muscular shoulders is leaning on crossed forearms at an open window just above the swinging pub sign, pushing his dark curls away from his face which, I very begrudgingly have to give him credit for, is very easy on the eye. In fact, now that I can see his whole face, he's actually quite hot. If you like that kind of thing, of course! Dark, handsome, strong jaw and that same devilishly brooding twinkle in his amber eyes, framed with dark lashes and brows that I was pondering on earlier for the Duke of Hastings. Although the Duke would never have the same sardonic grin on his face that Jack has stuck on his right now.

'Yes...' I clutch the top of the beer barrel to steady myself. '...thank you. And,' I gasp, trying to catch my breath, 'you should keep that dog under control,' I instruct, grabbing my bobble hat that has fallen off onto the sand. I brush myself down and shove my chestnut curls back into a scrunchy swiped off my wrist and then start to walk off.

'Er, you forgot something!' Jack yells, still killing himself laughing. I stop walking. After inhaling though my nostrils and swallowing hard, I momentarily close my eyes, open them, turn around and smile sweetly as a cover for my frustration and overwhelming desire to stick a loaf of bread on the hook of the bungee cord and lasso it up to that window to swipe the smile right off his cheeky face.

'What's that then?' I say, flinging a hand on my hip with far more cocky sass than I intended. I cringe. Next he'll be telling everyone how rude I am, and the people pleaser part of me absolutely hates the thought of that.

'The bike!' And he nonchalantly lifts an index finger to point towards it, doing that tilting head thing again as if my discomfort and dishevelled look are giving him maximum amusement.

'Hmm... yes, I knew that!' I grab the bike and go to march off again, which is no mean feat when you're trudging like a Sherpa through thick sand with a heavy load by your side.

'And that!'

I stop for a second time.

And turn around.

His face is full-on trying not to crack right up and he

even lifts a balled fist to cover his mouth to try and hide the fact as he whirls the pointy index finger again.

'The crate,' he nods. 'I saw you put it on top of the barrel table.'

So he was actually spying on me!

'Hmm, if you must know, it's a gift for Rita. I made some bread and baked treats for her because she's kind and thoughtful and considerate towards others. Unlike you!' And this time I muster up every iota of energy within me and power off like a motorised dune buggy lifting my bike up off the sand for added speed.

And I definitely do not look back.

Absolutely not...

Chapter Eight

Vowing to myself not to give Jack and his super sardonic smile another nanosecond of my headspace, I walk on for a bit, counting units of five as I inhale in and out in an attempt to gather myself and soothe my wounded pride. I'm frustrated with myself for caring about what a complete stranger thinks of me, and hate that however hard I try, I seem unable to not care. I'm still simmering when my mobile rings inside my good pocket; the ripped one is now flapping about in the breeze by my jean-clad thigh with the matted fleece lining of my coat hanging out all straggly and vagabond-like as I walk alongside my bike. I look like a right state and can wholeheartedly see why a workman giving the street lights a lick of paint gives me a wary up and down look as I cross over the road.

'Yes!' I snap to take the call, after pulling a woolly mitten off with my teeth and pushing the phone up to my ear, distracted and only just managing to resist doing a big huff too as I swiftly shove the mitten into the basket beside the bags of bread.

'Whoa! You OK, hun?' It's Patty, and it instantly irritates me that she's talking to me like she's a twenty-something millennial and I'm her best gal pal on a night out, and not a sixty-two-year-old mother to me, her daughter, at all. The one who is desperately trying to get herself together and make a happy, and very normal life for her children so they can have a lovely, cosy Christmas and live happily ever after. Honestly, my mother is about as sensitive and self-aware as a sledgehammer at times, with her oblivion to what's going on outside of her own bubble. I'm properly fed up now as the feeling of optimism from earlier fades in a flash.

'NO! Actually, Mum, I'm not all right.'

'What's happened?' she asks, and her voice softens in concern, which in turn softens my heart and I take a beat to swallow down the irritation and start again.

'I'm sorry, Mum. I'm just not having a very good day. Well, I was until a few minutes ago. But not now…'

'Oh, hun, what you need is a n—'

'Mum, please, I don't need a new man,' I jump in, determined to fend off another one of her Sugar Daddies R Us promo chats.

'Actually, Bridget, what I was going to say is that you need a nice treat. I've been thinking… and, well,' she pauses for effect, 'I've decided that I maybe should have made a little bit more effort to help you out with the deposit for a new home when you were so desperate and one step away from ending up on the streets with your babies and all your pets—'

'Oh, Mum, forget it, it's done now,' I jump in again, smarting at her overly dramatic depiction of my circumstances, like it's Dickensian times and I was one step away from ending up in the workhouse with my poor little Freya having to feed filthy old bed sheets through an old-fashioned mangle, while the boys go barefoot as they're shoved up chimneys to earn a single crust of bread to eat for the whole day. 'Honestly, we're all OK. We have a roof over our heads,' *just about*, I mutter to myself, thinking of the cracked plaster on the bedroom ceiling, 'and the little beach house is actually very lovely. Cosy and comforting, and it's on the shore right by the shipwreck where Te—'

'Yes, yes, I know all that, sweetie. But what you really need… is a new wardrobe!' she announces, sounding like a game show host delivering the details of the jackpot prize. 'A boost! And there's nothing better than a little makeover to make a girl feel brand new.'

'Oh, Mum. It's a nice thought,' I try again, politely, knowing that it's futile to protest outright. When Patty puts her mind to something then there really is no stopping her. She's like a lioness circling a baby goat in one of those David Attenborough wildlife shows, waiting for the optimum moment to sink her teeth in, lock her jaw and latch on until the little goat concedes defeat. Poor Derek never stood a chance; she was all over him within a hot minute of his first swipe right on the dating app. 'And I'm very grateful, Mum, but any money coming my way is going to need to go towards getting the Mini fixed, as there's obviously something seriously wrong with it. The car wouldn't even start today! And the beach house needs patching up, the garden clearing, the bedroom ceiling looking at by a professional, and there will be school uniform to buy, for when the children start their new schools, not to mention Christmas presents for them all too, of course.'

I inhale sharply and let out a long breath as the enormity of it all hits me. What was I thinking, putting just a few pounds away here and there? I should have saved much harder when I was still working the café. The savings tin is never going to be enough to cover it all, and selling the odd loaf here and there won't even pay for one pair of plimsolls for Freya, let alone the man-size trainers and smart black shoes that the boys need. No, I need to come up with a much better plan. And fast! Or I'll be gluing the soles of their old school shoes together like they did in the olden days at this rate.

'Yes, yes I get all that, Bridget,' Mum carries on. 'But sometimes in life you have to stop and take a breath and just put yourself first,' she tells me in a sing-song voice. 'And like I said, my treat,' she adds, and I wonder if she even heard me mention the car or the beach house or any of the other far more pressing priorities that really need to come before me having new clothes. 'So I've sorted it all out for you. Pop along to Carrington's and go to the customer services desk and they will take care of you. Five hundred pounds is there with your name on it! Well, not exactly your name – it's in my name, um… oh, what I probably really mean is … that it's Derek's name on it, as my credit card is maxed out at the moment. Just a temporary cash flow sitch! Because the fabulously festive garlands I had to have to go around the salon doorways were far more costly than I had anticipated. But you can't put a price on panache, can you, darling? Not when it comes to business.' She pauses to do a tinkly laugh and then I can hear what sounds like her taking a noisy slurp of a drink – her signature pornstar martini cocktail, no doubt. 'But Derek doesn't mind. You know he sees you like a daughter and—'

'Five hundred pounds!' I parrot, completely flabbergasted. 'I can't spend five hundred pounds on a new wardrobe.' My mind is racing as a fresh wave of panic pours over me. 'I'm ever so grateful, but I couldn't possibly—'

'What, is it not enough?' she says, sounding alarmed and then, 'I know fashion costs, but, babes, you can't put a price on looking your best either. And if you want to get set up with a new life like you told me you do, then a capsule wardrobe is an absolute must. It's an investment in *you*!' She expels a big puff of air as if to punctuate her point. 'Honey, I feel for you, I really do and I wish I could be there to give you a hand in picking out a few dazzling pieces to mix and match, but you know it's not all that easy for me to pop back and forth now with the Brexit thingamajig. Besides, Christmas is our busiest time of year. Everyone needs nice nails and brows for the festive seas—'

'Mum, thank you. It's very generous, but, honestly, if you're just doing this to help me meet a man...' I venture, as it's flaming obvious that this is her intention. And I feel let down. What hope is there if my own mother thinks I can't be happy unless I have a man in my life? '...then it's pointless. I'm—' But she cuts me off before I can tell her about the fiasco with Jack and that the last thing I need in my life is a man – not one like him, or any other man for that matter, having a laugh at my misfortune. No, I have enough to deal with without factoring in a new relationship that could end up in more heartbreak, and that wouldn't be fair on the children either. But why am I even thinking about this right now? I want to get on and share out the sample bags of baked treats and get back to the beach house for a nice sit down and a Baileys hot chocolate by the fire.

'Oh, babes,' Mum says, 'don't give up hope. Even the other Bridget got her man in the end. A decent one too. A lawyer! Fancy that. A Colin Firth lookalike – younger, of course,' she clarifies. 'And you'd like that. You know how you love all those period dramas! And there's still time, sweetheart... You're only thirty-four so if you get a wiggle on then you could even have another baby, if that was a stipulation for him. You don't want to leave it too late and end up with the menopause being a deal-breaker for him on the baby front.' I actually move the phone away from my face like they do in the movies and stare, aghast, at the beaming face of my completely bonkers and quite frankly, raving fruitloop of a mother as my mind is blown. Is she for real? I must have been teleported back to the 1950s or something! And with Christmas garlands around doorways, and all this talk of festive nails and brows being the number one priority, life sure is very different in Patty World!

'Mum, I have to go. Olly is calling me and I've left the children home alone for the first time and... well, bye. Love you!' And I press to the end the call, wincing at the white lie coming from my mouth, because Olly isn't calling at all, but... for crying out loud. And for the second time today! FML, indeed!

But then, hang on... A sudden thought comes to me. I

can't help wondering if it's possible to buy a load of clothes and then get a cash refund that I could use to pay to fix the car or call in a builder to check out the crack in the bedroom ceiling. Or maybe they sell school uniform now in Carrington's and I'm suddenly desperately racking my brain trying to remember if they used to have a uniform section or not. They'll definitely sell Christmas presents though, so I could use the money for that instead of buying clothes for me.

Arghhhh!

Now I feel dreadful for having such devious thoughts and being such a terrible and ungrateful daughter. And poor Derek... Well, not exactly poor – he's a multimillionaire – but that's not the point. Patty is still playing him like an absolute giant fiddle.

With all these thoughts muddling around inside my head, I send a text to Olly's phone to check that the three of them are OK. He replies within moments.

Yes, all good. Freya is happy playing with Snuggles and Chewy. Can we eat the rest of the mince pies?

I laugh to myself as I type a big YES and add some kisses and a few sideways laughing emojis. I'm just about to put my phone away when it pings again.

You are such a mum!

Charming! Well, silly me. I forgot that only old people and uncool 'mums' use the sideways laughing emojis – according to my teenage twins – and so I make a vow to try harder next time and leave off the emojis! Or perhaps I should just carry on using them to provide the boys with even more laughs. But I'm happy that the children seem fine and now that I have a bit more time and several bags of bread still to distribute, I decide to make my way over to the sailors' church, Our Lady Star of the Sea, to see if I can find Vicar Joe. Maybe I could say a little prayer for Patty while I'm at it because she seems to have lost all grip on reality these days...

Chapter Nine

It's like turning the clock back as I cycle along the promenade with the peppermint-green railings, past the bandstand and streetlights with their magical gold-lit bunting, reminiscing and remembering this exact same cycle ride on the way back from the beach in the school summer holidays.

On a whim, I decide to do a little detour past the sea cottage that Mum and I lived in before I moved away and she relocated to Marbella. The winding, hilly street is flanked on both sides with a higgledy-piggledy collection of little multicoloured pastel cottages and is so narrow that I have to dismount my bike and push it instead, or risk riding into a pedestrian or an oversized lorry trying to navigate the tiny tight bends. I smile on seeing so many cheery and twinkling Christmas trees in the small bay windows, homemade holly and crimson berry wreaths on the front doors, and make a mental note to see if I can find somewhere to get a tree to have in the beach house. The children will love it, Freya especially, and we can bake biscuits and make silver foil-covered stars on string to hang like baubles as we do every year. Yes, this could be a very cosy Christmas indeed, if I put my mind to it and come up with more ideas of how I can organise things on a tight budget. And don't let the likes of Jack get inside my head or my mother take over with her completely bonkers bananas world view.

I walk on and turn into the street where I used to live and see that it hasn't changed one bit. It still has a narrow pavement lined with terraced sea cottages with a variety of suitably nautical name plaques on the front doors. Some of the houses have little shingle-covered front courtyard gardens with a length of chunky rope looped between wooden posts at the perimeter. There are even a few houses styled with sailing-themed items: an old wooden oar stood at a jaunty angle by a door with Christmas lights twirled around it; the helm of a pirate ship propped against a plant pot; signs saying 'Gone to the beach'; and many seashells and pastel-coloured starfish made from plaster too. Slowing down, I reach my old childhood home and smile at the lovely, cheerful yellow front door, now with a jaunty red-berry holly wreath in the centre. The door was a boring black when

Mum and I lived here. It had a brass mermaid door knocker that I used to love and I'm pleased to see that it is all shiny and still in place.

I decide to leave one of my sample bags of baked treats by the door as a gift and gesture for old times' sake. I've put a little Christmas card inside with my details on so they can get in touch if they like my bread and would like to buy some more. But just as I go to place a bag on the step, the front door opens and it startles me. I end up dropping the bag and one of the mince pies tumbles away. Luckily, it remains in the wrapper and so, after propping my bike against a nearby lamppost, I quickly pick the mince pie up and go to pop it back inside the bag. On second thoughts, better safe than sorry, the last thing I want to do is give a complete stranger food poisoning or whatever from a pavement germ on the wrapper and end up with a bad reputation before I've even got to the part where people pay to buy my bread, so I shove the mince pie in my good pocket instead.

'Oh… um, so sorry to bother you,' I gabble as I gather the bag back up and end up dangling it from my outstretched hand. There's a man standing in front of me wearing a red-nosed Rudolph Christmas jumper with a white baby's muslin slung over his left shoulder and a harried look on his face.

'No worries. I saw you through the window,' he says,

glancing down at the state of my forlorn coat, his eyebrows knitting in wariness, before quickly motioning sideways with his head towards the house, 'so thought I'd catch you before you knocked on the door and woke the baby up – just got him down to sleep, you see.' He shakes his head and sighs. 'But I think you must have the wrong house though – we're not expecting any deliveries. Try next door; I know they're partial to a fish and chip supper delivery, but hang on... oh dear, that looks like bread you have there.' A beat of realisation flickers across his face. 'Ah, you're not delivering from the fish and chip shop at all, are you?' He rubs a hand through his already messy hair. 'Never mind me gassing on, I've been up all night – teething!' He then quickly adds, 'The baby. Not me.' He grins bleakly and shakes his head.

'Oh dear, I know what that's like. I have twin boys and a girl.' I nod and smile sympathetically as I lower my arm so the bag is now dangling by the side of my thigh.

'Do you really?' he says, smiling now and seeming to relax a little as he puts his hands on his hips. 'We have twin girls and a boy – he's the one teething. The girls are older, fourteen, and a whole different ballgame.' He rolls his eyes.

'Ah, yes, same age as my boys.' I grin and reciprocate the same look of mutual understanding and empathy as a parent of teenage twins. But then feel I'm doing my boys a disservice as Olly has been fairly happy since we got here; even Oscar has been less sullen. Maybe the change of scenery and fresh start is having a positive effect on then. Or maybe they're just volatile teenagers and will be back to being lazy and moody tomorrow. Who knows! That's hormones for you… the roller coaster ride of surprise that keeps on giving.

'No way!' he laughs. 'I'm Ian, by the way, and I'm guessing you must live locally, with the roads all iced up and nobody getting in or out of Mulberry? I was just listening to the radio and heard that the main road in is a complete no-go now with all the black ice. Treacherous apparently, and one of the supermarket delivery trucks has had a skid and is now blocking the top of the cliff road completely, so nobody is getting to Stoneley anytime soon. The recovery truck can't even get up there to tow it away.'

'Oh, I didn't know that. I've just been cycling around after coming along the coastal road,' I jump in, wishing I hadn't bothered him now as he's clearly wired from lack of sleep.

'Never mind. We'll just have to rely on the food hall at Carrington's, I guess. "Where life is sweeter…"' he beams, referring to the shop's strapline. 'So, whereabouts do you live? Don't think we've met before and I know most people around here.'

'Oh, I live further along on the beach, in the yellow

beach house on the end. But I used to live here, actually.' I point to the house behind him and grin tentatively, hoping he doesn't wonder what on earth is going on with me turning up at my old home like this.

'What *here*, here? As in, this actual house?' He widens his eyes and broadens his grin.

'Yes.' I nod. 'It was a long time ago. I grew up here, and, well, I moved away and now that I'm back I thought I'd pop by to er, um… well, I'm not really sure, to be honest.' I find myself waggling the bag up in the air again as the words, 'I made too much bread and so I've got some sample loaves here if you'd like to try one,' come tumbling out of my mouth.

'Oh,' Ian does a double-take as if trying to take it all in and work out exactly what's happening here. 'Well, even nicer to meet you in that case,' he says, slowly. A short silence follows.

'Would you like some bread?' I ask awkwardly, and then promptly follow it up with, 'Sorry, I sound daft, don't I? What I meant to say… is that I was out delivering my bags of surplus bread and thought I'd come and see what my old house was like now. I was about to leave a gift for you on the doorstep and leave quietly without disturbing you.' I smile gamely. 'But I dropped the bag, and, well, here we are.' I bob from one foot to the other wishing I'd just stuck to the plan and gone straight to the sailors' church. I could have given all the bags to Vicar Joe to distribute – he's bound to know who'd like them – and I'd be on my way home now and not bothering poor Ian who hasn't had a decent night's sleep in ages, it would seem.

'And then I stuck my oar in by pulling open the door,' he laughs, seeming not to mind my intrusion and so I let out a little sigh of relief.

'Phew! I am sorry, though. I probably shouldn't have come here and—'

'Of course you should have. We love living in this house and being so close to the beach. We moved here a couple of years ago and so I can imagine you have wonderful fond memories of when you lived here too. I would invite you in to have a nose to see what we've done to the place, but probably shouldn't, what with the baby sleeping.'

'Ah, it's very kind of you, but I couldn't intrude. It's lovely that you're happy here too and you're right, I do have some wonderful fond memories. Anyway, I should probably get going. My brood are home alone for the first time today and will have eaten their way through the contents of the whole fridge and all the kitchen cupboards if I don't get back soon,' I explain.

'God, yes, what is it with teenagers and this obsession with snacks,' he says, laughing and shaking his head. 'In my day we used to have a bit of toast and be quiet about it, but they make such a song and dance of it with their

Insta-perfect styling – I found one of my girls doing a full-on film shoot with a tripod and lighting too – of her breakfast cereal with a side of blueberries!' He laughs and I nod in agreement. 'Well, it was nice to meet you.'

'You too.' I go to walk away but then, remembering the bag still in my hand, I turn back. 'So would you like to sample the bread? I baked it myself – white sourdough. But I shan't be offended if you say no. There are some biscuits and mince pies... um... *one* mince pie,' I correct, 'inside the bag too. To help spread a little Christmas cheer,' I explain.

'Oh, well, if you're sure?' he eyes the bag keenly. Smiling, I nod to confirm. 'But let me pay you. I can't take a lovely-looking sourdough loaf from you for free,' he adds. I hesitate, feeling a bit awkward now as I've just rocked up here and I didn't exactly envisage selling bread door to door like a travelling salesperson. It seems a bit cheeky to take a payment, but then I think of Freya's plimsolls and... but no! I quickly decide that it's better to offer the sample in the hope of building future custom.

'This one is on the house, as they say, and if you like it... I'd appreciate you coming back for more. Deal?' I grin, wishing my cheeks weren't on fire as I catch him glancing down at my raggedy coat pocket.

'OK,' Ian says, slowly, 'then absolutely. It's very kind of you. I love a mince pie so I'll be sure to keep that for myself before my lot get their paws on it and start setting up lights and tripods just to take a picture of it. And Pearl, my wife, will be over the moon. She loves a nice sourdough loaf and was only saying yesterday that she couldn't get hold of one in the supermarket as the bread section had been completely wiped out with everyone stocking up for the holidays. And now with the road blocked, I guess she won't be getting back to the supermarket again anytime soon.'

'In that case, enjoy!' I hold out the bag for him. Taking it, he smiles and nods his thanks and then, as if something has suddenly come into his head, he says, 'Hang on... You're not Bridget by any chance, are you?'

'Yes, I am! Sorry, I didn't even tell you my name. How do you know?'

'Amazing. OK. Hold on a sec. Stay right here, I'll be back,' he says excitedly. After putting the bag on the carpet in the hall by the inside of the door, he dashes off back into the house, returning moments later with a folded piece of paper in his hand. 'I think this letter belongs to you!'

'Oh, what is it?' I ask, baffled, as I take the folded piece of paper from his outstretched hand.

'Pearl found it under a floorboard in the bedroom. Maybe it slipped down through one of the cracks. It's from someone called Ted and it's addressed to Dear Bridget... to you, and, well, sorry, we didn't mean to be nosey or anything, but it's a love letter. That's why we kept it safe. Pearl's an old softy for stuff like that and so...' He shrugs his shoulders before pushing his hands into his jeans pockets. 'It's nice for you to have it back, I guess.'

'I... *really?*' I start, stunned, and find myself clutching my mitten-clad hands around the letter and pressing it to my chest like it's a precious, priceless piece of art or something. Which it actually is to me, as I can see one of Ted's pencil doodles – a beating heart with a smiley face – on the corner of the piece of paper.

'I don't know what to say.' And I truly don't as a sudden surge of joy choruses into my heart. A moment of silence descends until a woman's voice calls out for Ian and he waves goodbye before thanking me again for the bread and closing the door behind him. I manage to mutter a dazed, 'Thank you,' and a 'I can't tell you how much this means to me...' as I stow the letter carefully away inside my good pocket for safekeeping. And after climbing back onto my bike, I ride away with my heart still soaring at the prospect of reading Ted's words and seeing one of his cartoon caricatures once again.

Chapter Ten

B ack home, and after feeding Chewy and Snuggles and helping Freya clean out their hutch, I've come out onto the deck with a mug of my warm mulled wine, toast, a blanket, and a hot-water bottle to sit in a deckchair and watch the plump sun set over the sea as I rest my aching legs and sore backside from all the cycling I did today. The sinking sun is a gorgeous, tawny colour making the sea shimmer into a liquid rainbow of red, gold, and green that is completely mesmerising and very restorative indeed. I inhale the exhilarating salty night air before taking a big bite of the hot sourdough toast with butter and strawberry jam. I discovered earlier, after finding out that the little two-slice toaster on the kitchen counter doesn't actually work, that toast made on the hotplate of the Aga is the very best kind of toast. Crispy on the outside and deliciously warm and chewy on the inside, Aga toast is now my new favourite and number one at the top of my go-to comfort-food list.

I let out a sigh of contentment and contemplate calling Lorna to see how she is, but after glancing at my watch and realising that it's Tuesday, I remember that she'll be having her virtual date with Liam and will no doubt be tucking into a taco right about now. So I take out Ted's letter instead and read it again for the umpteenth time. There's no date on it but I figure it must have been written soon after Ted and I first met as he mentions our calamitous tumble on the tiles in Santa's grotto and asks if the bruise on my backside has faded yet. I smile at the carefree and charismatic style of Ted's words, the innocence we had back then as teenagers with our whole lives ahead of us – or so we thought. But the letter isn't maudlin at all. In fact, it's a joy to read. A comfort. Even if Ted has 'borrowed' some of the words from that well-known Elton John and Kiki Dee song. Well, he certainly managed to win my heart, but the strangest thing is that I don't remember ever reading this letter. I have a vague recollection of us messing around doing karaoke and singing the actual song during a raucous night at The Hook, Line & Sinker many moons ago, but Ted was never a big letter writer. He must have been trying to impress me at the start, when we first met. He was dyslexic and shied away from writing and sending cards, which makes this surprise letter even more precious. Drawing pictures and thoughtful gestures were more his style. And back then, when we first started dating, he would often turn up with a little teddy bear or a packet of sweets, like my favourite strawberry bonbons, which he'd then end up scoffing before I could get a proper look in, as we watched TV and had a cuddle in my bedroom with the door ajar. Patty, for all her pushing me on the man front, was actually very prim back then and would only allow Ted into my bedroom if the door was left open.

I put the letter away inside my diary for now, figuring I can have another read later on as I write up my entry for today, when I'll definitely be grinning all over again at this unexpected turn of events. It really feels like serendipity, to have gone out with my bread samples and festive treat gifts and to have come back with the best gift of all for myself in return. And it's been a wonderful day. I loved meeting Mack, and it was nice to chat to Ian too. I remember reading somewhere that connection is a magical thing, restorative and can make all the difference to our mood, so Mack is certainly right to get his daily fix. It's a shame that he has to rely on going all the way to the supermarket in Stoneley to make it happen, but then I suppose it's a good thing too for him to keep active. Either way, I'm going to make sure I pop by his sea cottage with more bread in a few days' time and look forward to hearing more about Dotty. I also loved seeing my old childhood home; it gave me a good feeling too, a sort of calmness and a sense of coming full circle, being where I belong, anchored in this lovely little seaside town where people are friendly and the memories are fond. Mostly. I pedalled on to old Mrs Grace's house to say hello and see if she'd like a bag of bread and she was very gracious and pleased to see me but couldn't help herself from still going on about her flaming gladioli plants that have been 'nowhere near as good as the originals that you ruined,' is what she said, and I felt bad about it all over again. It's funny how a fleeting comment or moment can take you straight back to that younger self inside. I felt like a seventeen-year-old again, naïve and a bit clueless, but thinking I knew it all and was totally invincible. But Mrs Grace and I parted on good terms and she told me not to be a stranger and to pop by another time, especially if I had a loaf going spare because she had also got caught up in the big bread shortage scandal. Although, she was very vocal in telling me how determined she is to root out the greedy culprits stockpiling for the holidays and put a stop to it right away.

I then went to the church and met Vicar Joe, a bearded man in his mid-forties maybe, with a kindly manner and a rich, reassuring voice. If Rita hadn't told me I would never have guessed he used to be in a band

and sang on *Tops of the Pops*. He was very unassuming and delighted too when I told him about my bread-making, promising to share the baked goods out right away to the parishioners that can't get out to the supermarket either. He's also asked me to call in to the church again as soon as I do another big baking session as there's a small community café and shop in the building next to the church and they would very much like to buy some bread and mince pies to add to their menu and restock their shelves. It feels so wonderful to have a purpose and know that I can make a small difference by helping out and in turn earn money from bread-making. Although I'm a long way off from earning enough to cover the car repairs and sorting out the bedroom ceiling and all the new school uniform, at least it's a start. Vicar Joe also told me how it works here now with Christmas trees. Apparently, there's someone who collects them from a Christmas tree farm over in Tindledale and then delivers them around Mulberry for a very modest price. Vicar Joe has taken a note of where my yellow beach house is and promised to pass it on to the delivery guy, so I'm hoping we could have a tree very soon and the countdown to Christmas really will be on.

Smiling, I watch the boys who are busy cleaning up an old rusty fire pit that they found in the garden. Freya is running around on the sand giggling with Henry in hot pursuit, weaving in and out of the solar lights on little poles that the boys also found in the garden and have now pushed into the sand on either side of the wooden boards to create a marvellous magical grotto vibe to our new home here on the beach. The tide is coming in so the wooden shipwreck has almost faded from view now and so I lift my mug of mulled wine as if to say cheers to Ted and thank him for the lovely letter.

I've just sat back in the deckchair when I hear what sounds like the chugging of an old diesel engine. I glance up and away from the shore and see the glow of car headlights on the coastal road in the distance and heading this way. Moments later, and the engine sound has stopped; a car door slams and now another light is coming across the sand. I lift my blanket and stuff the hot-water bottle inside my coat and wander down the wooden path to see who it is, but I'm dazzled by the flashlight that is near blinding me now. Henry spots it too and must assume he's suddenly become some kind of fearsome guard dog as he starts barking, which is completely out of character because he's the soppiest and bounciest golden retriever there ever was. But still, he hurtles off at full pelt, barking all the way to see who has the audacity to approach his family in their new home.

'Henry!' Oscar bellows and before I can stop him, he's run off after the dog, closely followed by Olly. I manage to scoop an arm around Freya just in time before she follows her big brothers and her beloved dog into the beachy darkness. The flashlight is coming closer now and I can hear the boys chatting to whoever it is.

'Mum! Come and look at this,' yells Oscar, followed by a long whistling sound from Olly. 'It's beginning to look a lot like Christmas,' he adds in an enthusiastic voice, making a change from his usual one of complaint.

'What do you mean?' I call out, walking towards the light and wondering if this is what I hope it is. That our Christmas tree has arrived. I make a mental note to thank Vicar Joe profusely for delivering on such a prompt service. A fizz of anticipation floods though me at the prospect of cranking up the festive tunes and making the decorations to go on the tree, lifting Freya up to pop the fairy on the top, as per our Carrington family tradition ever since the boys were babies.

But the feeling swiftly dissipates as fast as it arrives.

Blooming typical!

Jack is standing in front of me dressed in mud-splattered black jodhpurs, knee-high riding boots and some kind of checked padded lumber jacket with a white fleece collar. There is the biggest and bushiest, lush pine tree slung over his left shoulder and the same sardonic grin from earlier spread across his *Bridgerton*-esque broodingly good-looking face with deep chocolate-brown eyes…if you're into that kind of thing of course!

'Where would you like it?' he asks, plonking the tree upright on the sand, his left hand grasped around the trunk in the middle to stop it from toppling over. There's a beat of silence as our eyes lock and I swear he's challenging me to come up with some kind of quip as a continuation of our run-in earlier on today. Keen not to give him the satisfaction, especially in front of the children, I smile and glance towards the house, but then figure here is as good as anywhere. I really don't want to be beholden to Jack by asking him to take the tree right up to the house. No. Not when we're perfectly capable of dragging it there ourselves.

'Oh, here is fine, thanks,' I say, doing my best to be amicable.

'Look, it's no trouble to take it over to your house.' His eyes are flashing as if actually wanting me to disagree, which is, quite frankly, completely ridiculous. He even shakes his head in a really annoying way, like I'm being deliberately difficult or whatever.

'Sure. But like I said, here is fine.' I'm unable to help myself from countering.

'Really?' he laughs. 'Why would you want it left here on the beach in the sand when I can easily take it right up to the house for you?' he says, his Irish accent becoming stronger. He shakes his head some more and I swear I can see the hint of an eyeroll. An actual eyeroll! RUDE. My jaw drops open at his sheer audacity. What difference does it make to him where I have my tree? But I clock the boys both staring at me as if they too are now wondering why I won't let Jack take the tree over to the house. Only Freya and Henry are oblivious as they run in circles around and around Jack and his tree. Suddenly, Henry stops running and starts sniffing Jack's jodhpurs and boots.

'Ah, that'll be Sinead's scent he's picked up on,' Jack says in a far more chilled and friendly way as he gives Henry's head a quick stroke.

'Sinead is your funny dog!' Freya stops running around and comes to stand next to me and opposite Jack.

'That's right, she is,' Jack tells her. 'The one you met in the dunes the other night… when your mammy was having a…' He pauses and looks me straight in the eye as if daring me to try and stop him from regaling the whole embarrassing tale all over again. I can even see his mouth twitching at the corners as if, yet again, he's trying not to laugh. I inhale through my nose and swallow down my frustration. He really is the most irritating person I've ever met! Why doesn't he just drop the tree off, tell me how much I need to pay him, and then go away again? It's as if he's always there and having a laugh at my expense – first in the sand, then earlier when he was leaning out of the pub window, and now here he is again. I swear he's appeared in my life just to wind me up on purpose.

'A comfort break!' Freya finishes the sentence for Jack, and to give him his due, he does actually display a modicum of consideration, as he smiles and changes the subject by asking Freya about her dog instead, to which she replies, 'His name is Henry. And I've got two guinea pigs too,' she says proudly.

'And what are your guinea pigs called?' Jack asks easily, letting the tree fall onto the sand as he crouches down and rests his elbows on his knees so he's the same height as Freya, which is also considerate.

'Chewy, because he looks like Chewbacca. My brother, Olly, picked his name, and the other one is called Snuggle. I picked her name because she loves snuggling,' Freya informs him, seeming very articulate and grown up, until she wipes her nose all the way across the back of her coat sleeve. I groan inwardly, but decide not to say anything about it and spoil her moment.

'Well, they sound like very fine names to me,' Jack nods encouragingly, not seeming to notice the spectacular nose wipe and I feel my irritation by his presence subsiding slightly.

'And my mummy's name is Bridget,' Freya adds. There's a short silence as Jack glances up at me.

'And that's a very fine name too,' he says to Freya, but holds my gaze a little longer than necessary as if he's actually flirting with me. Feeling suddenly discombobulated, I look away and stare out across the sea instead.

'Where is Sinead?' Freya enquires, her little face

peering into the distance behind Jack to see if his dog is somewhere on the beach.

Another short silence follows.

'Ah, she's in my truck over in the wee car park,' Jack tells her.

'But why did you leave her there?' Freya sounds disappointed.

'Well,' he starts, pausing momentarily for effect, I can only assume. 'I didn't want her to push your mammy over again...' As I look back to him, I see that he's still looking up in my direction. 'You see, I'm very kind and thoughtful like that!' And he actually does the head tilt thing again, the edge of his lips lifting into a smile and all the while holding my gaze until I can't bear it any longer and end up looking away first. Again. Dammit! The feeling of irritation at his presence makes a monumental return. I fold my arms and instantly wish I hadn't as it causes the hot bottle to shoot downwards and literally whoosh out from underneath my coat before landing on the sand at my feet with a big plop.

'Jesus, what the feck was that?' Jack yells, his Irish accent broadening as he instinctively goes to bounce back up into a standing position, but ends up toppling backwards before he manages to get to his feet. Freya near leaps right out of her skin too while the boys glance at each other before giving me a collective look of WTF! I've clearly embarrassed them yet again. I'm just about to reach down and pick the hot-water bottle up to show them all there's absolutely nothing to be alarmed about, when Henry does his usual trick of a running flyby swipe, wrapping his mouth around the woolly cover of the hot-water bottle before proceeding to prance around like he's suddenly the cockiest cock of all the walks there ever was, with his tail at full mast and wafting in delight, and with the hot-water bottle swinging jauntily from his gripped jaw. I give Freya a hug to check that she's all right, but in her usual stoic way she gives me a hug right back before brushing it all off and going after Henry, giggling all the way. The boys meanwhile are still gawping at me and Jack is pushing a hand through his hair and trying to play it cool like he's Danny Zuko in *Grease* when the T-Birds clock his over-the-top reaction on seeing Sandy again in the parking lot. And for some reason, this makes me see Jack in a very different light.

Human.

And not completely heartless and hell bent on winding me up for no good reason with his stupid head tilts and silly sardonic smiling at my expense.

There's another dimension to him... or so it would seem. He's clearly bothered by what I think of him. Even if it's only that he just looked like a prize plum in front of me as he rolled about on the sand. Ha! Now he knows what it's like. I don't laugh at him though, like he did when it happened to me. Twice! Oh no. But I do say, 'Oh,

Jack, you forgot something.' I make sure to keep a straight face as I point the toe of my left boot at the wallet that has fallen out of his back pocket.

'Yes, I knew tha—' He stops talking and checks himself before adding a more heartfelt, 'Cheers!' as he picks the wallet up, then after a short silence, adds, 'Guess I deserved that?' He shrugs, shaking his head with a wry smile on his face this time.

'Guess you did!' I lift one shoulder and grin right back. And there's a moment where neither of us says anything as we properly size each other up for the very first time. Then it's Jack's turn to look away first before smiling, a nice genuine smile I notice. He looks like he's about to say something more, but Freya and Henry come hurtling back in between us and I have to intervene before the water bottle ends up being ripped in two as part of their tug-of-war game.

'OK, that's enough,' I say, and Olly manages to get hold of Henry's collar so I can take the hot-water bottle from his mouth. I let him go and he dashes back inside the house, presumably to drink some water as I'm sure his cheeky run-around antics have made him work up quite a thirst.

'Mummy, can we decorate the tree?' Freya asks, changing focus again.

'Of course we can.' I give her shoulders a squeeze before she dashes off towards the house in search of

Henry. 'Boys, can you get the tree into the house, please?'

'What, now?' Oscar groans and lets out a massive huff of indignation, clearly back to his default setting of a perpetually put-out teenager.

'Yes, now, thank you, Oscar,' I say, and turn back to Jack. 'Thanks for bringing it over. How much do I owe you?'

'Ah, it's no problem!' He holds up a palm.

'Oh, no, I couldn't possibly—' I start, but he cuts me off with a shake of the head and another shrug of his shoulders.

'Call it a housewarming present,' he says, pushing his hands into his jacket pockets, and then it happens again... the head tilt and the start of a smile at the corners of his mouth, and then I wonder if maybe it's just his way. Perhaps it's just a thing he does and isn't meant in a cocky way at all, because he doesn't seem to be laughing at me right now. But no, he was definitely laughing at me earlier, I'm sure he was. He even had a fist over his mouth to try and stop himself. Hmm. But then he leaves me in no doubt. 'Look, I'm sorry about earlier, at the pub. I shouldn't have laughed at you like that. It was bad of me. Will you forgive me... and my lunatic dog? I'm trying to train her to calm down, but, well, you can probably guess that it's not going so well.' He lifts one eyebrow.

I hesitate, but then quickly relent, figuring it's no big deal in the grand scheme of things and it would certainly make my life a little easier to clear the air so I'm not boiled up with irritation by his presence or trying to avoid bumping into him, which could be problematic with Mulberry being such a small place. Plus, I came here to start afresh, not to enter in to some kind of silly tit-for-tat feud with the local pub barman slash Christmas tree delivery person. And it was considerate of Jack to leave Sinead in his truck, although completely unnecessary as I'm sure Henry would have loved to have got involved in her exuberant play and taken the focus of her attentions away from bodyslamming me and trying to lick me half to death or whatever. And not to mention the attentive way Jack just chatted to Freya about the guinea pigs, and then bringing the tree all the way out here and now calling it a gift is very kind too. But then what about him gossiping to Rita – and the whole pub, no doubt? I ponder for a moment longer, wondering whether if I saw someone in the sand dunes with a Christmas-themed knicker-clad bottom stuck up in the air, I'd be likely to have a laugh about it later on with Lorna? It takes me precisely one nanosecond to realise that of course I would. So I come to the conclusion that it's really not that big a deal. I'm not a hypocrite and I'm going to get over myself and give Jack a second go.

'OK, then. Sure, no hard feelings.' I shrug back. 'I'll

forgive you. And Sinead. But on one condition? Actually, two!'

'Er...' He eyes me suspiciously, but his smile has widened. 'Go on...'

'Well, firstly, you tell me why you're wearing jodhpurs and riding boots on a beach?' I point to his legs.

'Ah. I was at the stables, near the Christmas tree farm earlier, riding my horse,' he says, nodding, and I nod back thinking, *fair enough*.

'And the second condition?' he lifts his eyebrows.

'You forgive me right back. I was rude to you, ordering you to keep your dog under control and then running off like that the other night and then again in the pub garden.'

'Say no more about it. I shouldn't have approached you in the dunes on a dark night – I get that I startled you.'

'Yes, you did. Plus I was embarrassed, but then comparing you unfavourably to Rita today was a bit harsh,' I add, swallowing as I will my cheeks not to flame.

'Well, yes that was a bit harsh,' he agrees, 'but then who can blame you? I probably was enjoying it a bit too much. But it was damn hard not to laugh. The look on your face when you skidded over... A mixture of bewilderment and then fury... it was damn funny.' He shakes his head and laughs harder.

'OK, it wasn't that funny,' I say, but can't help laughing too as I replay the scene inside my head.

'Draw a line under it?' he asks as he stops laughing. I nod in agreement. 'Good. Because we're going to see a lot more of each other.' And the head tilt and smile thing happens again.

'Are we indeed?' I lift an eyebrow, wondering where this is going. I'm curious at his audacity, because he is definitely being flirty now. There's a beat of silence and, OMG, he's doing that figure-of-eight thing – looking at my lips and then back to my eyes. The thing that Lorna and I have discussed at great length and in great depth whilst watching period dramas where all the devilishly brooding cads do it to make the damsels swoon. And hang on a second… does Jack think I'm going to actually be seeing him… as in, like a date or whatever? *But no! No, no, no* is my immediate knee-jerk reaction. My mind races at the prospect of him asking and every instinct in me wants to dash back to the house and never see Jack's face ever again. *Please don't ask me.* I'm not sure. And I… well, I just don't know. And I don't want to have to think about this. My husband is there. In the sea. What would Ted think? Arghhhh. My head feels like it might explode, there are that many conflicting thoughts whizzing around inside it right now.

But then Jack adds, 'The choir!' and I gawp like a goldfish before doing a gigantic sag in relief.

'Yes! Yes, yes, yes!' is what comes out of my mouth followed by a massive smile.

OK, to be honest, it's more of a completely crazed Ronald McDonald style clown grin on my utterly relieved face. Jack's forehead instantly creases in confusion. No doubt wondering why I'm behaving in such a bizarre way. Perfectly understandable, because I'm wondering too. But *of course* Jack means the choir. He obviously belongs to it too. I've got the wrong end of the stick. Jack is just passing on the details for the choir from Rita. Of course he is. I should have known that. And never have I been happier at the prospect of singing in front of a load of people I've never met. And that's saying something, as I'm still scarred with mortification from that Spice Girls karaoke stint in the pub all these years later.

'Oh… well… OK,' Jack says slowly, a hint of wariness winging into his eyes now. 'This here has all the details for logging in, the password etc. and a few tips on what to expect. Oh, and I think there are some song titles on there too in case you want to have a look at them beforehand to get a feel for the lyrics.' After putting a gloved hand inside his jacket to retrieve some pieces of paper, he hands them to me.

'Thanks,' I say, taking the bundle. 'I'll… see you on Wednesday then. Yes. At the choir. Online on the screen,' I add, flapping the papers around in the air to make it perfectly clear, all the while cringing inside as I sound like a complete fruitloop.

'Er, cool, yes, see you there. At the choir. Online on the screen,' he repeats, looking at me strangely. 'Oh, and Rita wondered if you're up for making some bread rolls to go with our takeaway roast dinners?'

'Oh, I—' I start.

'It would really help us out and Rita said that potato and rosemary sourdough loaf you delivered earlier was top drawer. She was delighted with it and said to pass on her thanks for such a thoughtful gift.' He does a chef's kiss with his fingers which makes me feel chuffed to have received such a compliment. 'Since Jilly's bakery in the market square closed down and our wholesaler retired we've been winging it with supermarket supplies but—'

'Ah, yes, I heard about that,' I jump in, delighted to be talking about bread instead now, one of my favourite things where there's no possibility for any misunderstandings. I know where I'm at with bread!

'So, you'll help us out, then?' Jack asks, seeming to relax a bit too now. 'Rita will pay you for them; she usually does cash on delivery,' he adds, as if attempting to persuade me. But I don't need any persuasion as I'm grateful and completely flattered that Rita has declared my bread of a high enough standard to give to her paying customers. And she will pay me. For making bread. A short silence follows as the impact of what this could mean sinks in.

'Yes! I'd absolutely love to,' I beam, but then quickly caveat with, 'I'm not a proper baker or anything though. What kind of… volumes is Rita thinking?' I tentatively check, feeling elated but a little apprehensive as a trillion or so things immediately whirl around inside my head. Like buying all the ingredients for starters, and what about the Aga? It's a temperamental old beast – the main oven flame went out twice last night when I was baking. Luckily I managed to get it back on sharpish, but what if it conks out completely? And the lack of freezer space. But then maybe I don't need a freezer if I bake the rolls and get them to Rita right away. But then what about delivery? How many bread rolls can I fit inside my bicycle basket? I'd really need to get the car fixed…

But then I take a breath and will myself to stop panicking. I don't even have all the details yet; it could be just one or two dozen bread rolls in which case it's easily doable and no big deal at all. But still a fantastic chance to put my passion into practice and do something that I love. I'll figure out a way to get the car back on the road, and money to buy the ingredients too… I've only got one bag of flour left and the children's Christmas presents and new school uniform has to come first. I wonder again about going to Carrington's to see what I can sort out there. But then, what will Mum say? She's bound to want to see my new capsule wardrobe!

'Rita said she'll call by tomorrow when she's walking Skipper to go through numbers with you,' Jack says, bringing me back on point.

'Fab,' I beam all over again to cover the swirl of emotions I'm feeling right now. 'Well, in that case, I'll look forward to seeing her. Thank you. And please pass on my thanks to Rita too. I love baking and, well, I can't tell you how much this means.' Jack looks at me and his mouth opens, but he doesn't say anything. Instead the curious look lingers there mingled in with the head tilt and smile. A kind smile. Neither of us says anything. But it's Jack who talks next.

'Logs!' he says, sounding distracted. And it's as if some kind of spell has suddenly been broken. 'The fire pit.' He points to where Olly and Oscar are over by the house beside the fire pit that they've filled with scrunched-up pieces of old newspapers, presumably found somewhere in the house or the storage shed in the garden too.

'Ah, yes, they've been cleaning it up,' I say, stating the obvious.

'They need logs. Newspaper won't work. I have some logs. Dried-out old off-cuts from the Christmas tree farm in the truck. I'll get a load for them,' he says, sounding distracted. After gesturing with his thumb over his left shoulder back towards the little car park area where his truck is, Jack turns and walks away. 'See you in a bit,' he then calls out.

'Er, yes, sure. See you in a bit, Jack,' I call after him, before drawing my coat in tighter and wrapping my arms around my body into a hug as I wander over towards the house and wait for him to return…

Chapter Eleven

The following afternoon the house is heavy with the glorious scent of Christmas, blending perfectly with a fabulously festive and extremely comforting carol service floating from the radio. The evocative aroma of pine from the Christmas tree, always an instant nostalgic reminder of happy Christmases past mingles with the citrusy orange, cinnamon, spice, and all things nice from the baking session that's already underway. I've got my hair tied back in a big curly bun and my apron on over a Christmas-pudding-patterned jumper with the sleeves rolled up and my cheeks are rosy-red hot. I might even have a sweaty top lip. I've definitely got a sweat-drenched back. But in this moment, as I bustle around the kitchen checking on this and tweaking that, I couldn't be feeling any happier, even if the Aga is belting out enough heat to power a supersized sauna, the boys are bickering over whose turn it is to sit on the bit of the sofa that doesn't have any lumps or bumps, and Freya is hurtling around after Henry causing chaos as always.

Rita popped by first thing, shortly after breakfast time on her way back from walking Skipper, and said that not only would she like a regular supply of bread rolls, but she also asked if I could bake some loaves for the essentials boxes that they're planning on delivering around the local area while the clifftop road in and out of Mulberry is frozen and too treacherous to travel on. Apparently the gritter truck from Stoneley couldn't even get near it last night so now it's completely out of bounds for all the people who rely on the bus or a supermarket delivery. Plus, Rita said she would love to include some mince pies in the boxes too, and so I've made a head start and already have ten loaves proving, another two already baking in the Aga ovens, and three dozen mince pies cooling on wire racks on the kitchen table. Well, one dozen is on an actual cooling rack; the rest of the mince pies are on clean tea towels queuing to take a turn on the rack as I only have the one, which reminds me to add 'wire racks'…

I've started a list of things I'm going to need if I'm going to do this properly and supply The Hook, Line & Sinker with bread and mince pies. *Supply!* Did I really just say that out loud inside my own head? I actually can't believe it and had to check twice with Rita when she asked me to 'supply' her with more bread. Rolls, and mince pies too. And she wouldn't take no for an answer when I explained that I'm not actually a proper baker or anything, and so I wasn't sure it was fair for her to pay me as much as she has suggested – which is the going rate apparently – in case I couldn't give her consistency. Sometimes my bread doesn't turn out as well as I intended and she could very well end up with a wonky-looking loaf or a mince pie with a very soggy bottom. But she said that she was prepared to take a chance on me and to see how it goes because she has umpteen roast dinner bookings already lined up for this Sunday, and they've all opted for the bread roll option, plus they already have seventeen orders for essentials boxes, with bread being the main staple. And with the supermarket inaccessible, she couldn't let her regulars down, not this close to Christmas, which reminded her… would I make some mince pies too? She's letting me have some catering-size boxes of eggs, milk, and packs of butter to get started with and the rest I've come up with a plan for. I've phoned the customer services desk at Carrington's to see what baking supplies they have in their food hall and remembered they used to have a little home-baking section with muffin trays and pastry brushes, cake tins, and cupcake cases etc. I'm going to need some more wire cooling racks for starters, plus tins, stones, and banneton proving baskets plus large bags of flour, a big bottle of olive oil and another box, at least, of rock salt and several jars of mincemeat too. The woman I spoke to assured me they have plenty of supplies and cooking essentials, with home-baking having become so popular in recent years with everyone loving *The Great British Bake Off* and so they've actually expanded their selection of kitchen items. But they have absolutely no freshly made bread – they're having the same problem as Rita.

Luckily, Louis has been fed and is growing even bigger, although I've separated him into four so that I can feed each of them and end up with a much bigger supply of sourdough starters. By the sounds of what Rita said, I'm definitely going to need a bigger supply. The people of Mulberry love their bread! That's what she said when I asked about numbers. So as much as I can bake, she has assured me, will most definitely be eaten. Plus, of course, I want to make sure Mack is looked after too, and Vicar Joe's parishioners. I'm going to drop off some more loaves to the church on Sunday too so nobody has to go without this Christmas. I couldn't bear to think of that. So it's looking like it's going to be a very busy Christmas indeed, and I'm so delighted and very relieved to have another opportunity to earn some much-needed money.

'Mum, will you tell him?' It's Oscar, and he's got hold of Olly's sleeve and is trying to drag him off the sofa.

'But he's been here all day. It's my turn,' Olly yells,

shoving his brother's hand away to yank his sleeve free. 'Now look what you've done! You've ruined it,' he says, inspecting his sweatshirt.

'OK, that's enough. Honestly, I thought you two were over this silly bickering.' I take a deep breath and push my sleeves up further, feeling slightly swimmy in the roasting heat now. 'You've both behaved like such big grown-up boys since we got here.' And as soon as the words come out of my mouth I cringe, realising that I'm talking as if they are a pair of toddlers, forgetting that they're fourteen, for crying out loud. And I have absolutely no defence when they both stop wrestling and turn to look at me with flabbergasted faces that swiftly turn to disdain before eventually settling on something that looks like pity mingled with a tinge of fear that I might have actually lost the plot completely. Oh god. I've embarrassed them again. There's a beat of silence, but then eventually we all collapse into a fit of roaring laughter.

'Ah, you're such a big grown-up boy,' Oscar manages mid-chortle, in a silly baby voice to Olly as he goes to grab his sleeve again.

'And so are you, you giant noob,' Olly counters, standing up now and pulling his twin into a headlock.

'Get off me! You're the noob. I'm a million times better at gaming than you are!' Oscar says, trying not to get strangled by the crook of his brother's elbow. Henry thinks it's play time and starts jumping up and trying to lick Oscar's face, which of course makes Freya scream with giggles.

'OK, OK, that's enough,' I yell, wiping the tears of laughter from my eyes. 'Nobody is a noob, whatever that is!' And for some reason, this makes us all start laughing again. The commotion goes on until I can't bear it any longer and end up flinging the front door open wide and shooing all three of them, plus Herny, outside onto the beach, grateful for the cooling, salty sea breeze that rushes in to calm everything down.

As I wander back to the kitchen I ponder on how nice it is to see them all laughing again, even if they are laughing at me, because there was a time when nobody laughed, so it makes me feel even happier to see these small shoots of change. It's like my little family is a shattered plate of precious china and the pieces are slowly being glued back together again to make a new plate – the same but different and ultimately stronger, I hope. I smile to myself as I rotate the mince pies and sprinkle sugar over the ones going onto the wire rack, contemplating the plan I came up with earlier. I've decided to talk to Mum again about the capsule wardrobe, and explain to her that if I use the money she's kindly organised for me to have at Carrington's to help buy Christmas presents and school uniform for the children and supplies to invest upfront to get my fledgling bakery business up and running, I can then use the money I make selling baked goods to update my wardrobe at a later date. Otherwise, I will just have to try to avoid the topic with her or have a good rummage through my current wardrobe and convince her that it will all do. It's crazy anyway as it's not as if I'm going anywhere or seeing anyone where I might want to wear anything other than my thick winter coat and jeans, because it's wintertime here, in case she's forgotten. Plus, the clothes I already have are fine for me.

Mulling it all over, I've been pottering around in peace for an hour or so when Freya comes running back inside the house.

'Mummy, there's a lady here,' she says, flushed from playing with Henry while Oscar and Olly clean up some old deckchairs that they've moved onto after doing such a good job with the fire pit. Jack dropped off the logs as promised, before getting back to the pub and the boys got a roaring fire going and so we sat around the mesmerising golden flames and had a lovely evening all together. Freya even fell asleep on my lap, her little cheeks all red and toasty hot from the warmth of the fire. But she's too big for me to carry her all the way up to bed like Ted used to, so Olly stepped in and quietly took her upstairs instead.

'Oh, is it the lady from this morning? Rita. Has she returned with the baking supplies?' I say vaguely as I wipe my hands on my apron and check on the loaves in the Aga. Almost ready to come out. Another twenty minutes or so and they'll be golden! But then I remember that Rita has my number now so she would probably just call if it was something to do with the bread or mince pies.

'No, it's a different lady. Olly said to come and get you,' Freya licks a chubby finger and goes to wipe it in the sugar across the top of one of the mince pies on the cooling rack.

'Er, excuse me, no touching! Remember, sweetheart, what I told you this morning. These mince pies aren't for us to eat. Now, come and show me where this lady is.' I shoo her away from the table and towards the front door.

'Oh, I'm so sorry to bother you.' There's a woman with a lovely pastel-pink faux fur coat on, a cascade of shiny black curls bobbing around her shoulders, and a warm smile on her face. 'I'm Pearl,' she says, and waves from a distance over by the wooden slats leading down to the sea. 'Ian's wife? You kindly gave us a loaf of sourdough,' she prompts when it's obvious I can't place her. 'At least, I'm hoping I've come to the right place. Ian said you mentioned a yellow beach house on the end. And so here I am.'

'Ah, yes, of course... that's right,' I say, returning the grin. 'I'm Bridget. And I hope the bread was OK?'

'Yes, absolutely, it was.' Her grin widens as she nods

to confirm this. 'In fact, I've come to see if by any chance you might have another loaf, please, that I could buy from you to give to my neighbour? She's elderly and on her own, you see, and can't really get out to the shops after having a fall on the ice and bruising her hip... and so I popped a round of toast into her, made from your bread, and she was over the moon. When she returned the plate earlier, she said she had never tasted bread like it. And I agree with her. It really is delicious.'

'Ah, well, thank you. That's so lovely to know, but I'm afraid I don't...' I hesitate. But ever the people pleaser, I'm instantly fretting, especially seeing as she's come all this way and now looks so disappointed. Plus, what about her elderly neighbour who can't get out to the shops? I feel concerned for her as it can't be much fun being on your own indoors, so I wonder if I could give her one of the loaves in the Aga and then make another one for Rita. I've got time, and enough dough, as Rita isn't expecting her bread and mince pies delivery until tomorrow and the bread rolls aren't due until Sunday to go with the roast dinners, by which time I'll have got over to Carrington's and collected my order for more flour and wire racks and all the rest of it.

'Oh well, never mind,' Pearl says. 'I thought it worth asking as it really was excellent sourdough. Maybe another time? I could call by and place an order, you know, to give you a bit of notice,' she smiles and waves as she goes to walk away.

'Actually,' I call after her, wanting to help and realising that I could do it after all. 'I can let you have one loaf. You've come all this way, and, well… but it's still in the oven. If you don't mind waiting for it?'

'Ooh, yes please, that would be wonderful,' Pearl turns back, 'I can certainly wait. How long will it be?'

'About twenty minutes or so. And then the loaf will need some cooling time, but you're very welcome to take it and let it cool down on your way home.'

'That sounds even better. Lovely warm bread – my neighbour will be delighted. She was telling me how she used to love eating hot bread with butter straight from the oven after baking with her mother when she was a child. She's getting on now, has no family of her own left, and gets terribly lonely, so her childhood memories are very precious.'

'Then it's the least I can do.' I smile, happy to give a spark of joy to an elderly lady.

'And you can wait here if you like,' Olly says, offering Pearl one of the deck chairs that he's already cleaned up.

'Can we light the fire pit, Mum?' Oscar asks.

'Please, don't go to any bother on my account,' Pearl says, settling herself into the deckchair. 'I'll be fine here. This coat is remarkably warm and cosy,' she says, wrapping the gorgeous pink coat further around her as she snuggles into the chair.

'It's no trouble at all,' I tell her, before turning to Oscar and Olly and telling them they can get the fire pit going as long as they make sure Freya and Henry are nowhere near it when they're playing. 'And I'll make you a cuppa too, if you like,' I offer to Pearl.

'Well, if you're sure?' Her eyes light up and I nod. 'Then that would be very lovely indeed. Thanks so much.'

Twenty minutes later and the bread is ready. Pearl and I have had a wonderful chat about the parenting of twins as we got cosy around the fire pit.

'There you go.' I hand Pearl the bread wrapped in a tea towel for the journey across the beach back towards Mulberry and to her neighbour's home.

'Thank you so much,' she beams, stowing the loaf under her arm. 'Ooh, it's beautifully warm and smells just like utterly cosy, joyous comfort! I shall enjoy the walk back home even more now.'

She glances at the bread and I smile, slipping the very welcome payment into the pocket on the front of my apron before gathering up her tea mug and plate. I offered her a mince pie to munch on while she waited, keen for her feedback as a taste tester because it's all well and good that my children love my mince pies but if I'm to be paid for them then I need to be sure they are of a good enough quality. Luckily, Pearl gave a firm yes and a thumbs up.

'Well thanks for calling in, and it was nice to meet you and get some impartial feedback re the mince pies, plus of course I'm extremely grateful to you for keeping the letter from my husband, Ted.'

'Oh, there was no way I could get rid of it and I have to say that I thought it extremely serendipitous that you came by with the bread and we were able to reunite the letter with its rightful owner. It's like something out of a romance novel, or a film. Just lovely that the sender of the letter all those years ago went on to marry you. He was clearly falling in love with you back then and so I imagine he's very happy.' She beams and casts an eye towards the house. 'Sorry, I forgot to ask after Ted. Is he here? I bet he was surprised to see the letter turn up after all these years,' she adds, her eyes still twinkling in the smile. There's a moment of stillness. I can hear Freya laughing from over by the deck, and so, knowing that she's out of earshot and the boys are busy by the fire pit, I swallow, glance downward, and I'm just about to tell her, remembering the promise I made to myself after meeting Mack, when she adds, 'Sorry, I'm prying, and maybe it didn't work out after all.' Her cheeks flush. 'But I just assumed…' She pauses. 'Well, I saw your wedding ring and lovely vintage emerald engagement ring – I'm a jewellery designer you see, so I'm always on the lookout for unusual designs,' she tells me, and not wanting her to feel uncomfortable I gently explain. 'I'm so sorry, Bridget. That must have been very hard for you,' Pearl then says softly. 'The children too,' her voice going even quieter.

'Yes, yes it has been… but,' I pause, looking for the right words before settling on. 'I have hope, much more than I did before we moved here and so much has changed already, so it feels… sort of right, and promising, if that makes sense.' I smile as I contemplate what I've just said.

It does feel right. It's hard to explain, but already I can feel a shift. The children seem calmer too. More content. The twins are less obsessed with losing themselves in their online games and much more interested in doing other things. Outdoor stuff pottering around in the garden and cleaning up and repurposing the treasure they find there, like the little sailboat they dragged out from underneath a load of overgrown hedgerow that they want to sand down and paint. It's beyond repairing to resume its actual sailing days, but it will make a great seating area, they reckon, for filling with blankets, bean bags and cushions and lounging around in by the fire pit to enjoy their new favourite hobby which is telling jokes and making up elaborate stories about pirates and smugglers bringing all kinds of contraband ashore back in the olden days.

'It certainly does make sense. And good for you.'

Pearl nods. 'I know we've only just met but you strike me as a lovely, kind, warm-hearted woman and so it's important for you to find your harmony so you can go forward with your life – to find what really works for you. What makes you happy, ignites your passion, and allows you to thrive... and it's not always what we think it should be.'

'That's a lovely thing to say, thank you. You seem very wise. *Find your harmony*, I like that.' I nod thoughtfully, making a mental note to bank this for further pondering on later. Most likely when I'm pottering around baking in the stillness of the night when the children are in bed. Or sitting out here by the fire pit knitting Freya's scarf for her Christmas stocking.

'I didn't mention that I'm also a therapist,' Pearl says, but then quickly adds, 'not that I was trying to "therapise you", as Ian calls it when I get philosophical.' She shrugs. 'Sorry if it came across that way,' she adds, looking concerned.

'Oh, it's fine,' I assure her, liking her even more.

'Phew. Well, I'd better get going and drop off this bread. My neighbour said she'd love a nice bacon sandwich with a cuppa if I was able to find you and manage to buy a loaf for her.'

'Ooh, don't we all. What's your neighbour's name?' I ask, thinking of Mack.

'Glynis. Why do you ask?'

'Just that I know somebody else who loves a nice bacon sandwich. And he also likes a nice chat. He's on his own too and I'm guessing he's around the same age as your Glynis so maybe we could introduce them? They might be good company for one another,' I suggest.

'You know, that sounds like a very good idea. I'll mention it to Glynis,' Pearl says.

'And I'll mention it to Mack too,' I smile, warming to the plan, because nobody should feel lonely. I know what it's like, at night time especially; it's the worst feeling in the world and is one of the reasons why I bake in the evenings. Much better than lying awake with a busy head full of thoughts that always seem a trillion times more intense in the middle of the night.

'Marvellous. It was really nice to meet you, Bridget.'

'You too, Pearl. And please do just call – you have my number – if you'd like more bread, or perhaps we could have another cuppa together some time,' I venture, having really enjoyed her company. It was so refreshing to talk about normal day-to-day stuff, like twin parenting, how our respective children are holding out for snow this Christmas, books, baking bread, knitting and, well, just general chit chat that didn't involve Ted and how I'm coping, followed by a sympathetic smile before changing the topic to me moving on and meeting another man – something that has definitely dominated the conversations I've had this last year. Not that there's anything wrong with that. I know they just want me to be happy, and I truly appreciate all the kindness Lorna has shown me – Mum too, in her own way, if we forget about the Sugar Daddies R Us thing of course. But it was just lovely to feel light and unburdened by the shadow of grief without being tiptoed around, to feel normal for a little while. A new normal, if you like, with a new friend. It feels like starting afresh, and exactly what I was hoping for by coming here.

'I definitely will,' Pearl says. 'Baked snacks and a good natter sounds like the perfect treat to look forward to and you have my number so if you need a hand with anything – babysitter, dog walker, school stuff, or just a general chat about our delightful teenagers,' – laughing, she shakes her head and I do too – 'then just give me a call. I know how hard it can be to build a new support network when you relocate to a new place.'

'Thanks, Pearl. I appreciate it.'

'See you soon, Bridget, and good luck with your bicycle bakery.'

Feeling happy, I head back inside. Bicycle bakery… Mmm, I like the sound of that. Yes, it has a nice ring to it. Maybe I don't need the car after all. I certainly don't have the money to pay to get the Mini looked at, let alone repaired, and Pearl did say something about happiness or thriving maybe not being what you think it is. So perhaps the bike is all I need for now… and I have an idea. I head to my crafting box to see if I still have the wooden stamp set with tiny letters and a pink ink pad. I want to see if I can design something to stamp on my paper bags to make them look more professional. A pop of excitement bubbles inside me as I realise that I'm one step closer to realising my dream of setting up my own little bakery business, and I have the perfect name for it too: Bridget's Bicycle Bakery.

Chapter Twelve

'Hey, girl! Is that you?' someone calls out from across the market square.

I've just dropped ten loaves of bread and all the mince pies off to Rita at the pub – it's surprising how many loaves can fit inside a bicycle pannier, and the answer is five, to be precise. And so I was over the moon when Oscar found a pair of faded old khaki-green bicycle panniers in the back of the shed. They were covered in cobwebs and had salty white tidemarks on them from the damp sea air, I guess, but I managed to clean them up and cover them in a pretty strawberry-print piece of fabric from my crafting box. They fit perfectly on either side of my old bike to transport the bread in, and with the mince pies in the wicker basket at the front it's worked out absolutely fine. Rita did call to say that Jack is happy to come and collect the baked goods sometimes, if he's not busy in the kitchen cooking the lunchtime menu. Apparently, he's not only the barman and Christmas tree delivery person, he's also the chef at the pub too. But after thanking Rita – or should that be Jack? – for the kind offer, I explained about my plan to move more and feel fitter and I have to say that the ride along the coastal road today was a little easier than it was the first time, so it's a step, or a pedal rather, in the right direction.

'Bridget, babe. It is. OMG, it's you! Long time no see, babycakes.' I stop walking and turn around.

And then I see him.

'EDDIE!'

I do a double-take. The last time I saw my wickedly acerbic and completely camp friend from the Carrington's days, he was about to jet off to Los Angeles to film a TV chat show.

'Wow. How are you?' I ask, taking in his impeccable look: blonde hair in a side parting and super slick and mischievously sparkling blue-green eyes framed by perfectly cultivated eyebrows. And with his beautifully manscaped face he doesn't look a day older than he did when I was a Saturday girl all those years ago. In fact, he actually looks younger, if that's even possible. He's wearing a beautifully tailored cashmere coat with a dazzling diamante-encrusted grey wool scarf and matching grey leather gloves.

'You know me, sweetpea.' He presses the tips of his gloved fingers to his lips before offering out a flamboyant flurry of air kisses. 'Always dazzling!'

'Well, I can see that!' I call back, pushing my bike across the square until I'm standing opposite him. 'Look at you! All perfect. You put me to shame,' I say, on seeing him glancing down at my flappy pocket and vagabond-style coat which I tried to repair with a safety pin on account of not being able to find my sewing kit, but the coat looks worse than ever now. 'I had a bit of an accident, got pulled over by a massive dog…' I grin, and after glancing and widening his eyes at the state of me, Eddie waves a nonchalant hand in the air as if he can't bear to hear more on such a dull matter. I stifle a laugh on seeing his character hasn't changed one bit either – still as imperious as ever. But there's no malice in Eddie, just a perpetual display of utter exasperation.

'That's the Bridget we know and love,' he laughs. 'You always did like to take a tumble. Do you remember that time in Santa's—?'

'Ha ha, yes, I remember it very well,' I jump in and shake my head. Trust him to open with that. 'So how come you're here and not in LA or wherever it is I thought you lived these days?' I grin again, thinking what a blast from the past he is and I wonder if he knows how the rest of the gang are doing. He was very close with Georgie and Sam so it would be great to hear about them.

'Oh, darling. It's been horrendous. Wait till you hear this!' He pauses as if composing himself to impart completely shocking news. 'You know, I'm actually trapped in this tiny town that time forgot!' His eyes widen in disbelief as he shakes his head. I can't help laughing at his outraged audacity – he always did see himself as destined for so much more than Mulberry-On-Sea. Even as a schoolboy he was convinced that some kind of crazy accident had occurred and he had been swapped at birth with a global superstar's baby and should rightfully be growing up somewhere far more luxurious and glamorous.

'What do you mean?' I ask, seeing the look of utter disdain that darts across his rolling eyes.

'Exiled!' he adds dramatically, followed by a curt nod, 'Banished from being in my actual main residence in the Hollywood hills of LA until all the renovations have been completed. Yes, here I was enjoying a little me time on my yacht that's moored up in the harbour over there when a call comes through from my manager and he says, "the contractors have asked that you don't come back, darling, until they've finished laying the marble floor"… or whatever it is that's taking them an absolute eternity to do. And, apparently, my design ideas are slowing the whole project down. So now here I am until who knows when.' He shakes his head back before tilting one shoulder forward.

'Oh, Eddie, surely it's not that terrible.'

'Hmm, you try sleeping on a tiny cabin bed…' He pauses as if to check himself. 'Well, it's a double, so at least that's something, but, still, it's a fraction of the size of my actual bed in my actual home,' he tuts. 'My back is all twisted up like a gnarled old apple tree. It's intolerable.'

'What you mean? Don't you have one of those new apartments overlooking the harbour?' I ask, vaguely remembering hearing this on bumping into one of the old gang when I was here on holiday a few years back.

'Yes, the penthouse with a panoramic wraparound view,' he clarifies, just in case I had forgotten how fabulous his flat is. I pull a confused face, wondering what the problem is then, but he soon tells me. 'My live-in Spanish housekeeper, Valerie, is currently enjoying it with the rest of her large *familia*!' He shakes his head and lifts his arms up before dramatically dropping them back by his sides as if in utter defeat. Then, his voice softening, he explains, 'In a rare moment of utter compassion and kindness, I offered my apartment to Valerie so she could invite her family to come and spend Christmas with her. I said they could all stay for as long as they like, never envisaging that I wouldn't be allowed to go back home.'

He folds his arms this time. 'So here I am, on my own without any of my people. Apart from the yacht crew. Even my husband, Ciaran, is back home in LA, and so I can tell you, Bridget, sugar pie, that it's very nice to see you. A familiar face to brighten my day!'

'And you too, Eddie,' I say, stifling another laugh that's in danger of erupting from my mouth at any moment. Poor Eddie having to slum it on his luxury yacht.

'Thank you. I knew you'd understand,' he adds in all seriousness. I can't contain it any longer and so after a kind of strangled choking noise comes out of my mouth, I laugh out loud. And I can't stop. Eddie blinks a few times as I then manage to compose myself enough to ask what he's doing wandering around here if he hates the place so much, which is inexplicable in itself as Mulberry is such a lovely little seaside town.

'Wouldn't you sooner be on your yacht, Eddie, than pottering around out here in the street if you don't like this lovely little town?' I ask.

'Oh no! The crew and their incessant chat about tedious stuff like protein shakes and kale juice recipes is doing my head in, darling. No, I'm on my way to Carrington's to take refuge in a large latte from their Christmas-themed log cabin café they have set up next to the reindeer pen. It's the only thing that's getting me through.'

'Well in that case, I'll walk with you,' I say cheerfully. 'I'm on my way to Carrington's now to pick up an online order.'

'Oh.' Eddie looks startled now at this sudden change to his expected plan. 'Are you really?'

'Yes, that's right. Baking supplies, and to see if they sell school uniform and—'

'Come on, you can tell me about on the way,' Eddie cuts in, clearly not at all interested in the trifling details of my shopping list. 'I want to hear all about you and what you've been up to since you escaped Mulberry with that red-hot man of yours, Ted.'

On arrival at Carrington's department store, I find a lamppost to lean my bike against. I see there's a lovely little log cabin outside with twinkling fairy lights around the roof that's serving mulled wine, hot chocolate, coffee, and cakes to take away. Christmas carols sung by a choir are coming through speakers into the street and there's even a little herd of reindeers wandering around by the bandstand that has a nativity scene set up inside it with bales of straw dotted around for people to sit on and soak up the cosy festive atmosphere. It looks gorgeous and feels incredibly Christmassy. Freya would love to see this, so I must remember to pop back another day and bring her with me. She was keen to stay at home today with the boys, no doubt because she didn't want to miss out on her share of the plate piled high with misshapen mince pies that I didn't think were of a good enough standard for Rita to put into the Christmas essentials boxes that people will be paying for, so I left them out for the children to snack on instead. Plus a written reminder on the kitchen table, as always, to not go upstairs and to make sure one of them calls me immediately if there's a problem of any kind. Oh, and absolutely under no circumstances are the boys to light the fire pit. Definitely not!

Eddie leads the way over towards the log cabin, stands in front of me, and yells, 'Surprise!' before stepping to the side so the two women making coffees and manning the tills can see me.

'BRIDGET!' they scream in unison. And there in front of me are my old friends from my Saturday job days, Georgie and Sam. Both women are wearing black aprons with the Carrington's logo in gold embroidery written across the bust area and have their sleeves rolled up ready for business.

'OMG, how are you?' Georgie smiles, offering me a platter containing a selection of pretty miniature cupcakes, and, before I can answer, Sam, with her corkscrew blonde curls bouncing around her shoulders, fills a mug with mulled wine and hands it to me.

'On the house,' she beams, holding out the paper cup, which I take gratefully. 'It's so good to see you, Bridge, and you must have some of these cute little red velvets too. My signature cakes and Georgie's favourites, as always.'

'Thank you,' I say, cupping my mitten-clad hands around the cup for warmth. 'I'm very well,' I say, catching Eddie's eye. I told him about Ted and after giving me another flurry of air kisses followed by an enormous hug he said some of the most beautifully heartfelt and caring words I've ever heard. Underneath all his posturing, Eddie is a real sweetheart and full of compassion. He gives me a kind look and a little nod of support, but Georgie and Sam already know about Ted and sent flowers for the funeral. 'It's so lovely to see you both, although I thought you were living in Italy these days, Georgie?'

'Ah, yes, Tom and I spend a lot of time there but I miss Mulberry,' she says, her eyes sparkling on mentioning her gorgeous partner, 'especially at Christmas time, so I'm here staying with Dad and Nancy. Are you here for Christmas too?' she asks, going to box some of the lovely little cakes up for me. Freya and the boys are going to love them, if they last that long... I might very well eat them all on the way back home as they look that good.

'No, well, yes, I am, but not just for Christmas... I've

moved back to Mulberry. We're living in Ted's parents' old beach house now.' I grin before taking a sip of the deliciously comforting mulled wine; it's got more of a kick than mine has, and is spicy with a hint of cloves and a thin slice of orange bobbing about in the cup. It's a nice touch and I'm going to try it in a mug of my brew at home for an added splash of decadence the next time I'm sitting on the deck looking out to sea.

'Well good for you,' Georgie grins. 'We must get together when we can. Maybe cocktails one evening or a stroll on the beach for a proper good catch-up?'

'Yes, I'd love to.' I nod and grin back. 'And if you fancy coming out to the beach house then we can light the fire pit and I'll warm some mince pies. It'll be just like the old days,' I add, thinking that I'd quite like that. A carefree time with old friends and plenty of laughs sounds perfect.

'Can I join you? It'll be so much fun,' Sam says over her shoulder as she froths some milk into a jug at the coffee machine. But then stops moving and properly turns to look at me, and with a face full of compassion she softly and very tentatively asks, 'and we could toast Ted and talk about the good times?' as if feeling her way. A little silence follows, the four of us united in quiet contemplation until, after taking another sip of the mulled win, I nod.

'Yes. To Ted. You know, he'd have absolutely loved

the thought of us all toasting him and talking about him. And he'll be with us in spirit as the beach house looks out onto the old shipwreck.' They all nod and smile contemplatively, visibly relaxing on seeing that I'm OK. It's OK. They don't need to tread carefully around me. We can talk about Ted without it being sad or awkward or me crumbling into a trillion little pieces unable to even string a sentence together properly like I was the last time I spoke to Georgie and Sam shortly after the funeral. Yes, it feels nice to be with people who knew Ted from the old days, to have that shared experience of him. Lorna loved Ted too of course, but didn't meet him until much later on so it's not really the same. And of course Mum knew Ted, but because she didn't think he was good enough for me, she hasn't ever been interested in hearing about him so there wasn't ever the opportunity to have a laugh with her about the good times I had with him; but then again, at least she doesn't tread carefully around me. Ted's parents do. And I to them. And that's heartbreaking, but maybe one day soon we'll get to a place where we can all relax and chat about Ted together with joy and fondness, and maybe even crack a joke or two again. Ted's dad is actually a brilliant joke-teller and was forever making Ted and me crack up with his slapstick sense of humour and so I look forward to the day when he is able to do that again. It would be nice for Freya, Olly, and Oscar to see the fun side of their granddad again and hear about the daft things their dad got up to from someone other than me.

'I can't wait. I've missed you, Bridge, and I'm so happy you've come back to us,' Georgie says kindly, even though I made zero effort to keep in touch. I didn't even return her calls in the months after the funeral, but seeing her today, it's as if we had just spoken yesterday. It brings to mind that old adage of good friends being like stars: you don't always see them but you know they're always there.

'Me too,' Sam says, and then with a quizzical look on her face she adds, 'I don't suppose you're still baking these days, by any chance, are you?' and does pleading eyes.

'Sam!' Eddie jumps in, 'you can't launch in with a request for loaves when our gorgeous girl has like literally only just returned to us. I know you're desperate for bread, like the rest of Mulberry is, but... standards, darling,' he quips, giving her a disparaging gaze. 'At least give her a moment to catch her breath and settle back into the quiet life in this tiny little town.'

'Oh, Eddie. We all love Mulberry and, deep down, I think you do too! And besides, we're down to our last few loaves and you saw how big the queue was five minutes ago. They'll all be back tomorrow and want sandwiches, and you know what people are like when they're hungry,' she laughs. 'And you can't blame me trying. Bridge bakes the best bread and that's the end of it.' Sam turns to look at me and then after giving Eddie a snippy look, Georgie joins in.

'Do you remember all those years ago when you made sandwiches for us all to have on the beach and none of us could believe you had made the actual bread yourself too, because it was that good? Georgie grins. 'And you were only thirteen or something like that.'

'Yes, I do remember. What a day that was.' I smile and shake my head, thinking fondly of us lazing around in the sun having a laugh on the beach and eating cheese and crisp doorstep sandwiches washed down with lurid blue Slush Puppies from the ice cream shop when we were supposed to be at school! Patty went mad when a teacher spotted us and marched us back to our respective homes. 'And yes, I definitely am still making bread,' I say, sipping more of the mulled wine.

'Oh that's brilliant. Would it be possible to have as much as you can spare please?' Sam says, her eyes dancing in glee and relief. 'I'll pay you of course.'

'Well, I'll do my best,' I hesitate, and then tell her about the request from Rita at the pub.

'Of course, I understand. The essentials boxes must come first. The elderly and vulnerable need the bread more,' Sam's voice tails off.

'But I'm sure as soon as I've got myself organised and into a proper little production line in my home kitchen then I'll be able to bring you some loaves. Or maybe I can ask Jack to drop them off. He works at the—'

'Oh yes, we all know Hot Jack who works at the pub,' Eddie interjects, flashing us all a very dreamy look.

'Ah, yes Hot Jack!' Sam laughs, nudging Georgie who flutters her eyes and clasps a hand to her chest like she's the lady in a period drama swooning over her intended. I laugh too, suddenly feeling transported back to those Saturdays in Handbags and Accessories when it was so much fun and life was most definitely simpler, when it was all about who had a crush on who and what outfits we were going to wear that evening. And again, it feels nice and comfortable to be back. That may not sound very exciting or aspirational, and Patty would probably think I'm bonkers – she couldn't wait to move away either, just like Eddie – but I reckon there's a lot to be said for feeling that you're exactly where you belong.

'Yes, Hot Jack,' Georgie echoes.

'So how do you know Hot Jack?' Eddie fixes his eyes on me. And with them all staring in my direction I suddenly feel like a rabbit caught in the headlights. I go to talk but hesitate and then my cheeks flush.

'OMG, is he the reason you've moved back here?' Georgie asks.

'No! Oh no, definitely not,' I quickly say, shaking my head to immediately put them right. 'Of course not. I don't even know Hot Jack… Oh, um, what I meant to say was, just Jack. He's not hot or anything.' They all look at me blankly now as if I've just sprouted another head. 'Er… well, I guess he is if you like that kind of thing, of course, but not my cup of tea.' I pause to see them all leaning in a little closer and for some reason I get a sense that they don't believe me. Eddie even has one eyebrow lifted as if scrutinising me for clues of my true feelings.

'Stop it!' I laugh, going to bat his arm with my gloved hand, but he ducks backwards and so I end up flapping like a bird about to take off. 'You're incorrigible and just as annoying as you always were,' I say, pretending to be cross. 'What I meant was that I could ask Jack if he might drop a batch of loaves to you because I'm also baking for the pub and he's offered to collect from me as my car isn't working and, well, it's hard work with that big bike, and…'

But it's no use. I can see that the old gang are just as fun and lighthearted and silly with their teasing as they always were, all tilting their heads to one side and giving me that look. The same look I got when I first met Ted and, admittedly, I did go on about him at any given moment, but I don't fancy Jack. No, it's a ridiculous notion, although I can't deny that I'm enjoying this banter. It makes me feel light, and alive, and dare I say it… free.

Free from the grief that at times does feel like a ton weight sitting heavily on my shoulders. I'll always love

Ted, of course, but something is definitely shifting. I can feel it within me. It's as if coming back here to Mulberry is helping me find a place for him. Whether that's on the shipwreck in the sea or in a section of my heart, he's no longer consuming all of my waking thoughts, or indeed my dreams, with no proper place to go or emotion for me to attach to it all. In fact, last night was the first time I dreamt about Ted without feeling panicky. Yes, it felt wonderful and restorative. Calm. We were walking together in a field, chatting and laughing, and it was comforting. I woke up feeling as though I'd had a marvellous catch-up with an old friend. So maybe I'm finding my harmony, as Pearl calls it, now that I've found home. Settled. And my new relationship with Ted, for that is what it is now, can move onto a more settled phase too.

'Whatever you say, sweet cheeks,' Eddie says, and I give him another look.

'I'm more than happy to have Hot Jack deliver the bread,' Sam adds as I finish the last of the mulled wine and drop the paper cup into the bin to the side of the pop-up café.

'Just call me,' I say to Sam. 'Do you still have my number?' And she fishes inside the pocket on the front of her apron. After retrieving her phone she quickly scrolls and then turns the screen towards me so I can check the number.

'Bridget the Baker?' I laugh on seeing how she's stored my name in her contacts list.

'Well, that's how you were first introduced to me – do you remember? It was in the Carrington's canteen. Georgie brought you over to the table to join us for lunch on your first Saturday.'

'Oh yes, that's right.' Georgie nods. 'Friends ever since… and it really is so good to see you again, Bridget.'

After confirming that the number is correct and pointing over towards the main doors of Carrington's department store, where I'm heading next to collect my online order, I say my goodbyes, returning a few more air kisses and hugs from Eddie.

I'm beaming from ear to ear as it sinks in that I have another customer for my fledgling little bakery business, and wasn't it lovely to see my old friends again?

Chapter Thirteen

Back home, and after lots of complaining from Freya about it being bedtime, she's finally conceded defeat and, after giving Chewy and Snuggles a goodnight cuddle, has gone off to sleep. The boys are cosy with blankets wrapped around them in the sailboat and telling each other spooky ghost stories as they toast marshmallows on the fire pit. I'm sitting on the deck with my usual hot-water bottle, blanket, and a plate of Aga toast plus a mug of festive Bailys hot chocolate, and casting off the knitted unicorn scarf for Freya's Christmas stocking. She's going to be delighted with it, I hope and think, as I cut the end of the wool and stitch it in before holding up the glittery pastel pink, yellow, and blue striped scarf to check it over. Satisfied, I fold the scarf carefully and stow it inside my knitting bag for safekeeping and ready for wrapping in tissue paper later on – which reminds me, I must find the box containing the children's Christmas sacks and stockings to hang by the fire, as we do every year. Even Henry has a stocking that we stuff with treats and a new squeaky toy that has usually driven us all mad by the time Boxing Day comes around.

I glance at my watch and see that it's nearly time to log in to the choir and find out if I can sing a sea shanty, although I'm wondering how Henry and the boys are going to react when they're treated to my tone-deaf warbling. But it seems quite fitting to be joining a sea shanty choir outside on the beach with the twinkling glow of the Christmas tree lights looking all pretty through the window next to Ted's sparkling star lantern. The row of outdoor lights flanking the wooden walkway look pretty too, as does the cosy dance of the gold and red flames in the fire pit. The tide is out so there's just a gentle hush from the velvety sea as it trickles back and forth over the sand; the wind has dropped too so it's blissfully calm and serene out here tonight.

OK, only a few minutes to go so I finish up my toast, place the plate down on the deck, and wrap my fingers around the mug of hot chocolate for reassurance as I follow the instructions from Rita and tap the keyboard to join in. Moments later, and as if by magic, there's an actual choir of people on the screen of my laptop in little squares with Vicar Joe in the sailors' church standing by a bookcase. He's thumping the top of the bookcase with the heel of his right fist as if to give a beat to count everyone in to start singing. And that's not all. There are about twenty-five people in the choir – mostly men with deep rousing voices – and they're all wearing hats! Nobody said anything about a hat. And we're not talking about just any old hat. No, these are peaked sailor-style hats, like the one Mack was wearing, and hold on... I swipe across to the next screen and see that some of the men and a couple of women are wearing pirate-style tricorne black hats with a resplendent gold braid trim and I'm suddenly transported back to that field trip in school to the beach when we learnt all about the history of smuggling in seventeenth-century Mulberry-On-Sea. Wow! Some of the sea shanty choristers are wearing black jackets with gold buttons and OMG, it's Jack. *Hot Jack*, as the Carrington's gang calls him. And if I'm being totally honest, I can see now exactly why they think he's hot because Jack is on the screen in front of me looking like he's literally just ridden a stallion across the cliffs all the way from *Bridgerton* or stepped out of an equally romantic and sizzling period drama where he's playing the devilishly handsome highwayman. Jack is standing by the bar of The Hook Line & Sinker wearing a white ruffled shirt with the ties undone to reveal a flash of a dark-haired and very solid-looking chest. His brown curly hair is wild and his legs are clad in tight black breeches and long leather boots. He's also thumping the heel of his right fist on the wooden bar top making a pint glass full of beer slosh precariously. Everyone is chatting and laughing and generally having a fun time until Vicar Joe stops thumping, glances at his watch, gives me a welcoming wave and then asks everyone to stop talking and follow his instructions with some vocal limbering up exercises. After everyone has gone through a series of oohing and ahhing and stretching their faces into funny shapes, the actual singing starts.

A Christmas carol but sea-shanty-style.

'God Rest ye Merry Gentlemen.'

And by the time they reach the tidings of comfort and joy bit I am completely mesmerised. Not only by the singing which is utterly entrancing and emotional and rousing. Yes, very rousing indeed! I even have to discard my hot-water bottle as it's suddenly become very hot out here on the deck. I take a sip of hot chocolate and fan myself with the corner of the blanket that was tucked underneath my arms and wonder if I dare FaceTime Lorna and turn the phone to my laptop to let her have a look at Jack. Sorry, Hot Jack. Because he actually is. But on second thoughts, absolutely not. He's looking directly at me now. Singing and thumping his fist. And he has that smile in place with the tilting-head thing. He lifts his free hand up and I instinctively glance over my shoulder to see who he's waving at. But he's shaking his head and frowning now, like he's baffled about something. My cheeks flush nonetheless. He's moving now, walking around the other side of the bar to sit on a stool so I can only see the top half of his body, his hands hidden from view.

Rita must be in another section of the pub, upstairs in a private part away from the bar as she's sitting on a sofa with a lovely brightly coloured crocheted blanket across the back and a log fire to the side of her with a twinkling Christmas tree in view too. She has a chubby grey cat draped across her lap, a glass of red wine in one hand and a sheet of paper in the other, presumably with the lyrics for the songs written on it. She looks as if she's thoroughly enjoying herself as she sings away, gently swaying her glass from side to side in time to the beat of the song.

A message pops up in the chat section on the screen. A private one just to me.

Good to see you, B x

Oh, it's from Jack. But why is there a kiss? I push my hair back away from my roasting-hot cheeks and go to type a reply, and hesitate. Are we allowed to send messages during the choir practice? I'm sure I saw something in the choir information pack that Jack dropped off, politely asking choir members not to message during the practice sessions as it can be distracting for other members. Well, it's certainly distracting me, that's for sure. I take a mouthful of hot chocolate and pick up my own sheet of paper with the song lyrics on, figuring I should at least make some attempt to join in. But I'm scared! Feeble, I know, but what if I really do sound ridiculous and they all roll about laughing? Or worse still, expel me from the choir for being too awful and in danger of ruining their wonderful sound? And it really is a wonderful sound. Soulful. Just beautiful and very emotional. Nostalgic too. It conjures up thoughts of sailors and simpler times. Community and kindness and kindred spirits all looking out for each other in the good times and bad. Much like Vicar Joe and Rita and Jack are doing with their essentials boxes and making sure nobody is forgotten about. Including newcomers like me and my family and making sure we have a Christmas tree. I think again of Jack bringing the tree and how kind and generous it was of him to gift it to us. The lovely pine-scented logs too. Especially after we got off on the wrong foot to start with.

OK. I'm going to go for it and sing. After three. One, two, three…

I check the paper just to be sure I'm at the right place. Yes, that's right …

'Tidings of comfort and joy,' I sing in a very quiet voice and I'm just limbering up for the next line when another message pops up on the screen. Jack again. And I can see now that he's got his hands out of view underneath the bar so that the rest of the choir can't see that he's messaging me from his mobile. Hmm, he may be kind and generous, but daring too! And for some reason this appeals and I find myself warming to him more.

Why aren't you singing? x

I'm curious to see another kiss. I put down the mug of hot chocolate and pull my laptop closer on my lap to type a reply.

What do you mean? I am singing.

I hesitate again, this time with my finger hovering over the x key. Should I add a kiss too? It seems a bit strange. We've only met a couple of times and it's not like we know each other or anything, so it's a bit forward, but then again I'm very out of touch as I only ever message Mum and Lorna and of course I always put a kiss. I can't remember the last time I messaged a man that wasn't Ted. Apart from in a professional sense, like a plumber or the window cleaner for example. In fact, I don't think I've ever messaged another man in any kind of social or romantic sense as sending text messages on mobiles weren't really a thing back before I met Ted as a teenager. Or maybe adding a kiss to his messages is just Jack's way. Like the head tilt and sardonic smile thing he does. Perhaps he signs all his messages off with a kiss, and I'm thinking about this too much. I decide to go for it and add a kiss too. What harm can it do? It's just a pleasant courteous thing to do and, besides, the people pleaser in me doesn't want to look offish if I don't, or old fashioned and behind the times like my darling twin boys already think I am. Not that I'm feeling pressured to reciprocate with a kiss. Not at all. It's just, well... I actually don't know, but I do know that I'm starting to get a tension headache from wondering what I should do. Arghhhh. Right, get a grip, Bridget. It's just a kiss in a message. No big deal. So I press send. I cough to clear my throat and lift the paper up higher to hide my face. Moments later, there's another message. I peer around the side of the paper.

Really? Your lips aren't moving. Are you shy? x

No x

Are you sure?

And this time he's added a wink emoji before the kiss. 'Cheeky fucker!' I say, *out loud*, forgetting that the whole choir can hear me. I cringe as a few people on the screen suddenly look left then right as if wondering who on earth just ruined the gorgeously soulful humming. It's a quiet bit to start the next song that Vicar Joe is doing while everyone else is silent. Except me! Shit. Another message. This time it's a group message from Vicar Joe reminding us all to mute ourselves at the start of each new shanty so as not to distract the group with 'inadvertent background noise' when he's teaching and showing us a demo of how the singing should sound. Oh god, I forgot about that; it was in the instructions too. I quickly tap the mute button and deliberately avoid looking at Jack as I can see out of the corner of my eye that his shoulders are bobbing up and down as if he's killing himself laughing. Typical. I've shown myself up again. And he's loving every minute of it, again, as another message pops up.

> Charming! Do you insult everyone like that or just me? What happened to us drawing a line? x

I don't hesitate at all this time and rally a reply right back.

> Stop teasing me then x

A few second pass when he's thinking of a comeback, I assume, and I have to admit I'm impressed that he can sing and type at the same time, because he really is singing – his mouth is moving, unlike mine which is set in a pursed line as I wait for his quip response, no doubt.

I can't resist x

Well try x

I've typed the words but haven't pressed send yet when another message pops up.

I can't. I'm a cheeky fucker x

I almost choke on a mouthful of hot chocolate because I guess I walked right into that one. I ponder for a moment and pretend to be singing and making sure I'm moving my mouth too as I try to come up with a suitable retort, but it's no use and so I plump for the obvious.

Sorry, that was a mistake x

I put my laptop at a distance on the little wooden picnic table to the side of me, resolved to focus on the actual singing as I look the other way towards the fire pit on the sand. It is choir time after all and not 'swap flirty

202

chat messages with Hot Jack time'. I sing on for a bit after Vicar Joe demos a new Christmas carol – a sea shanty version of 'Silent Night', and then does the thumping and humming thing to count us in to join him. Jack is singing too, although he looks a bit disconcerted on the screen; his head is bowed as if he's still looking at his phone and keeps glancing up. I'm getting into the swing of it now and the boys are looking back from the fire pit with puzzled looks on their faces. Oscar is standing up. And OMG he's giving me, aka his embarrassing mum, a Wayne's World double thumbs up! He's impressed, and that's saying something coming from him. My heart glows as I see both of my teenage boys clapping and grinning now, genuinely so, and in a pause at the end of the chorus I wave at them and then inhale a big lungful of crisp, salty sea air mingled with the woody scent of the logs crackling and flickering on the fire pit. Taking in the scene set out before me, I feel content. Happy. Cosy. And perfect timing too as the song reaches the 'all is calm, all is bright' bit.

Out of the corner of my eye I see another message pop up and can't resist glancing across at the screen to see what it says.

Apology accepted and sorry for teasing. Can I make it up to you? x

I read the message twice. What does he mean, make it up to me? And then I glance across at the boys to see if they're still looking in my direction as I feel very clandestine typing my response. But I'm also very curious to know.

What do you have in mind? x

Three dots appear on the screen so I can see that he's typing and I realise that I'm holding my breath in anticipation. Instinctively, I take a quick look out to sea and wonder what would Ted think, if he was watching over us or whatever he may be doing right now. I don't feel panicky like I did the other night when I thought Jack was implying we'd be seeing each other – as in, going on a date. But I'm in no doubt now that this is definitely a flirtatious situation and I actually think I'm OK with it. Jack sure interests me. I reckon there's much more to him than first meets the eye – hidden depths, as they say... And here's the thing too: seeing him in normal clothes as opposed to bundled up in a giant coat, hat, and scarf covering up half his face – in pirate-slash-highwayman clothes, to be precise – and singing such emotionally tender songs is very appealing indeed. I know it's a bit shallow to go on looks and of course they fade in time in any case, but I'm not going to lie... I'm enjoying the flirt and the messaging seems far less daunting as I dip my toes back in the dating pool, if that's what this really is. But then another message pops up on the screen and it seems that this is very much what it is…

Can I see you some time? x

It seems weird seeing it there in black and white, and he's very bold. But I still feel clandestine, almost as if I'm cheating on Ted. I know this may seem dramatic as he's no longer here, and I knew Ted well enough to believe that he wouldn't want me to be alone for the rest of my life, as I would for him if I had been the one to die, leaving him alone. No, he'd want me to be happy. To find love again one day with someone new. Someone kind. Someone… just nice, and then as if Jack has read my thoughts, there's another message.

Maybe Christmas drinks and a barbecue on that fire pit of yours? Low-key! I'll prepare the food and bring it with me. My treat. Know you have a lot on with the bread-making x

I smile, thinking how thoughtful it is of him as I type out my reply.

Sure. Low-key sounds lovely. Thanks x

I press send, wondering what he'll prepare, but then remember that he's a chef so it's bound to be nice. What a treat to have a meal cooked by Jack as I get to know him more. And then something occurs to me: what will the children think? A moment of panic pulses through me. What if they aren't ready for this? How will they feel? Of course, their loyalty will always be to their dad but—

I stop, take a deep breath, and will my pulse to slow back to a normal rate. It's just a festive drink or two and a barbecue on the beach. Two new friends getting to know each other. I must stop overthinking the situation. It's not even a proper date-date, as in going to a restaurant on our own or the cinema or for a drink or whatever, but still, maybe the boys will actually enjoy it... Having someone to work the fire pit with them, and they're pretty infatuated with the whole fire thing right now, looking for more logs and making requests for giant marshmallows and hunks of bread to toast all the time. And as for Freya, I can let her stay up so she doesn't feel left out. I think that's important, especially as she seemed to get on so well with Jack. I wonder if I should mention it to him? That the children will be here of course. But as I'm pondering another message pops up.

Tomorrow night? I'll bring plenty of food for
everyone. What does Freya like, and the boys?
Burgers, bangers, freshly caught fish? x

I draw in another big breath as I reply, not anticipating it would be so soon. I thought I'd at least have a few days to get used to the idea and to chat it through with the children too – see how they feel about a man joining us for the evening. But then, I guess I should just take the plunge and go for it, live dangerously! Or on second thoughts maybe not dangerously, given my over-zealous imagination when it comes to envisaging accidents. So just cautiously with flair perhaps! Yes, this is much more me, and so I type my reply.

Sounds good. I'll bring the bread x

And then I quickly add:

My children will eat anything. Thank you.

And I add a laughing face emoji and press send before realising it's not cool. Oh well. That's me. The uncool mum. Guess Jack will have to take me as he finds me, old-fashioned laughing emojis and all. Which he does, as he replies with a simple kiss, a sideways laughing emoji and two baguette emojis, and suddenly I feel like a teenager all over again, flirting and having fun, and so I reply with a dinner plate emoji, a beach wave, and three baguettes, plus a Christmas tree and a snowman for good measure, realising that this is who I am now, someone who communicates through the medium of emojis! And I have to say that I quite like her. She's fun and light.

Vicar Joe is wrapping up the choir practice session now and everyone is lifting a glass as if to say cheers, so I lift my now empty mug and join in, thinking what a fun and eventful evening it's been. Who knew choir practice could be full of such surprises? I'm definitely a choir convert and swiftly make a mental note to get myself the pirate gear. Maybe Jack can tell me where to get a tricorne hat. With a feather. I fancy that! A big plume of hot-pink marabou floating from the rim. And how about a fake hook like actual Captain Hook, the pirate in the Peter Pan Disney film? The boys will be beside themselves when I'm warbling away dressed up like that. Embarrassing Mum overload! Bring it on. I haven't felt this light and upbeat in ages and it's very lovely indeed to have something nice to look forward to.

'Well done everyone, and great to have you join us, Bridget,' Vicar Joe says, and I smile.

'Thanks for having me.'

'Will you come back again?' someone shouts. 'Hope we didn't put you off with our dress-up pirate gear.' And they all laugh.

'Not at all. I was just thinking I need to get a hat and possibly a hook for a hand,' I say, and they all roar with laughter.

'I've a hat you can have.' It's Rita and she's doing a thumbs up. 'Jack can bring it over.' I'm sure there's a fleeting look of knowing on her face, almost as if she can tell that something has happened between the two of us. But before I have time to ponder further, Vicar Joe is talking again.

'And remember we have the over-seventies bingo festive special on Christmas Eve here in the church café. It's come around very quickly this year. Please let our older members of the community know and I'm very happy to help get them familiarised with using the technology if they don't want to venture out in the cold weather and prefer to join in online, and then of course we have the turkey dinner with all the trimmings to be delivered on Christmas Day, courtesy of Rita and Jack at the pub. So if anyone is free to help with the distribution, it would be very much appreciated, but I understand that you will all want to be with your own families…' There's suddenly a flurry of messages to the whole group from kind souls volunteering to help deliver the Christmas dinners to the elderly and housebound. I make a note to chat to Vicar Joe to see how I can help out too when I drop off more bread to him. The children will most likely complain about going out on Christmas Day, but I think it would be nice to do something to help others.

There's one last private message from Jack.

It's been fun, B. Look forward to seeing you
tomorrow night x

Smiling, I tuck my laptop under my arm and head
back inside the beach house to get on with some more
baking...

Chapter Fourteen

The following morning I can hear the buzz of chatter coming from outside. Henry is spinning in circles by the window in excitement to see who is there as Olly and Oscar come flying through the front door bringing with them a gust of crisp sea air. I'm in the kitchen, of course, and in my usual element baking and bagging up last night's big batch of bread loaves, plus some mince pies, cinnamon swirls, and mini stollen cakes with edible sprigs of green holly on top all ready to take to Vicar Joe; I figure his flock might like some extra festive treats in addition to a freshly baked loaf of bread. Freya has made some more very cute little Christmas tree decorations too so I'm going to pop those in the bags. Plus, I've set aside a bag for Mack and a bag for Pearl as she's been in touch to ask for a couple of loaves – one for her and Ian, and one for Glynis – and then I'll be going over to Sam at the Carrington's pop-up café to deliver to her after she phoned through an order of three white sourdough and three crusty brown loaves.

'Mum, there's lots of people outside asking if this is Bridget's Bicycle Bakery?' Olly says, pointing over his shoulder back towards the open front door.

'Ooh, really? Bridget's Bicycle Bakery?' A bubble of curiosity and excitement pops within me at the mention of an actual bakery-sounding business being linked to me. This is my dream after all. Could this really be happening? I need to investigate right away and so I put down the wooden spoon and mixing bowl that's tucked into the crook of my elbow and after wiping my hands on my apron and tucking a chunk of hair back into place, I follow the boys outside and onto the deck. There's what looks like a group of dog walkers milling around the fire pit as each of the six or so people has a lovely pooch of some kind, either sitting patiently at their heel and basking in the heat from the flames or scampering around on the sand. Henry is delighted as he near dives off the deck before hurtling across the sand, trampling over Freya's latest sandcastle creation, to join in the doggy mayhem, his ears flapping as he runs and his whole body wiggling from side to side in excitement. Soon he's part of the melee of chocolate, yellow, and black Labradors, a couple of cockapoos, a Jack Russell, a springer spaniel and an Alsatian puppy that's not quite got the hang of how this socialisation thing works yet as she's busy bombing around with a giant stick, sideways in her mouth that's twice the size of her so all the other dogs are giving her a wide berth to avoid getting bonked by the big stick.

'So sorry to bother you by turning up unannounced,' a woman with a lovely tartan coat says as she comes towards the deck. 'Pearl – she lives in the same street as me – mentioned that you bake the best bread and that you go out delivering on your bicycle, and then the women who've set up the Christmas pop-up coffee cabin by Carrington's said so too. And I know it's a bit cheeky, and, well, gosh, I didn't realise that there would be such a queue… Word has got around that your bread must be as exceedingly good as we've all heard it is. Do you by any chance have a loaf that I could buy?' She smiles before rubbing her mitten-clad hands together to keep them warm. 'And everyone else is here for bread too.' She nods and smiles at a very debonair man with thick white hair and a matching Santa beard, dressed in a black overcoat with a red scarf knotted at his neck and a jaunty sprig of festive gold tinsel fashioned into a flower shape and pinned to his lapel.

'Yes please, love,' he nods and gives me a cheery wave. 'Six loaves if you have them going spare, and Rita in the pub told me your mince pies are the bees knees so I'll have two dozen of those too if you can manage it. I'm Bill, by the way, and I run the little care home on the outskirts of Mulberry. My residents are very partial to an afternoon tea of sandwiches and cakes and with everyone stocking up for Christmas the supermarket is running out of bread in the blink of an eye these days and the delivery vans still can't get up the blasted cliff road, that's if you're lucky enough to get a delivery slot. I've been on to the council again this morning, but staff shortages mean the gritter trucks couldn't cover all the streets last night. I told them that Mulberry is practically cut off from civilisation with the main cliff road out of action and it's not practical for everyone to trudge across the sand dunes to get anywhere or to use the narrow beach road. Perfectly fine if you're riding a bicycle but not for a supermarket delivery truck' – he lifts his hands up in the air as if to punctuate his point, and a few of the others nod in agreement – 'but, anyway, it's not all doom and gloom. I think the lifeboat lads are going to take the 4x4 up there to the main cliff road later on and shake a load of gritty sand from the harbour across the tarmac after they've given it a good old going over with the shovels to get rid of all the ice. But still...' Bill draws breath and shakes his head before carrying on, 'Although please serve the others first as I'm not a queue jumper, never 'ave been.' He nods this time. 'I should have got my act together earlier as the others were all here before me.'

'Oh, it's OK, Bill. I don't think any of us will stand in the way of the older folks having a few sandwiches with their afternoon tea. Pay it forward and all that! Besides, I'll be in your care home one day and will be looking forward to a lovely afternoon tea so make sure you have plenty of bread for when my time comes,' the first woman in the tartan coat chuckles.

Olly and Oscar are stoking the fire pit now and setting up deckchairs for the crowd to sit in. Freya is having the time of her life chasing around with all the dogs and I'm doing a swift count up to see just how many people we have here looking for bread. A quick headcount makes it twelve loaves, if I give them one each and cover Bill's request too. I think it's probably doable and I'll still have some loaves leftover to take to Vicar Joe at the church.

'Yes, I think I have enough bread for all of you,' I beam, pleased that I went overboard on the baking again last night. After choir practice I had a definite spring in my step and so when the boys went to bed I poured myself a mug of mulled wine, put some festive music on, and treated myself to a big baking session that didn't end until just after midnight with the Aga ovens filling the house with the gloriously cosy scent of bread. There's a cheer as a few of the people settle into deckchairs and I'm proud of Olly taking a note of exactly the types of bread each person wants, using his phone to keep track as if he's working in a proper little beach café. Oscar, mind you, is looking disgruntled and if I'm not mistaken he's sizing up whether to pitch in or carry on being in his usual teenage sulk. A few seconds later, and his competitive streak gets the better of him and he strides over to a guy with a big hipster beard.

'I could bring you a latte too, if you like? To enjoy while you wait. The finest Columbian beans giving a smooth, rich taste...' he says, and I do a double-take, stunned at my son's temerity. Oscar sounds like he's suddenly turned into a proper barista. And since when did he talk about lattes? Or even know about Columbian coffee beans and smooth, rich-tasting coffee? He doesn't even like coffee! And I'm pretty certain that we don't even have any Columbian coffee in our house. Unless he means the jar of instant in the cupboard. Oh God, I don't want to get into trouble for misrepresentation or whatever it is. This impromptu beach bakery café will be closed down before it's even properly opened. But as Oscar turns to look over at me, I spot his eyebrows lifting and his mouth tilting at one side and I know that look on his face... He's up to something! But at least his scowl has faded for now so that's a good thing.

'I'll get on and start making up the orders,' I say, thinking I'm best not knowing what he's up to, as I dart back into the beach house and immediately grab some extra bags. Oscar is close behind me and he's filling the kettle with fresh water now, and oh my goodness, he's put the kettle on the Aga hotplate to boil. I stare at him, my mind boggling as I've never seen him willingly boil a kettle to make a hot drink for anyone before. 'What are you doing?' I ask, giving him a nudge with my elbow as I slip a white sourdough loaf inside a bag. 'And, Olly, let me see your phone screen so I know what breads to bag up.'

'Mum, we've got it all under control!' Olly says, and after scrubbing his hands with soap and warm water (another first I've ever witnessed for each of my boys) he's now sorting all the bread into orderly sections to make a mini production line. White sourdough loaves piled up at one corner of the table. Brown at another. Potato and rosemary next. Crusty white baguettes opposite, then mince pies and bread rolls, and cinnamon swirls all lined up in the middle.

'What is going on?' I bellow in a whisper voice, not wanting the people just outside the door to hear me and think I'm an amateur who doesn't even know what she's doing. Well, I am an amateur, I suppose, but I do have some catering experience from my time spent working in a café and I do have the proper food hygiene and safety certificates too, so I'm not a complete beginner.

'We're helping!' Oscar says, like it's the most obvious thing in the world and my jaw drops as I wonder where my sulky teenage son disappeared to? Who is this assertive, confident young man lining up mugs on the kitchen counter while his equally organised and capable brother is multitasking by looking at his phone to see the orders and then bags them up accordingly. The pair of them are operating like a slick production line in perfect synergy as they move around the kitchen handing cartons of milk, a jar of coffee (I knew it!) tea, and sugar to each other.

'Mum, you do know that we need to invest in a decent coffee machine if we're going to do this properly,' Olly says in a matter-of-fact voice as he stirs two mugs simultaneously with a teaspoon in each hand. 'We can't be serving up instant and charging two pounds a pop.'

'Two pounds?' I echo, flabbergasted. 'What do you mean two pounds?' I pivot on the back of my heel to look at him. But he rolls his eyes and shakes his head as if I'm the clueless one.

'For the coffee. Mum, it's the going rate! Well, that's pretty cheap for a takeaway coffee to be fair,' Oscar states.

'But we could charge more for the good stuff,' Olly responds, resting the chin of his nodding head on the knuckle of his index finger, just as Ted used to when he was mulling over an idea.

'Yes, and if we can operate a Bring Your Own Cup scheme then even better. Saves on washing up and protects the planet from pollution.' Oscar looks very impressed with himself now as he high-fives his twin. Meanwhile, my mind is completely boggling.

'Hang on a minute,' I manage to squeak, still flabbergasted. 'We can't just set up a bakery on the beach... or a café or whatever this is!' I lift my hands palms upwards as I swivel my head from one twin to the other, panic coursing through me.

'Why not?' they counter in unison.

'Just think of the money!' Oscar then adds, putting on an American New Yorker accent and shrugging like he's Don Corleone in *The Godfather*. I stare, stunned, and then slowly shake my head, trying not to smile as the proverbial penny drops. More money coming in means there's more chance of him getting the new, expensive games console he's had his eye on for a Christmas present. Oscar was never one to take his eye off the end goal. But then who can blame him? He's a teenage boy, and I know when I was his age my whole world revolved around dreaming of the latest must-have item.

'But there are regulations and things. Licences and insurance and, well, laws that have to be followed. Like selling instant coffee from a jar and dressing it up as some kind of fancy artisan blend or whatever.' I attempt to stare them down, but neither twin is in the least bit fazed.

'Then we'll research it all and sort it.'

'Sort it?' I drop my arms and fold them in front of me now.

'Yes, Mum,' Olly says, chivvying me out of the way. 'But right now, we have customers waiting, so please, chop chop!'

Chop chop! My mouth opens and closes in rapid succession like a guppy fish gasping for air. *CHOP flaming CHOP! Did he really just say that?*

He whips out a tray from a cupboard under the counter and starts loading the mugs of hot drinks onto it.

'Hmm,' I start, but swiftly realise that right now I need to just get on with it, so I do. 'Well... in that case, please be careful on the steps with the hot drinks. Maybe just carry two at a time and don't rush,' I call after Olly as he walks out of the house, my head going to thoughts of him slipping and scalding himself and... I close my guppy mouth and take a deep breath, pushing the panicky thoughts from my head as I try to get on with bagging up the orders. But then I remember there are several loaves in the Aga ovens that need bringing out so I grab the gloves and go to do that instead.

'Mum, it's fine,' Oscar says very calmly, and I stop moving. 'You can do this!' He steps forward and for the first time in a very long time he voluntarily gives me a big hug. I let myself sink into his embrace before rubbing his back as I used to when he was a little boy.

'You know, you're absolutely right! But you do know that even with selling lots of bread and cups of coffee I can't guarantee being able to afford the games console that you want. I'm sorry, love,' I tell him as I step back, then seize my moment to give him a quick big kiss on the cheek figuring it best to manage his expectations.

'Mum!' he rolls his eyes at me. 'I do know that, but we can at least try.'

'Sure, of course we can,' I agree, not wanting to crush his optimism.

'And if not this year then definitely next year. We'll have sold loads of bread and coffees by then,' he grins cheekily and I allow myself a moment to hope that he's right.

I smile and glance out of the window to see that all our customers are sitting around the fire pit chatting and laughing and cupping their mugs of hot drinks while the dogs are still playing, and it makes my heart sing to see such joy wrapped around our little delapidated yellow beach house. It brings to mind that old adage of things happening for a reason, because if we hadn't had to leave our last home that had become a place of sadness, then we wouldn't have found warmth and cheer here in our new home this Christmas. Or indeed, be pulling together in a perfect trio, working as a team to service our customers waiting on the sand for a loaf of freshly baked bread from Bridget's Bicycle Bakery.

'Right, I'd better get on and bring out the bread,' I say, slipping my hands into the oven gloves and pulling open the Aga door.

Chapter Fifteen

A gloriously restorative sunset shimmers like liquid gold over the ocean as I sink, gratefully, onto a big bean bag in the hull of the boat to relax with a blanket and the cosy heat of the fire pit. Seagulls are swooping and soaring, their wings an elegant silhouette in the evening sky.

I'm shattered – but in a satisfied and utterly content way after the rush earlier this morning to make sure our customers left here happy with a loaf or four tucked under their arms. I then cycled there and back to Our Lady Star of the Sea sailors' church to drop off all the bakes to Vicar Joe before pedalling on round to Pearl and Ian's house to drop off their bread and some extra mince pies as a thank you gift for spreading the word and sending more customers my way. Next I went to Mack's seaside cottage where he made me a lovely cup of tea that we drank sitting on a bench opposite his house looking out to the sea as he told me more about Dotty and how she loved this time of year, seeing all the children of Mulberry sledging down the snow-covered grassy slopes. We both mused on whether there was likely to be snow this Christmas, commenting on how the sky had seemed so ripe for it a few times recently, but there had been nothing yet, much to Freya's disappointment. It brought a smile to Mack's face when I described how it's the first thing she does each morning, to peep around the curtains hoping to see a magical swathe of snow across the grassy dunes. I also told Mack about Pearl's neighbour, Glynis.

'Poor dear, can't be easy on her own,' is what he said, when I mentioned she might love a bit of company if he was up for having an intro. Then added, 'well, I never knew that!' seemingly flabbergasted when I talked to him about the sea shanty choir and that it could be just the thing for him to revive the memories of his fisherman days. I told him he'd fit right in with his sailor's cap and deep tenor voice. He's agreed to dig out Dotty's old laptop and give it a go. Lastly, I called by Carrington's and dropped off Sam's bread order before popping instore to buy some Christmas presents and new school uniform for the children. I spoke to Mum and explained that if I could use the money she gave me to add to what

I've already earned from the bread-making then it should be enough to cover the cost and then I can focus on saving up to fix up the car, repair the house, and get the bedroom ceiling looked at properly. After doing her typical 'merits of meeting a millionaire' promo chat, she reluctantly came around and agreed that the children couldn't go without 'the good stuff', as she calls it. As long as I promise to treat myself to a new wardrobe when the bakery business takes off. It was actually very lovely, if surprising, hearing her have faith in me making it work. But not before she did a little quip about a handknitted unicorn scarf seeming so sad, totally not grasping the fact that Freya is obsessed with having one.

When I got home, Olly presented me with his 'Bridget's Bicycle Bakery business plan', which was pretty impressive, if a little long and extremely ambitious in the detail to expand through to every beach location in the country and possibly the whole world within three years! Needless to say, he wasn't overly impressed by my perceived lack of ambition when I explained that the Aga, with its multiple ovens and always-on ability, is fine for baking lots of loaves to service a fairly small beach community, but it's not an industrial oven that could cope with such a large-scale enterprise. Dropping off orders with little festive treats and tree decorations by bicycle and serving up coffees and tea on the beach is probably going to be the most I can do right now. I'd still like to have time for a cuppa with my new friends, Mack and Pearl, and my oldest friend too, which reminds me... I must give Lorna a call to see if she wants a hand drawing up the questions for the Christmas Eve quiz. So now I'm well and truly looking forward to a relaxing evening with a lovely mug of mulled wine and a hot-water bottle to soothe my aching legs and backside, the muscles in which I wasn't even aware of before now, are throbbing from all that pedalling.

'Mummy, Mummy, Jack's here, and he's got Sinead with him!' shrieks Freya, swiftly tossing aside a spade she's been using to dig a 'conservation pool' in the sand for a bucket full of tiny crabs swimming in seawater that she found in a rock pool. Henry, right on cue as always, cocks his head up from a settled sleeping position on a blanket beside me, and then after hurdling over the side of the boat in one swift movement he bounds over to greet Jack and Sinead, completely unfazed by the size of the enormous Irish wolfhound that's twice the height of him, at least. I'm very happy indeed to be sitting down inside the boat so I'm not bowled over again by the extremely exuberant dog. Mind you, Sinead seems considerably calmer this evening as she stands, beautifully behaved, beside Jack. But then I see why as Jack has her on a harness attached to a lead that is clipped to his belt.

'Hope it's OK to bring her? I didn't want to leave her

at the pub as Rita is out delivering the takeaway dinners tonight and she'll just wail the place down if left on her own, which is exactly what she did when I went to walk away from the truck to come over here,' Jack explains, arms full with a pile of silver foil-covered platters. A guitar case is hanging from a red strap across the back of the black leather flight jacket with shearling collar that he's wearing over a chunky Aran wool fisherman's jumper and Levi jeans with boots. His black curls are windswept around his face. He definitely suits the Hot Jack name, even if he does have the usual head tilt and sardonic smile in place. As he comes closer, I catch a whiff of a cool, fresh scent of sea salt and citrus. I smile inwardly at the effort he's obviously made and there's no denying a little frisson of physical attraction ignites within me.

Pushing the blanket back, I take a deep breath in anticipation of how the evening may turn out – and of how Freya, Olly, and Oscar are going to feel having him here. When I told them earlier that he was coming over for a barbecue, the boys just said, 'cool' and Freya was more interested in knowing if Sinead would be coming too, so I'm not sure if they even picked up on the date element of this evening. It does seem strange though having Jack here, when it's been just the four of us for so long now. But then, no, 'strange' isn't really the right word for how I feel right now. I'm not quite sure what it is, if I'm honest, only that I've never felt like this before. I'm excited, yes, but it's more than that. I guess it's just different. Nice too. Jack's presence immediately brings a warm, reassuring – exciting even – dynamic to our group here on the beach. Even the boys have stopped playing frisbee and are coming over to greet him and Sinead, and Oscar is instantly drawn to the guitar and comments that he loves playing too and can they do a 'guitar sesh' together by the fire pit later on? The epitome of cool as far as I can tell by Oscar's reaction when Jack shrugs casually and says, 'Sure, buddy, let's do it.' But before I can question or analyse my own feelings any further, it's Freya who answers Jack.

'Yes! You can bring her. Can't he, Mummy?' I nod and smile in agreement and go to say, 'As long as I'm not bowled over by her for a third time,' but then on remembering my decision to go with the flow, and because I don't want to make Jack feel awkward before the evening has even started, I close my mouth again. 'I love her,' Freya adds, flinging her arms around Sinead's neck as the dog that's the size of a donkey and almost as tall as Freya, flops to the ground, rolls onto her back and lets my six-year-old daughter tickle her tummy as she shrieks with laughter like it's the funniest thing she has ever had the pleasure of doing. The sound of her joy is an absolute delight, especially when I think back to how she has been over the last year. And then I realise that quiet, withdrawn little girl hasn't shown herself since we came here. In fact, I can't remember the last time I saw Freya looking sad and so my smile widens on seeing her carefree cavorting on the sand with Sinead.

'Good to see you, Jack,' I say, standing up and bringing my arms out from underneath the thick woollen festive red poncho I found at the bottom of a box when I was doing the last of the unpacking, meaning I could ditch the old, flappy-pocketed coat that has definitely seen better days; the fabric near disintegrated when I tried to patch it up with a needle and thread. I've put my best jeans on, added a light touch of makeup and let my curly brown hair flow around my shoulders.

'Good to see you too, B,' he nods, and a moment passes between us as he looks me up and down, seeming to draw me in, but not in a weird way – in a nice, casually appreciative way. 'You look...' He seems to hesitate as he glances at the boys either side of me, wondering perhaps what the most appropriate and acceptable compliment might be to say to their mum, before settling on, 'Great. Really great.' He nods some more, and I'm sure I spot a hint of a blush in his cheeks as the sardonic smile fades, to be replaced by a lovely wide, kind smile instead. 'And glowing!'

'Ah, that'll be all the cycling! It gets the blood pumping,' I reply, stepping over the side of the boat and then for some quite unknown, but completely ludicrous reason, I lift my arms so they're at right angles to my body, and then bend my elbows. I look like I'm the strong man in an old vaudeville circus act as I dip down at the knees and after puckering up my lips I squeeze my fists and take a look at my biceps, swivelling my head from side to side. There's a moment of silence and then a little piece of my pride suddenly shrivels within me as Oscar and Olly stare at me with that familiar look of utter horror splashed all over their disapproving faces.

'Oh, Mum,' Oscar even mutters under his breath as I slide my arms back down by my sides. Jack's amber eyes are fixed on me now as if he has no idea what to make of me. But he's still smiling, so I guess that's something. At least he isn't pegging it back across the sand as fast as he can to get away from the fruitloop standing in front of him doing a lame one-woman comedy act.

'Well… it, er, sure does,' Jack says, diplomatically, before adding, 'Your hair looks nice like that.'

'Oh, thanks,' I say, patting my curls and finding myself grinning like a teenager out on a first date, which I guess this is, in a way. Certainly the first date with someone new that I've had in absolutely years. 'You look great too,' I tell him. 'I love the jacket; it suits you. And you smell lovely.' I know that both twins are groaning inside. I just know them well enough to know without even daring to look in their direction. But at least they seem OK so far with Jack being here, and OK with me clearly being flirtatious in front of them. Oscar, for sure, would be sullen and making it obvious if he wasn't, so I let out a little sigh of relief and switch the subject back to Sinead.

'Well, I'm glad you did bring Sinead. Poor thing doesn't want to be left in the truck all alone and miss out on the fun,' I say, in a silly, smoochy voice as I crouch down next to Freya and tentatively go to give Sinead a tummy rub too. But then Henry seems to get jealous as he immediately shoves his head up underneath my left arm and goes to lick the side of my face to take my attention away from Sinead.

'Hey, Henry, calm down,' I attempt, but it's no use, and Henry takes this as a cue to give me even more affection. Then, with the speed of a blinking eye, Henry has knocked me over and I'm on my back with him practically on top of me, his front two legs standing on my midriff, making sandy paw prints all over my marvellous festive red poncho. Jack looks on, helpless to do anything to help because his arms are full, but I can see that he's doing his utmost not to laugh, probably figuring it's for the best after the telling off I gave him last time this happened in the pub garden. I expel a big puff of air as I manage to push Henry away from me and roll onto all fours (oh god) then attempt to get to my feet, which isn't easy when you ache all over from having cycled a trillion miles, or so it seems. I can barely put my legs together – I'm like a bloody cowboy having spent too long in the saddle – and I note that not one of my darling twins tries to help me up. No, they're both too busy bent double, laughing themselves into a flaming hernia!

'OK, it's not that funny,' I splutter, on eventually managing to untangle myself from the doggy jumble of Henry and Sinead, and make it back up into a standing position. 'What is it with dogs wanting to roll around on the sand with me!' I exclaim, brushing the front of my poncho and tidying my hair that's now flopped all over my face.

'They like you, and who can blame them?' Jack smiles, making my pulse quicken. 'Come on, let's get the food sorted out,' and he wanders off towards the fire pit like it's just an everyday occurrence seeing me writhing around in the sand – which, it suddenly dawns on me, it absolutely is… for him! The only time he's seen me and I've NOT been face-planting the sand is when I was safely seated during choir practice.

———

The sun has gone down completely now, and we are all full up from having eaten far too much of the delicious food that Jack cooked on a proper portable beach barbecue he brought with him and set up on the sand near the fire pit to create even more of a lovely, toasty warm vibe on this winter evening. We've polished off tasty prawn and chorizo kebabs, harissa sardines, and dirty burgers loaded with cheese and chilli that the boys gave a sterling ten out of ten plus plenty of nodding and thumbs up. We've had pitta pockets stuffed with crispy chicken, mayo, and salad that Freya declared her brand-new favourite food accompanied by a big buffet of sausages and crab cakes, salt and chilli butter-coated corn cobs in foil, fruit skewers, marshmallow s'mores to toast on the fire pit, and all finished off with tumblers of homemade Christmassy eggnog mocktails for the children and mugs of festive hot apple cider for me and Jack.

I'm back in a position of safety, sitting in the boat so I can't fall over, and Freya is snuggled up inside a sleeping bag with a pile of cushions with Henry and Sinead curled up either side of her. Both dogs are snoring loudly, much to Freya's amusement, as they sleep off their meat comas after each being allowed to have a couple of leftover sausages. Jack is sitting in a deckchair on the other side of the fire pit and Oscar and Olly have gone over to the little car park to pick up a bag that Jack left in the back of the truck, having offered to go for him as he's spent practically the whole evening tending the barbecue and making sure we all had enough to eat.

'Mmm,' I take a sip of the delicious hot apple cider.

'This tastes so good, Jack. The food was wonderful too, thank you. You're a great chef.' I grin, as he picks up his guitar and loops the strap over his head and into position.

'You're welcome, B.' Glancing at Freya, I see that she is asleep and so I decide to move the conversation on a bit.

'I've had a great time and hope we can do it again some time?' I suggest tentatively. It's been a wonderful evening and I would love to have another one just like this. Jack is good company, fun, and the children all seem to like him too.

'Sure.'

'Great. But on one condition?' I say.

'Go on. I'm beginning to realise you like your conditions,' he laughs gently, tweaking a few strings in preparation for playing, the moonlight and flames from the fire pit flickering a golden glow across his face that is deep in concentration.

'That I do the cooking next time. I can't let you do it all again,' I tell him.

'Sounds fair,' he says, but doesn't look up. Silence follows. It's a little awkward to be honest, just the two of us without the distraction of the children and the food to focus on. I'm not sure if he's just being polite. Now I can't help wondering if maybe he feels sorry for me on my own with the children out here on this isolated part of the beach in our rickety, ramshackle little beach house. It's hard to tell as the conversation between us this evening has mostly been lighthearted banter without much actual talking and getting to know each other, but I try again.

'So how come you're here in Mulberry, Jack? It's a long way from Ireland.'

'It's a long story…' He carries on strumming his guitar and I wonder if it's OK to ask more. I'm about to try again when he stops strumming, and after looking as though he's wondering what to say, he rests one hand on the top of the guitar and tells me. 'In a nutshell, I came here for love. Or so I thought at the time,' he says cryptically, and I drink more of the cider, willing him to continue. A few seconds later, he does. 'A big mistake, as my ex-girlfriend decided that pub life wasn't for her after all and went straight back home. We came over from Ireland together, Ciara to manage the pub restaurant and me as the chef managing the kitchen. An adventure, if you like, only it didn't work out that way. She had been seeing my best mate, you see.' He pauses and after taking a big chug of his cider, he carries on. 'They're married now, with a baby boy, living back home in Galway.'

'Oh, I'm so sorry, Jack. That must have been tough.'

'Ah, it's fine,' he says, quickly brushing it off, but I get a sense that the hurt still runs deep. 'Mulberry is a great place to be. I like it here and the choir and the community are a craic. Kind and welcoming too. Rita is one in a million. She let me stay on here after Ciara left and so now we manage the pub between us – she's been like a mam to me,' he adds, his voice softening slightly, and I get the impression that Rita helped him through what must have been a pretty hard time when Ciara left. A split is always difficult, but a betrayal from a best friend must be devastating.

'Yes, Rita is lovely,' I agree, thinking of the welcome box she left on the porch and how much it meant to me. Such a kind gesture from a stranger really lifted my spirit and signified a starting line of sorts, the mark of a new beginning.

'So what brings you here to Mulberry? And this close to Christmas too! It's an unusual time for a house move,' he says, giving the guitar chords a casual strum. I finish the last of the cider and place the mug down over the side of the boat and onto the sand. After taking a deep breath, I wonder if I should explain about having to leave our old house, and what happened to Ted, of course, and wanting a fresh start and to put my family back together again in time for Christmas. But I hardly know Jack, and if he is here tonight just to be kind because he feels sorry for me, then I'm not sure if I want to open up and share something so personal. Maybe I should wait and see how things go, but then he's shared something from his past that was clearly quite difficult for him. Before I can figure out my feelings any further, Freya suddenly pops her sleepy head over the top of the sleeping bag.

'My daddy died!'

Jack stops strumming and looks up at me, his eyes softening.

Silence follows.

I can see Freya's bottom lip wobbling and her forehead creasing as the enormity of what she's said out loud sinks in. Instinctively, I draw her into me in a big hug, rubbing the side of her arm to soothe and reassure her. I open my mouth to step in and say something, but the words won't come out. It's Jack who speaks next, quietly and tenderly.

'I'm so sorry your daddy died. I'm sure you miss him.' Freya nods as she loops her head out from underneath my arm to snuggle her face into Henry's fur and then Sinead's before sitting up and looking directly at Jack.

'He lives on a shipwreck in the sea now,' she tells him, in her usual matter-of-fact way, and Jack smiles kindly, looking at me and then back to Freya. 'But he's not cold because he has his dog that is called Jingle. She died when Daddy was a teenager, so she's in heaven now too and can give him a cuddle whenever he wants one.' I smile at the simplicity of Freya's thinking, and that she's remembered this from last Christmas when I overheard her having a heart-to-heart with Lorna who very patiently and gently gave her this comforting assurance.

Before any of us can say more, the boys are back and Olly has a black bin liner over his shoulder which he puts down on the sand.

'Jack, your truck is so cool. Can we go for a ride in it some time?' Oscar asks, flopping back into the boat on the other side of Freya with a massive grin across his face.

'Well, if your mam says it's all right, then sure, we can sort something out,' Jack replies, then, after pushing his guitar out of the way behind his back, he stands up, opens the bag and pulls out a gorgeous festive holly wreath studded with red berries and a lovely long red, gold, and green velvet ribbon. 'This is for you, B. To go on your front door.' He lifts the wreath up in the air.

'Oh, wow! It's wonderful and very Christmassy. Thanks, Jack.' I stand up too and walk over to him. He moves a little closer and I instinctively do too, wondering if I should give him a hug, but for some reason I hold back so instead he places the wreath on the wooden path and then pushes a hand through his hair before looking me straight in the eyes. I hold his gaze, thinking how thoughtful he is, and wonder if I was wrong to doubt him earlier. But the moment passes as Jack swings his guitar round and goes back to his deckchair by the fire pit.

'OK, who's up for a campfire singalong?' he says.

'Yes!' we all chorus, eagerly.

An hour or so later we've covered off all the Christmas carols, and drunk more cider and mocktails when Jack glances at his watch.

'Hate to spoil the party, folks, but I'm going to need to get going,' he says, pulling Sinead's lead from his pocket and standing up as if to go and round her up. Sinead and Henry, having awoken from their power naps are cavorting across the sand now, having the time of their lives, chasing and teasing each other with bits of soggy seaweed, and with no sign of running out of steam just yet.

'Oh, yes, sure.' I glance at my watch. 'I can't believe it's almost eleven o'clock.'

'You know what they say, time sure flies when you're having fun, and I've had a lot of fun tonight, B, but I've got an early start tomorrow in the kitchen.'

'When are you coming to see us again?' Freya asks, popping her sleepy head over the top of the sleeping bag again, her hair all fuzzed up as her woolly bobble hat slips off. Oscar reaches across and after retrieving the hat from the hull of the boat, slips it back on his little sister's head. The simple gesture of brotherly kindness makes my heart melt in this tender moment as Freya then kisses the back of his hand before saying again, 'Mummy, can Jack come to our Christmas Eve party?' A moment of silence follows as I glance at Jack who is busy packing his guitar away into its case. I'm not actually sure if he even heard what Freya just said. 'Mummy? Jack? Do you want to come to our party?' she tries again.

'Well thanks for inviting me, sweetheart,' Jack pauses, and he looks hesitant as if searching for the right thing to say and so I step in, not wanting him to feel that he has to accept Freya's impromptu invitation. Plus, it feels way too intimate and too soon – not that I'm thinking this is an actual thing between me and Jack or anything at all… I inhale sharply through my nose and try to slow my breathing as I feel way too panicky all of a sudden.

'Jack is probably busy, my love. Christmas is a special time for family and friends. I'm sure he has plans already or he might be worki—'

'I'd love to!' Jack jumps in, keeping his eyes fixed on mine. 'If that's OK with your mammy?'

I swallow hard, the panicky feeling building further, but on seeing Freya's eager face as she swivels her head to look at me, I find myself nodding slowly as I mouth, 'Are you sure?' over the top of her head and he does a resolute nod back. 'Yep. It's my turn to have Christmas Eve off this year so it would be a pleasure to join you.' I glance at Olly and Oscar to gauge how they feel about Jack joining us on what's always been a special tradition for our family, with Ted very much at the centre of it. Both boys are nodding –

Olly is even grinning and Oscar's face isn't scowling – so I take this as a sign that they are both OK with the plan.

'Sure, why not,' I say, quickly followed by, 'on one condition.' My children all look at me expectantly and Jack has a 'here she goes again with the conditions' look on his face. 'That I do the cooking. Our traditional festive buffet feast, and it's only fair as Jack has gone to a lot of trouble to cook for us all tonight.' Everyone nods in agreement.

'Works for me,' Jack grins.

'Oh, and there's another condition,' I say, as the boys go to start playing with the frisbee again. 'We all help clear up the plates and barbecue stuff and take it back to Jack's truck.' And as if by magic, each one of my children immediately jumps into action and starts helping. As the boys busy themselves piling plates up and packing away the portable barbecue, Freya stacks the plastic glasses inside each other, Jack and I go to round up the dogs. When the twins and Freya are safely out of earshot, Jack stops walking.

'B, are you OK?' he asks gently.

'Oh, yes, sure, why?' I stop moving too and turn to look at him, seeing his face full of concern.

'It's just, well…' He pauses as if searching for the right words, 'What Freya said earlier. I'm sorry, I didn't know.' He shakes his head and then looking down at the sand he adds, 'And I shouldn't have been such an arse when you first arrived here—'

'Hey, you weren't to know, and besides, it's good that you didn't know.'

'How come?'

'Well, you didn't tiptoe around me, being on your best behaviour or whatever, for starters…' I smile wryly.

'Hmm, well you can say that again. In fact, I did the complete opposite, like a massively insensitive oaf.' He shakes his head as if he's cross with himself now and he pushes his hands into the pockets of his jeans. 'But I'm not going to pretend, B. I am attracted to you. I was intrigued from the moment I first clapped eyes on you. And, to be honest, I can't stop thinking about you, but I totally get that I might have got this all wrong and, well, I guess what I'm really saying is that if you don't feel the same way and this is just a polite friendship thing… you know, if you're just being kind in agreeing to me being here this evening…' He pauses and I think of my thoughts earlier and how it seems that we've both misread things. 'Or that it's too soon, and then—'

'Jack. I've had a lovely time tonight and…' My voice fades as I can't find the words I want to say, so then settle on, 'I want to get to know you more. I can't promise anything, but I think I'm ready to find out…' I pause, and then add quietly, 'Ted died just over a year ago…' I glance down at the sand as my voice tails off.

'Do you want to talk about him? About what happened?' he asks, gently.

'Um, I'm not sure.' I hesitate, unsure of where to start, or how much to tell him. Will he want to listen to me talking about my first love, my everlasting love? Because that won't ever end; my love for Ted will always be there. 'Maybe not yet.' I lift my eyes to his.

'OK. But please let me know if that changes, yes?' He smiles.

'I will. I promise.' I grin, feeling lighter somehow. It's as if a burden I didn't realise I had has been lifted, shifting something between us. I can relax and talk about Ted when the time is right and that feels nice, comforting.

'Cool.' He nods pragmatically. 'And one last question. Are you sure it's OK for me to come over on Christmas Eve? I saw how you hesitated, but I can understand why now. I won't be offended. I get that it's a big thing. Christmas is, as you said, for friends and family.'

'Yes!' I laugh. 'Hundred percent. I want you to. We're friends, aren't we? New ones, yes, but we have to start somewhere, don't we?'

'I guess we do,' Jack grins. 'OK. In that case, I'll look forward to it,' he nods decisively.

'Me too.'

Chapter Sixteen

On Sunday morning I'm woken with a start when Freya flings back the curtains and shrieks, 'Mummy! It's snowing! Look. Look. Look at all the pretty snowflakes.' Rolling over and shielding my eyes from the shaft of dazzlingly brilliant bright winter sunshine, I yawn and gather myself before dashing over to stand beside her and revel in her glee. There's just something so magical about waking up to a confetti of pristine white snow fluttering all around. It's like we're inside a giant snow globe, glittery and mesmerising. Even the waves in the sea have softened to a gentle rhythm, like a penny pusher slot machine nudging coins of ice back and forth on the shimmering snow-capped shore. Freya claps her hands together in excitement before spinning around and swiftly pulling a jumper on over her nightie.

'Come on, Mummy, let's go outside and catch snowflakes on our tongues.' She's tugging jeans on now followed by a pair of pink socks.

'OK, sweetheart, just let me quickly get dressed too,' I beam, enthused by her joy. But then a prickle of panic sets in at the prospect of trying to cycle through snow into Mulberry to deliver the bread rolls to Rita. I don't want to let her down, especially as it's my first big delivery, but what if I'm unable to get to her? I wonder if Jack can come and collect the bread rolls instead? But then, on second thoughts, he's bound to be busy today with prepping the meals for the Sunday roast orders already placed. He's not going to have time to come all the way out here when there's a mountain of vegetables to peel and chop, and so it's probably best not to ask and put him in an awkward position.

I'm brushing my hair when my mobile phone rings on the bedside cabinet.

'Mummy, it's Jack,' Freya says, grabbing my phone and handing it to me.

'Oh, I was just thinking about you,' I say to answer, on autopilot as I mime a request for Freya to put her welly boots back down on the floor. She's found them from somewhere and plonked them on the bed and I can already see a streak of wet sand smeared across the My Little Pony face part of the pillow case.

'All good thoughts, I hope?' he says, with a tease in his voice that tells me he's smiling.

'Er, yes, absolutely,' I say, and it's true. I have been thinking about him. Quite a lot in fact since the barbecue the other night, and each time I've found myself smiling as I recalled the various special moments from that lovely evening.

'In that case, do you fancy coming sledging with me?' There's a pause before he quickly adds, 'All the children are out on the grass slopes having the time of their lives and I thought Freya might love it. What do you reckon? I remember her saying she was wishing for snow this Christmas. I bet she's delighted this morning.' He laughs.

'Oh, um, yes, thank you,' I say, smiling at his thoughtfulness. 'She absolutely would. Freya is beside herself already, but we only have a sprinkling here. What's it like there?'

'Thick snow. An inch or two already. Do you think the boys would be up for it too? I used to love sledging as a kid, but they might think it's not cool...' Jack laughs, sounding like a big kid himself now as he speaks faster, clearly excited at the prospect of going sledging.

'I'm sure they would. If I can persuade them to come with me when I drop the bread rolls off—'

'I'll pick you all up!' Jack says, like it's obvious he will. 'The coastal road is going to be covered in snow very soon as it's drifting your way. There's no chance of you all making it on foot and with a heavy bike to push through a blizzard. You'll be like explorers trekking to the North Pole by the time you arrive in Market Square, you know, with the icicles clinging to your eyebrows and all that.' We both laugh as we ponder this vivid, if dramatic, image inside our heads.

'Can you imagine? I can hear the grumbling from the twins already.' I shake my head at the thought, not even wanting to contemplate suggesting to them that we walk all the way to Mulberry in the snow. 'But what about the Sunday roasts?' I check.

'All prepared. Just the chickens and joints of beef to put in the ovens and Rita has offered to keep an eye on all that. Snow isn't her thing so she's very happy to cosy up in the pub kitchen and keep warm. Plus, I made an early start this morning. I had an inkling it might snow so we'll drop the rolls here at the pub, go for a sledge, and then I'll be back in time to plate up. See you in an hour or so?' he says. He has it all worked out, and it's very appealing not being the one in charge for a change.

'Well, in that case, yes please. That would be a great help and the kids are going to love it.' I laugh on seeing Freya bouncing up and down in front of me, clearly having got the gist of the conversation.

———

An hour or so later, we've dropped off the tray of bread rolls to Rita, who I'm delighted to say was over the moon with them, and immediately placed an order for four dozen more to go with the turkey roast and all the trimmings that the pub is doing for the annual Christmas Day special. We are now on the white-capped grassy slopes leading down to the sea, the curve of colourful beach huts pretty in contrast to the thick sheet of glistening snow. There are little groups of families and friends and an assortment of dogs all around us, the sound of laughter and happiness and joyful play making me feel nostalgic for my own childhood here when I did exactly the same. But there's a tinge of sadness too that Ted can't see this, can't be here with his children to enjoy it. I take a moment, inhaling through my nose and letting out a long puff of air that curls upward into the cold beachy air as I reach my hand down to give Henry a quick stroke behind one ear. Sensing my contemplation, I'm sure, Henry leans his body into the side of my leg as if to give me a cuddle before bouncing back into the snow, trying to bite it as he hurtles off to play with Freya and the boys nearby. Jack left Sinead at home with Rita, figuring her exuberance might be too much for everyone gathered here on the slopes today.

'Everything OK?' Jack says quietly, glancing up from his crouching position. He's primed to build the biggest snowball I think I've ever seen, his two gloved hands still scooping and shaping the snow as he looks at me intently.

'Yes, all good.' I nod, pinning a stoic grin on my face.

'Sure?' He does the head tilt, which I'm beginning to realise is definitely just his way.

'Yes, I was just reminiscing… and thinking of a picture we have on the mantelpiece of—' I stop talking.

'Go on. Please, I'd like to know,' he prompts, still shaping the snowball. 'Is it a picture of Ted?'

I nod, and look over to where Freya and the boys are messing around making snowballs and dropping them on each other's heads, much to Freya's amusement. Her big brothers are even kneeling so she can have a good go at getting her own back. Even Henry is joining in by trying to retrieve the snowballs Freya is throwing, the look of confusion on his doggy face is a picture as he tries to work out where the ball has gone as it disintegrates on impact.

'Yes,' I lift my eyebrows. 'A lovely picture of Ted as a boy, here, sledging on the slopes, smiling and happy and just so vibrant and alive…' I tell him, letting my voice tail off.

'B, that's a great image. And a fantastic memory to have. Please don't ever think you can't mention him. He was your husband. Your love. Your children's dad. How long were you together?' A short silence follows before

Jack adds, 'Sorry, I'll shut up. You said you weren't ready to talk ye—'

'It's OK.' I smile. 'We were together for years and years, since we were teenagers.' Jack nods slowly as if taking it all in.

'That's nice. And the same as my mum and dad. My dad died when I wasn't much older than Freya,' he says, keeping his voice low so the children can't hear him over the hubbub of the snow play and the sound of the sea.

'I'm sorry,' I say, and he stands up, leaving the snowball by his feet.

'Yeah, it was tough. But you know, the memories my mam shared about my dad made all the difference though. Kept his memory alive, sure it did,' he says, his lovely Irish accent growing stronger as he talks about the memories from back home. 'In fact, I think I probably know more about my dad – as in, what he was like as a person and all that – than I do about my mam. And she's still alive and thriving and well into her seventies now.' He nods and goes to pick up the massive snowball.

'That's interesting to know. I think I should probably talk about Ted more with the children.' I pause to ponder for a moment, and glance over again at the three of them laughing and having fun. 'It's a tricky one some days though. I don't want to upset them, you know.'

'Yes, I know. And I sensed that the other night when Freya told me her daddy had died. I saw your hesitancy, and the concern, and then the silence, and that's perfectly natural. It's tough to talk about. My mam was the same until we had a big bust up over it when I was a teenager, and a fecking pain in the arse. Cocky and inconsiderate was my specialty – you know the drill.' There's a beat of silence before he adds, 'Not much has changed, eh?' and tosses a tiny snowball at my left shoulder before giving me that smile again, raising one flirtatious eyebrow in his classic broodingly *Bridgerton* style. I'm not going to lie – it does make me melt a little inside.

'I wouldn't say that. You were actually quite lovely the other night.' I pause and then add, 'Very considerate,' while trying not to smile back.

'But I wasn't when you dropped off the crate for Rita!' He quickly ducks as I scoop up a big handful of snow and go to throw it at him. It misses. 'Bad luck.' He laughs gently.

'Hmm, next time you won't be so lucky,' I grin, enjoying the banter, and more importantly, the easy way we are chatting about something that is actually very serious and personal for each of us. But it doesn't feel that way at all with Jack. Instead it's easy and effortless. 'So what happened with your mum?' I ask curiously, not having ever met an adult whose dad died when they were a child. I didn't even know my own dad. He and Patty split up when I was a toddler and then she lost touch when he went back home to Scotland and we never heard from him again.

'It kind of built up,' Jack says. 'At first, we were both just sad, I guess, and neither of us said very much at all. We were a bit numb. But then the days and then weeks and months sort of drifted on until Dad was never really mentioned much at all. Then I felt that she was keeping him all to herself, if that's make sense?' I nod, knowing exactly how that feels. There have been moments when I've not wanted to talk about Ted and the memories we shared, as if by doing so they're no longer just mine to cherish; I have to share him somehow, and I don't want to. Selfish perhaps, but memories are all I have left. 'Mam didn't talk about him and if *I* did, then she clammed up, went quiet, and it made me question why.' He shrugs. 'Looking back through adult eyes I can see that I was just a lost kid, but still… I was pretty tough on my mam.'

'Ah, that must have been tough for you too though,' I say, hoping Freya and the boys never feel that way. I can't actually remember the last time I actively talked to them about Ted, what he was like and the things he enjoyed doing before he became their dad. I resolve to fix it right away because they have a right to share his memory too. It's not fair of me to keep him all to myself. And then I realise that sharing more of Ted with Freya, Olly, and Oscar can only be a good thing. It will keep his memory going for even longer as they take him with them on into their own lives and perhaps to their children, Ted's grandchildren, too. I turn to Jack. 'Thanks for bringing this up. It's been good talking to you.'

'Any time. It's good to talk, and I've made the mistake of not doing so in the past.'

'How come?'

'I've grown up a lot since, but, with Ciara, I was a bit of a closed book. Too focused on getting my chef training under my belt and then not making time for her when we first moved over here…' He pauses. 'But, come on, let's go and have some fun in the snow. I don't want to bring the mood down with all that stuff from the past. We can chat about it another time, if you like?'

'Yes, sure,' I nod, thinking I'd like to find out more about Jack. 'A heart-to-heart by the fire pit some time, perhaps?'

'Sounds like a cracking plan. Right, come on, do you want to do the honours?' He reaches down to retrieve the giant snowball and hands it to me. Then he steps back a few paces and lifts his arms up. 'Come on, give it your best shot!' He laughs. I take aim and after counting to three I hurl the snowball at him and it lands splat on top of his head. I stagger about laughing as he falls back into the snow, doing an angel with his arms and legs right at the moment Freya comes running over. Seeing Jack on the ground, Freya flings herself down near to him and makes her own snow angel. With my heart singing at the sound of her giggling, I wander over to where the boys are pushing each other over on purpose and wrestling with one of the plastic sledges that Jack brought with him for them to use.

'Can I join in?' I laugh.

'OK,' Oscar shrugs, nonplussed, but looks surprised as he stands up and I go to push him over into the thick snow. He's fast though, and manages to bounce out of reach before ducking back in between the three of us and going to push me over instead.

'You have to be quicker than that to catch me,' I joke as I jump back just in time, grabbing the rope of the sledge up from the ground.

'Hey, Mum, it was my turn next,' Olly says, and so I offer the sledge to him instead. 'It's OK, you can go,' he then adds, magnanimously, as he indicates for me to keep hold of the sledge.

'Honestly, it's fine. I want you to have fun,' I say, then after taking a breath, I add, 'Dad used to love sledging down these slopes.' There's a moment of silence as both boys stop moving around in the snow and for a second I wonder if I've said something wrong. Have I upset them? But then Olly grins and says, 'I bet he was a wicked sledger! Super fast.' I nod, swallow hard, and smile before continuing.

'Yes, you're right, he was. He scared the life out of me once. We were about seventeen, not long after we first met, and we came down here in the snow. I was on the front of the sledge, with him behind me and he pushed us so fast we nearly crashed into the beach huts.' I shake my head at the hair-raising memory. Both boys are enraptured, hanging off my every word, before Oscar gently takes the rope of the sledge from my hands.

'That's awesome! Dad was a legend,' he says, then after seemingly pondering for a moment, he adds, 'It's good to be back here.' And he actually cracks a smile.

'Do you think?' I say, then keep quiet as it's rare for Oscar to be candid and so I don't want to miss the moment by talking too much and making him clam up, because yes, it's good to talk, but it's also good to listen.

'Yeah, it's like a bit of Dad is still here. I saw that section of the sea wall on the drive here, the part where he fell off that time, do you remember? We were eating chips in the sun and a seagull swooped down and Dad toppled back onto the sand and his chips went flying everywhere. We couldn't stop laughing as loads more seagulls flew in and ate them all.'

'Ah, yes, I do remember!' I say. 'I'm surprised you do though, as you were only little – about five or six years old.'

'It's funny what sticks in your head.'

'It sure is,' I smile, handing him the sledge. 'Come on, let's have a go together!' And after plopping the sledge down on the snow, he sits on it and indicates for me to get on too and sit in front of him.

'Go on,' Olly says, 'I'll stay here with Freya and Jack. And take care of Henry too.'

Soon, we're flying down the snowy slope, the wind stinging our cheeks as we gather speed, and for one moment, just as I did all those years ago, I think we're going to crash into a beach hut. But just as his dad did before him, Oscar manages to swerve the sledge just in time and we end up coming to a halt on the wet sand, only missing the actual frothy waves from drenching us by a few millimetres. I jump off and give Oscar a huge hug.

'Thank you, my love.'

'What for?' He surreptitiously untangles himself from my embrace. I notice him smooth his hair back on seeing a very pretty girl in a figure-hugging sky-blue ski suit, a tumble of black curls tied up in a big pony tail, and fluffy ear muffs over her head. I smile as he suddenly seems so much older – and most definitely doesn't want his mum cramping his style.

'I'm not sure exactly. I guess, just for making the most of us coming back here. You seem happier.' He nods in agreement, but his attention is elsewhere and so I leave him to it.

I spot Pearl and Ian, and then further on I can see my old friends, Georgie and Sam, too, her little girls, Holly and Ivy (yes, they were conceived at Christmas time) looking adorable in matching teddy bear snowsuits, giggling and shrieking as they run around in the snow. Sam's husband, Nathan, is keeping a watchful eye on them.

'Hi, Bridget!' Pearl waves as I get closer to her. 'Lovely to see you here. I was just saying to Ian that it looks like our Lola over there…' – she pauses to point in the direction of where I've just left Oscar – '…is quite taken with your boy.' She laughs as I turn to see Oscar and the girl in the sky-blue ski suit chatting and seemingly flirting. He keeps flicking his fringe back from his face, just the way Ted used to when we first met, and Lola is laughing and twiddling a lock of her hair. Smiling, I think, *Good for you, Oscar*. Seeing him having fun and being a typical teenager is a tonic indeed after all he's been through. Hopefully it will cheer him up a bit and he'll be turning his frown upside down much more from now on.

After chatting to Pearl and Ian, and hearing how they've spoken to Glynis and she's up for having a cuppa and a chinwag with Mack, I say goodbye and go to make my way back up to the top of the snowy slope where I can see what looks like Freya and Jack having a snowball fight with Olly. I'm halfway up the slope when I see Vicar Joe wearing a navy duffle coat with a red handknitted scarf swathed around his neck and standing outside a pastel-pink-and-cream striped beach hut at the end of the second row. As I get closer I see that he's got what looks like a little hot drinks station on the go – there's a wooden trestle table by the door of the open beach hut with an enormous silver hot-water urn at one end and a couple of trays of white china mugs at the other. A Bluetooth speaker is playing Christmas favourites giving the snowy air a magical, festive feel and with Vicar Joe's Santa hat on his head it's definitely beginning to look a lot like Christmas.

'Bridget, how are you doing?' Vicar Joe says, clasping his gloved hands together before picking up a mug. 'Can I tempt you to a cuppa? We have tea, coffee, or hot chocolate to keep the snow revellers fuelled!'

'Oh yes, please, a hot chocolate would be wonderful,' I say, as he makes me a very welcome warming drink.

'There we are.' Vicar Joe places the steaming mug on the table before dashing back inside the beach hut. Moments later, he returns with a fresh batch of mugs which he arranges onto the trays.

'This is just the thing, thank you,' I say, lifting the mug that is cupped in my hands keeping them toasty warm. 'And I love what you've done with the beach hut. It looks just like an alpine wood cabin with the fern trees and the candy cane bunting,' I say, marvelling at the sight before me. Vicar Joe has made the hut look truly magical and for a moment I feel a fizz of anticipation for

Christmas, just as I used to as a child. You know, that moment each year when you feel festive for the first time. I missed it last year – I just wasn't in the mood – so I'm extra excited to have gained it back.

'Yes, it's become a bit of a tradition – hot drinks for the sledgers and the magic of Christmas,' he says. 'The traditional nativity scene is back in the church. Here it's about having fun and singing our favourite carols.' And for a moment, I think he's going to burst into a rousing singalong as he turns the volume up to Brenda Lee belting out the classic 'Rocking Around the Christmas Tree'.

'Well, I think it's a lovely idea. There's a real community spirit here today, it's so nice seeing everyone having fun, which reminds me, could I ask you a favour please?'

'Of course.' Vicar Joe nods.

'It's a friend, Mack, an older gentleman… He's on his own, you see, after his wife died. I've told him about the sea shanty choir and he's going to give a go, and I remember you offering to help out with the technical side of things. He has a laptop – well, his late wife did – and so he—'

'Say no more!' Vicar Joe holds up a hand. 'I'll make sure Mack is all set up. It will be a good opportunity to recruit him for our bingo too. The more the merrier!' He smiles. 'And we're very short on gentlemen. The bingo ladies are always bemoaning the fact.' He shakes his head and chuckles.

'Thank you. I think he'd appreciate it. You're very kind.'

'And so are you, Bridget. I'm hearing wonderful things about your delicious bread and baked goods. The community is overjoyed to have bread back on the menu and it makes all the difference to some of my parishioners.'

'I'm so pleased,' I grin. 'It makes all the difference to me too. Making bread brings me joy so everyone's a winner.'

'Have you always been a baker?'

'Well, no not really. I've always liked to have a go, but I really got into it as a kind of therapy, I guess.' I take a mouthful of the deliciously creamy hot chocolate.

'In what way?' Vicar Joe asks, pouring himself a mug of coffee. I take a breath and try to think of the best way to explain it to him. I don't want to talk about grief, not today; I want it to be about having fun and sledging and looking forward to Christmas; drinking hot chocolate and doing snow angels.

I settle on, 'It's soothing, and keeps my thoughts from wandering. The act of kneading and shaping the dough is incredibly satisfying, as is the sense of having created something from scratch. Not to mention the completely comforting aroma of freshly baked bread. One whiff of that warm, cosy scent and I know everything's going to be all right. It lifts me.'

'I see. How fascinating.' He nods, as if deep in thought, and then he comes right out with it.

'And does everything feel all right now?'

A short silence follows.

'Yes, I think it does.' I nod and my smile widens. 'And thanks again for this. I'll just finish up so you can have the mug back.'

'Oh no need – take it with you. You can pop the mug back next time you're passing by the church, if you like.' He smiles kindly.

'In that case, thanks again.'

'You're very welcome. It's been nice chatting to you, Bridget. You seem like a very wise person.'

'Ah, I'm not sure about that. Just muddling through like everyone else.'

'And making a difference! Kindness and community, that's the key. And faith too.' He smiles gently. 'We are very grateful to have you join our community.' He nods and offers me a tin of candy canes. 'For the children,' he says, then adds, 'or their parents,' and winks. We both laugh as I take three, one each for Freya and the boys, before hesitating. 'Go on, the peppermint canes are very nice stirred into the hot chocolate,' he suggests, dropping his voice as if letting me into a secret. 'I'm very partial to one after a long walk on the beach.' He gives the tin a little shake.

'In that case...' I take one of the green-and-white striped canes and pop it into my pocket. 'And thank you. It's been lovely chatting to you too, and I'm very grateful to be a part of the community.'

After telling Vicar Joe where Mack lives, I wave goodbye and make my way up the rest of the slope to join the others, smiling and thinking how different things seem now compared to how they were when we first came here, full of uncertainty about the future. But not anymore. I can feel buds of optimism blooming within me, unfurling more and more each day, and with Bridget's Bicycle Bakery keeping me busy and a sense of community, the sea shanty choir, and new friends, the future is now looking a whole lot brighter. And meeting Jack too. He's definitely growing on me. I think it's fair to say that he's gone from being the most irritating person ever, to actually very pleasant and, dare I say it, exciting to be around. I look ahead and see Olly and Freya having fun. Henry too. Oscar is there now, with Lola, and the joyful scene before me makes my smile widen. Yes, coming back here was the right thing to do. My children seem happier and I'm beginning to feel whole again.

Chapter Seventeen

It's Christmas Eve and the four of us are in the cosy open-plan kitchen and living area. The log burner is comforting as it crackles and wheezes away, mingling the scent of pine with a scrumptious seasonal aroma of warm bread, mince pies, sausage rolls, and fruity rich Christmas cake. Carols are playing on the radio as I put the finishing touches to our mammoth festive feast for us all to enjoy when we join Lorna and her family for the virtual quiz. The boys have loaded up the fire pit outside, now that it's stopped snowing, and have spent the afternoon gathering driftwood and building a log mountain big enough to keep the fire going for the whole of the Christmas period and on to at least the end of January, or so it seems. There's certainly no danger of any of us going cold on the beach with all the hot-water bottles and blankets to snuggle into, although it's a gloriously still night now that the wind has dropped and the tide is so far out that only a calm, soothing shushing noise of the waves rippling back and forth can be heard in the distance. The boys have dotted fire flame torches and candle lanterns down the length of the wooden walkway so the whole area in front of our beach house is illuminated and magical-looking, even if it does resemble an aviation landing strip out there. But as Olly rightly told Freya, Santa is certainly going to know where to land his sleigh tonight! Her eyes were like dinner plates on hearing this snippet of magic and she immediately set about sweeping the last of the snow from the wooden walkway and making sure the 'Santa Stop Here' wooden sign that Ted made for her a few years ago was stuck firmly in the sand just to be sure.

'OK, so what have you decided to choose?' I call out to Freya. She couldn't contain her excitement any longer and so I've decided to let her and the boys open one present early. But now Freya can't decide which one to go for, typically. She's spent the best part of the last half an hour oohing and ahhing and pressing and touching the tip of her index finger to the corners of the shiny red and gold festive wrapping paper. Of course, her big present is tucked away out of sight so as to be a surprise for tomorrow – a pink plastic dog-grooming parlour, complete with a little sink that has an actual shower hose that can sprinkle real water, a hairdryer and two very cute soft toy huskie puppies with fluffy coats all ready to be shampooed. I think Freya is going to love it and I was so pleased Mum could see the merits of me getting it for her. I figured it was far more important for Freya to feel happy than for me to have a new capsule wardrobe.

'Mummy, Mummy, can I choose this one please?' Freya eventually decides and goes to haul a big, round squishy present that arrived a few days ago from Ted's parents in Australia.

'Sure you can,' I tell her, decanting the last batch of mince pies onto a cooling rack. I take my apron off and hang it over the back of one of the kitchen chairs and go over to the twinkling Christmas tree in the window next to Ted's star lantern.

'Boys, can one of you give me a hand to bring this out please? Carefully, so the tree doesn't topple over?' I've got my hands around the present but am struggling to manoeuvre it free. Oscar comes to the rescue and gently pushes it from the other side until I can lift it out. 'Right, there you go!' I say to Freya, her eyes dancing in delight and her mouth forming a big O shape as she takes in the sheer size of the surprise present.

'Want me to help you?' Oscar offers, but Freya instantly shakes her head vehemently. I don't blame her – she wants to cherish the full unwrapping experience for herself, and so carefully tears at the paper. Tentatively at first, but then excitement gets the better of her and she goes for it, ripping the rest of the paper away until she can see what's inside.

'Look! Look! Mummy, Oscar, Olly. Look at it. I'm in love,' she declares with full drama as she presses her face into the biggest grey and white soft toy koala bear that I think I've ever seen. The boys and I all laugh gently on seeing her glee, with her arms wrapped tightly around the koala's head in a hug, and for a moment a lump forms in my throat. Her moment of happiness is everything and when I think back to how she was on Christmas Eve last year, I can't tell you how special this is to see. I inhale sharply through my nose as I lean down to kiss the top of her head, drawing in the scent of her strawberry shortcake shampoo.

'Wow! It's amazing,' I tell her as she turns to check that I'm looking at how completely perfect the koala is. 'Granny and Granddad have chosen the best gift for you, haven't they?'

'Yes. And I love them too.' Freya nods. 'Can I see them on the laptop to say thank you?' she asks, still clutching the koala's head.

'Well, yes you can, darling. It's a lovely kind thought but it's the middle of the night in Australia right now. Let's call them tomorrow on Christmas Day like we always do.'

'OK,' Freya says, then, 'there's something else!' And

she lifts the koala's leg up to find a reindeer onesie complete with antlers on the hood and an elasticated red nose. Seconds later, she's stripped off her jeans and jumper and is pushing her legs into the onesie. Jumping up, she slots her arms in and zips herself up before pulling the hood up. Olly laughs. 'Ah, you look so cute, Freya.' He tweaks the antlers and lifts her up to see herself in the mirror above the fireplace. She squeals and then does a whinnying noise like a horse, making us all collapse into fits of laughter.

'Reindeers don't whinny!' Oscar shakes his head and I'm pleased to hear a lighthearted tease in his voice instead of the critical, chastising one he had seemed fond of until more recently.

'Yes they do.' Freya is adamant and treats us all to another burst of whinnying with extra high-pitched neighing now too.

'Shush with the neighing and look at this,' Olly tells her. 'There's something here for Henry.' He opens up what looks like a matching reindeer dog coat in brown faux fur; it has a hood and antlers on too.

'Ah, he's going to look so cute too,' I say, going to round Henry up to try the coat on, but just as I go to find him, I hear him bark and then see through the window that Jack has arrived with Sinead bouncing along beside him. She's spinning in a circle now in excitement on spotting Henry bounding out the front door as I open it to greet Jack.

'Merry Christmas!' Jack announces, handing over a large brown paper bag. He has a crimson-red fluffy Santa hat on his head and the same, now familiar, twinkle in his amber eyes. He's wearing a silly Christmas jumper with black jeans and boots

'Oh, wow, thank you. Merry Christmas to you too.' I smile and look into the top of the bag. It's crammed full of enormous carrots! I laugh and raise my eyebrows.

'They're for Freya,' he explains, like it's the most obvious thing in the world for him to be bringing a six-year-old a big bag of enormous carrots.

'Um… thank you?' I hesitate, clearly missing something here.

'For the reindeers! I thought Freya might want to leave out a carrot snack for them tonight. I used to love that part of the Christmas Eve traditions the most.' He grins and I catch a glimpse of the boy that he used to be and it dawns on me that he really is a big kid at heart. All that sardonic smiling and cheek at the start was perhaps a bit of a front as he's looking sheepish now, hesitant and unsure, feeling foolish like he's made a mistake. But he hasn't at all. It's a perfect gift for a six year old who is beside herself with excitement on the night before Christmas.

'Thank you. This is such a thoughtful gift, Jack.' And

we both lock eyes and seem to freeze for a moment, as if neither of us is sure what to say or do next. An awkward silence lingers and I'm not sure what he's expecting from me. Eventually, I speak, 'Freya is going to love these carrots.' We both grin and nod like a pair of coy teenagers. Then, right on cue, Freya appears at my side in her reindeer onesie, and after thanking Jack, she toddles off with both arms around the big bag in search of a bucket to put the carrots in next to the 'Santa Stop Here' sign, 'So the reindeers can eat them while Santa brings the presents in,' she explains earnestly.

Later, Jack and the boys have got the fire pit roaring and have dragged the kitchen table out onto the deck where it is now laden with all kinds of festive buffet treats that I bought from the Carrington's food hall. Cold cuts of roast beef, ham with a honey-mustard glaze, slices of turkey, sausage rolls, coleslaw, potato salad, pork pies, piccalilli, crisps, cheese balls, cranberry and brie, plus stilton and a trillion or so homemade mince pies, mini stollen cakes and gingerbread biscuits that Freya decorated in her usual splattering of red and green holly-shaped sprinkles. Taking prime position in the centre is a rich Christmas fruit cake complete with snow-white royal icing over marzipan, and a robin and more holly leaves with tiny red berries too that took me several attempts to get just right. But it was so worth it to see Olly and Oscar's faces as I carried the cake out to the table. It's their favourite, and so I've also made two additional smaller individual Christmas cakes. They're all wrapped and ready to pop on the top of their stockings as a little extra treat. They might not believe in the magic of Santa anymore but that's not going to stop me from creeping into their bedroom in the middle of the night and draping bulging Christmas stockings across the ends of their beds. Tradition is important; I love the familiarity of it and found it a comfort in the darker moments after Ted died – and think the children did too. I also like to think they'll carry on with the traditions when they have their own families one day.

I'm just finding a space for the big batch of warm straight-from-the-oven crusty bread rolls when Olly bellows, 'Mum, come on, Aunty Lorna is waiting for you.' So after checking the table is just how I want it, I grab my mug of mulled wine and dash down the wooden walkway and step into the boat, instantly sweltering from the furnace-like heat radiating from the fire pit.

'Phew, that's better,' I puff, loosening my thick woolly scarf. 'No danger of us feeling the cold tonight, is there!' I can't help laughing on seeing Olly and Oscar's bright-red faces that are coated in a fine sheen of sweat as they each do a running leap before landing on bean bags in the boat. Jack is lounging on a deck chair to my left and Freya is still frolicking on the sand in her reindeer onesie with Henry and Sinead in hot pursuit.

'Right, is everyone ready?' Olly asks, and we all nod and clap and shout 'Three, two, one, it's Christmas quiz time!' Another tradition we seem to have adopted over the years. Jack lifts his can of Guinness up in the air and then looks sideways at me just at the same time as I do. He winks and smiles and it makes me glow. Lorna appears on the screen.

'Hello, my loves. How are you all?' she says, looking amazing as always. She has a sparkly gold party dress on and her blonde hair is piled up into a 60s-style beehive, her eyes twinkling, and then it dawns on me. I know that look on Lorna. She's smitten. I surreptitiously lift the blanket over my lap to create a little tent of discretion in which to WhatsApp her. Silly, I know, but we enjoy the side commentary – it's become our thing over the years. I finish typing and press send.

SMITTEN KITTEN

I add the kiss emoji and, in an instant, she has messaged back.

Never mind me. When were you going to tell me that
Jack is properly period drama hot!!!

She's added three flame emojis which completely
match my own flaming cheeks on reading her reply. I
flick my eyes between my phone screen and then up to
the laptop screen that Olly has set up on top of a box so
we can all see each other. Lorna is soon joined on the
screen by her mum and dad from their plush upper-deck
stateroom on the cruise ship. Then Lorna's sister, Amy,
and brother-in-law, Bill, appear. Bill, as always, is ready
with his egg timer and clipboard of questions. Plus, Liam
is on the screen now too wearing blue scrubs and sitting
on the single bed in the on-call room at the hospital. I
lean forward to get a good look at him, liking his kind
eyes and the way he glances to his right where Lorna is,
and then blows her kiss. After blowing a kiss back to
him, Lorna looks directly at me and lifts one eyebrow as
if to say, 'Well? I'm still waiting for your answer!' before
grinning like a looper and swivelling her eyes to where
Jack is. Thankfully, Jack is oblivious to Lorna's scrutiny
as he's got his head down to pick up the tennis ball that
Sinead has just dropped at his feet. We're just settling
down and waiting for Bill to ask the first question when
another message from Lorna appears on my phone
screen.

Now, please don't be cross with me. I know Patty
can be outrageous but she asked if she could join
us tonight as a surprise for you and the children. It is
Christmas after all and she wants to make more of
an effort. She has promised not to mention Sugar
Daddies R Us xxxx

I hurriedly type a reply, wondering if Lorna has gone out of her mind. It was a disaster the last time Patty joined in the Christmas quiz. Five years ago it was, and she came over from Spain to spend the holidays with us. Well, she didn't actually stay in our house, she booked herself into a suite at a luxury five-star hotel nearby and then turned up with a carrier bag full of pastries and mini pots of jam that she had purloined from the breakfast buffet. Patty then got too tipsy on her signature pornstar martini cocktails, tried to make the children drink champagne because 'all the continental children do', then flirted outrageously with Lorna's boyfriend at the time, before ending up in A&E at midnight on Christmas Day with a suspected fractured arm after she fell over Lorna's lovely vintage bar cart. Then, when Ted went to pick her up from the hospital, she told him he was punching above his weight when he married me! I press send and chug down an enormous mouthful of mulled wine.

Whaaaat? Have you forgotten what happened last
time?

But it's too late and Patty and Derek appear on the
screen seated on gold stools at what looks like a
traditional Irish bar inside the games room at their villa,
complete with whiskey, gin, and vodka optics on the wall
and a green clover motif on a mirror, next to which is a
framed print saying Murphy's Irish Bar above a pint of
Guinness. I gulp and close my eyes before inhaling
sharply and silently praying that she doesn't start on
Jack. I should have warned him at least… if I had known!
Another message from Lorna pops onto my screen.

Sorry. I can see you're fuming. I should have told
you. I can always disconnect her if she gets too
much xxxx

I reply,

Hmm! Not fuming! More panicked

And then quickly follow with,

Oh, here we go!

Mum is waving a little Irish flag and looking like

she's about to speak. I push the phone away, wishing I could hide underneath the blanket with it too.

'Hello, my darlings!' she shrieks and blows a multitude of air kisses with both hands, looking like she's guest presenting *Ru Paul's Drag Race*. She's wearing a jewel-encrusted scarlet-red kaftan with matching red marabou-feather-trimmed bell sleeves and her hair is backcombed to within an inch of its life, giving her the biggest beehive I think I've ever seen. 'Merry Christmas to you all. I'm so sorry I can't be with you in person this evening, but I'm raising a glass to you all,' she adds in her best Lady Bountiful voice. 'Now, where's my precious baby girl? My favourite granddaughter!'

'Granny!' Freya, who seems to have suddenly developed supersonic hearing, comes charging across the sand from over by the buffet table, where only two seconds ago she was obliviously singing and dancing and pressing yet another mince pie into her mouth. But she adores her granny and can't wait to see her, and of course I don't want to spoil that for either of them, so I let my guard down a bit and give Mum and Derek a wave with a big smile and a cheery 'Merry Christmas to you both too'. If Mum wants to make more of an effort then it's only right that I do too. I don't want to be bracing myself every time her face appears on the phone screen. I know she means well, even though she was pretty mean to Ted. But I can't change any of that now and so perhaps

Lorna is right; it is Christmas after all. A time of peace on earth and goodwill.

'There she is!' Mum shrieks some more and after flinging the flag away she claps her hands together. 'Oh my goodness, look at you being so adorable.' Freya waves and then still in her imaginary reindeer character she prances around whinnying and making us all laugh. 'And my two handsome boys!' Patty turns her attention to Olly and Oscar now and I see them smiling politely but can also tell that they're bracing themselves for her to come out with some kind of embarrassing innuendo as always, something no fourteen-year-old boy wants to hear from their granny. Right on cue, Patty delivers. 'I bet the pair of you feature in all the girls' dreams! Some of the boys' dreams too,' and she does a ridiculously exaggerated wink. I shrivel a little inside as I drain the last of my mulled wine.

'Mum! Derek!' I swiftly jump in to try to steer the spotlight away from Olly and Oscar who are now muttering about needing to go and fetch more logs to add to the already toppling pile. I give Olly's thigh a quick pat as if to telepathically reassure him that I've got this and will deal with his outrageous granny and get us on to the actual quiz a-sap, as he likes to say.

But it doesn't work out that way and Patty turns her attentions to me and Jack!

'Ooh, Bridget, is that your Jack sitting in that

deckchair there next to you?' she says, leaning right up close to her camera as if to get a better look at him. I open my mouth to explain that he isn't *my* Jack but she powers on regardless, adopting a ludicrous-sounding Irish accent. 'Jaaaaack! Now you are quite the snack!' OMG. My heart sinks. She deepens her voice to a provocative purr and I want the sand beneath this boat to suddenly open up into a big sink hole that I can crawl into. 'May the leprechauns dance over your bed and bring you sweet dreams!' she keeps on, lifting her cocktail glass up and sloshing the contents over the side as she does a big tick of approval in the air. Help. I slide further down on the bean bag wishing I was anywhere but here right now.

'Jack, I'm so sorry,' I swiftly whisper out of the side of my mouth as I glance at him. But he doesn't seem fazed in the slightest and lifts his pint of Guinness up in cheers, seemingly taking it all in his stride.

'Sláinte!' He laughs. 'Good to meet you, Patty. I can see where Bridget gets her good looks from.' He winks at me, and, as if by magic, my mother is now simpering like a silly, lovestruck puppy. She's even put her drink down and is making a heart shape with her hands.

'Oh, Jack, you and I are going to get on like a house of fire! You do know that Derek is Irish too. He's from Dublin. Do you know it?'

'Sure. I know Dublin pretty well,' Jack nods, easily.

'Well, my husband, Derek, do a little wave, darling.'

She nudges poor Derek who does as he's told before placing an arm around her shoulders and giving her a big squishy kiss on the cheek. Mum giggles and pretends to be bashful as she pushes him away and whispers something about putting a pin in it until they're alone later on. OMG, now there's an image of their parent no daughter wants inside her head. 'Yes, Derek has a very large family there. The Murphys. Maybe you know them? His sister is Shona Murphy and—'

I can't help myself and have to jump in again. 'Mum, Dublin is a big city. Jack doesn't know every single person in Ireland… just because he's Irish.'

'Oh yes, I know that, sweetie. But you never know. You'd be surprised. When we flew to Barbados for our honeymoon, the woman who was lounging on her bed in the opposite suite… they have suites in First Class, you see,' Mum pauses to let this revelation sink in. 'Yes, her daughter was married to a man that went to school with Derek's Shona. Fancy that!' A stunned silence follows. It's Lorna's mum who speaks next.

'You used to go out with a boy from Dublin! Didn't you, Lorna? Do you remember him? A lovely lad… and you were ever so upset when he dumped you to go and do his police training.' She turns to Lorna's dad for clarification.

'That's right, dear. But I don't think he was from Dublin though,' he says, his forehead creasing as he tries to recall exactly which town in Ireland the ex-boyfriend was from, before adding, 'Let's get a top-up before the quiz starts.' They both get up and wander off-screen.

My phone screen lights up. It's a message from Lorna.

TIME TO DISCONNECT?

Ah, but your M&D aren't here. We can't start the quiz without them

I'm teasing her, and then try not to laugh on seeing Lorna's look of exasperation as she shakes her head and stuffs a large lump of breaded brie with cranberry glaze into her mouth. But my smile soon freezes as Patty has turned her attentions back to Jack now and I curse myself for revelling in my best friend's discomfort because I've missed what Mum actually said… something about her baking skills. But the screen freezes momentarily. When it comes back on, Liam says he's going to get a coffee, Derek is making more cocktails behind his bar, and Bill and Amy are fiddling with their lighting, so it's just Lorna, me, Jack and Patty chatting now.

'Yes, that's right, Jack, Bridget gets her talent from me,' Mum says. 'I used to love baking crusty rolls and croissants for her when she came home from school. The house would smell all lovely and cosy, just like you imagine the celebrity homes in *OK* magazine do. And they are very simple to make, especially if you go for the part-baked option. Just take a roll or a croissant out of the freezer and pop it in the oven.' I pull the blanket up even further until it's almost covering my cheeks that are flaming like a pair of plum tomatoes. I steal a glance at Jack who has a look of utter astonishment mingled with 'my mind is completely boggled' stamped all over his face. I bet he's never met anyone like my mother before! He goes to speak, but isn't quick enough as Patty is on a roll now. 'But you don't need me to tell you, Jack, not with you being a chef and all. And I have mentioned to Bridget that she needs to sort out her wardrobe. She's going to upgrade it as soon as the bakery business takes off. I imagine you have all sorts of fabulous red-carpet celebrity chef events to take her to?'

'Mum!' I splutter, with far more of a hiss than I actually intended and so after pausing and taking a big inward breath through my nose, I tell her, 'Jack's not a celebrity chef! He's—'

'Not yet, sweetie! Not yet. But he could be very soon. We all have to start somewhere and from what I can see on The Hook, Line & Sinker website, absolutely everyone loves Jack's food. Five-star rave reviews all over the place for his famous roast dinners.'

'Whaaaat? I can't believe you looked him up!' I say, in a whisper-shouty voice, not even daring to look in Jack's direction. My pulse is racing. This is typical Patty, and I bet she thinks this is her 'making an effort' to be nice to Jack. A wealthy celebrity chef, I guess, is on a par with a pilot, shipping magnate, or property tycoon in Patty World.

'Oh, but you have to these days with catfishing and all that going on. Jack doesn't mind, do you, darling? Not when my Bridget is such a stunner.' She doesn't wait for him to reply. I shake my head and give Mum another look of utter disbelief. Lorna is making big eyes at me now and shaking her head too, her finger poised, no doubt, to press the disconnect button. But it's Bill who brings this cringefest to a close as he taps his watch and butts in with an officious, 'OK, that's probably enough chit-chat now, thank you. We need to get on with the quiz as we have a very tight time schedule,' and after flipping his varifocals from the top of his head down to his eyes, starts reading out the first question. I seize the moment to escape and after asking the boys to be joint captains of Team Carrington – it's their specialist subject in any case: gaming – I hotfoot it over to the buffet table to pile up a plate of all the food to feed my muddle of emotions with right now.

I'm busy strategically balancing another mince pie at the top of my mini food mountain, figuring I might just sit on my own on the deck for a bit and stuff my face, when Jack appears.

'Are you OK?' he asks gently, placing his empty glass on the table.

'Um,' I manage through a mouthful of sausage roll.

'Your mum sure is a craic.'

'That's one way to put it.' Silence follows as I finish the sausage roll. 'I'm really sorry, Jack.' I look away.

'What for?' he asks, picking up a mince pie and taking a bite.

'Well… her calling you a snack, for starters!' I wince.

He laughs. 'I'm taking it as a compliment.' He lifts his shoulders nonchalantly, then polishes off the rest of the mince pie. After pondering for a bit he adds, 'It is a good thing, yes?'

'It is, yes,' I nod, remembering the women saying it about one of the guys on *Married at First Sight Australia*. 'It's a flirty compliment. It means she thinks you're hot, although it's all kinds of wrong for my mother to say it to you. Not that you aren't hot,' I quickly add. 'You are!' I stop talking and wish my face wasn't like a furnace right now.

'Thanks. I'm happy you think so.' His smile widens. A short silence follows, before Jack continues, 'Patty was right about one thing though…' His head tilts as he moves closer and touches the back of my hand that is resting on the edge of the table next to my plate. I look at him and he holds my gaze as he adds, 'You are a stunner!'

He lifts one eyebrow as his fingers brush the back of my hand, sending a sizzle of pleasure straight up my arm. Neither of us speaks and time seems to stand still as Jack's hand moves up my arm, coming to a rest at the nape of my neck. On realising that I'm holding my breath, I manage to exhale and then smile as a small gasp escapes from my lips. I want to speak, to reassure him as his eyes linger, looking, searching to see if this is OK. A medley of emotions flood through me, but the words won't come out.

Instead, a sense of fear swirls up inside me, mounting into panic and then when the words do come out of my mouth, they are harsh and rude, my fear turning to anger and it's too late as I end up saying, 'Stop it! No, Jack. What do you think you're you doing?' I turn my face away from his and after swiftly holding up my hands to break free from his embrace, I shake my head, tears smarting in the corners of my eyes as my face burns, my bottom lip stinging as I bite down so hard I'm sure I can taste the metal of blood.

'But, I thought—'

Jack stops talking and after staring at me with what looks like horror mingled with confusion and hurt on his face, he steps back and away from the table. After pushing a hand through his hair, he opens his mouth as if to say something more but seems to think better of it and then, shaking his head, he mutters, 'I'm sorry,

Bridget,' and then something about it being best if he leaves me to it. And before I can work out what just happened to me, Jack is going. He's got his hands in his pockets and his head down as he walks away across the sand…

Chapter Eighteen

It's Christmas Day in Mulberry-On-Sea and we are delivering hot roast turkey dinners with all the trimmings to the elderly and vulnerable members of the community who aren't up to cooking for themselves. I volunteered to make a mountain of mini Christmas puddings to go with the dinners and they're all packed into the bicycle panniers and wicker basket, along with pots of fresh cream and brandy butter that Rita has batched up in the pub kitchen. All the people we've delivered to so far have been over the moon to have their turkey dinner brought to them, with some saying this is the best Christmas they've ever had. Vicar Joe and his church workers are here too, as are members of the sea shanty choir, standing in the middle of Market Square, dressed in full pirate costume, their black tricorne hats decorated in red, gold, and green tinsel. They are singing a medley of festive favourites and the atmosphere is buzzy and uplifting with people milling around.

There's a lovely sense of kindness and community, making it very easy for me to get swept along and be outwardly jovial too, as a cover for my sadness at the way things deteriorated last night with Jack. I ended up going back to sit in the boat and join the quiz with a made-up story about him having to return to the pub to deal with some kind of unexpected last-minute thing. I did send him a message later on to apologise and he replied saying that it was fine. But I know that it's not really. Far from it. And he's been very cool with me today, looking through me as if I'm not here. I'm exhausted from lying awake in bed for most of the night, staring at the bloody big crack in the ceiling and trying to work out why I reacted the way I did when he was about to kiss me. I thought I was ready to give things a go with Jack, but it seems that when it came down to it, perhaps I'm not. Or maybe I was more embarrassed or annoyed than I realised by the way Mum carried on, because I can't stop thinking, how come she could be nice to Jack but didn't bother making the same effort with Ted? It doesn't seem fair. Although one thing I did manage to work out in the middle of the night is that part of me felt a bit guilty. Not because of the attraction to Jack, but because I was having a good time with him. Having fun, feeling excited. Living life!

But whatever it was, for now, I need to put a smile on my face. It's Christmas Day after all and Freya, Oscar, and Olly are here with me; the last thing I want is for them to pick up on anything being untoward. I want to make the best of it so my children have a wonderful day, and I'm proud to say they joined me with only the minimum of fuss, and didn't even complain about walking along the coastal path to get here. The boys even helped with bagging up all the bakery orders of fresh bread, more mince pies, mini stollen cakes and some colourful Christmas crackers that Freya and I made from tissue paper and cardboard with handwritten jokes inside for our customers to have as a little festive extra to go on their dining tables. This is a first for the boys on Christmas Day. Last year they didn't emerge from their bedrooms until lunchtime and then silently wolfed down their Christmas dinner before burying their heads back into their phones. It was a sad time for us all, but it makes this year all the more special. Henry is here with us too, dressed in his new festive red-and-white snowflake-patterned sweater that I knitted for his Christmas stocking and Freya has tucked the little hood with reindeer antlers over his head to keep him warm and protected in the snow. He looks incredibly cute and I think he knows he's the star of the show today with an extra charming wiggle to his gait as he trots along in front with his tail wafting from side to side. Several people have already stopped to fuss him, and one elderly lady, on seeing Henry from her window, dashed out with a sausage wrapped in bacon – or pigs in blankets as they're called – especially for him. Henry lapped it up, sitting at her feet and endearingly tilting his head to one side before giving her a paw and inhaling the sausage in one greedy gulp. Anyone would think we never fed him the way he carried on.

'OK, everyone, so here is the last batch of deliveries to go out.' It's Rita, wrapped up in a lovely chocolate-brown teddy coat and standing in the doorway of The Hook, Line & Sinker kitchen with a clipboard in one hand and a pen in the other, ticking off her list of names and addresses to make sure nobody is missed. 'Bridget will pop her Christmas puddings inside the boxes and then they're good to go, so thank you everyone and Merry Christmas. And please, each of you help yourselves to a bowl of Jack's delicious roast potatoes, and the soup warmer has hot apple cider in too.' We all chorus back our Christmas greetings and thanks for the thoughtful snacks and then Vicar Joe waves his hands in the air to get everyone's attention.

'I'd just like to add my thanks to all of you for helping

us out with the deliveries today, to Rita and Jack for their time and cooking skills. Not to mention the apple cider that smells wonderful, very cosy and Christmassy.' We all clap and I steal a glance at Jack who is standing nearby, but he doesn't even look in my direction. 'And a special thanks to our newest neighbour, Bridget, and her Bicycle Bakery. I hear there's always a gathering of eager bread lovers over at that end of the beach these days.' Smiling, he nods and gestures in my direction. 'Thank you for coming back to Mulberry-On-Sea when we all needed you… and your delicious bread and baked treats. Especially the mince pies!' He pauses to pat his middle. 'You sure have made life sweeter.' There's a ripple of laughter and I blush as everyone claps and nods in agreement with Vicar Joe. I'm thrilled on hearing them say they like my mince pies too as well as the potato and rosemary sourdough, or are partial to a sausage roll.

'Ah, it's my pleasure,' I say. 'Well, it's always been my dream, in fact, to bake, and now I can, every day, so thanks to all of you for making this come true. And I agree with Vicar Joe, life is sweeter here in Mulberry-On-Sea, because of all of you, so thank you too for making me and my family feel so welcome.'

'Yes, and please come to Bridget's Bicycle Bakery whenever you like. We have plenty of seating and a brilliant fire pit and can even make coffee and tea to have while you wait for your fresh-baked bread.' Oscar is talking now and we all turn to look at him, with me feeling very proud of the change in him. He's gone from sulking and fighting me at every opportunity to being my biggest champion, just like Ted was, and I know he would be very proud too of the young man he is becoming. Olly too. And Freya. I look to each of my children in turn and feel my heart soar, and then a calmness comes over me. They made it. It's been a long journey for them, this last year or so, but I truly believe that they are out the other side of it and have hope and happiness once again to see them onwards. Of course, they will always shoulder the burden of grief but they have something more now to balance and sustain them too, for whenever that wave returns.

After the boys and I have shared out the Christmas puddings, pots of cream and brandy butter into the boxes, Rita motions me to a box at the far end of the table.

'This one is for Mack. I thought you might like to take it to him.'

'Oh yes, please,' I say, thinking of the tissue-wrapped Christmas present in my crossbody handbag. I've knitted him a navy fisherman's jumper and Freya has made a card with a lovely picture of him in a boat with a Santa hat on and a fishing rod in his hands, an enormous mackerel dangling on the end of the line.

Once all the boxes have been loaded, the children and

I head along to Mack's cottage and after placing the box on the little wall by the front door, with the present next to it, I ring the bell. Moments later, Mack is here with an enormous grin on his face as we sing that festive favourite carol, 'We Wish You a Merry Christmas'. We've just reached the 'glad tidings' line when Henry wriggles his way forward and sits expectantly at Mack's feet.

'What have they got you dressed up in, boy?' Mack shakes his head as he gives Henry's antlers a tweak and we all laugh as Henry nudges the box with his nose, no doubt thinking he might get to eat the lovely turkey dinner inside. 'Er, no chance,' Mack says, taking the box inside before returning a few minutes later. 'Does he like biscuits?' Mack asks, holding up a Rich Tea, but before any of us can answer Henry is sitting once again, drooling and sweeping his tail from side to side in anticipation. 'I take it that's a yes,' Mack laughs, and I nod to say that it's OK and so Henry scoffs the biscuit in one big, greedy gulp before standing up and swishing his curly tail some more, making his antlers bob about.

'Can you open the present please?' Freya says, bouncing on her heels in excitement. Talking of which, she screamed with joy on seeing her Pet Grooming Parlour at the crack of dawn when she woke up eager to see if Santa had indeed 'stopped here' by the sign on the sand and the reindeers had eaten all the carrots. Of course they had, and carrot crumbs were left scattered around, much to her delight. The boys and I exchanged knowing looks and inwardly congratulated ourselves on having had the foresight to stash the carrots in a cupboard as soon as she had gone to bed.

'Oh, Bridget, this is marvellous. Thank you very much, dear,' Mack says, holding up the jumper. A misty look moves into his eyes on reading Freya's card and I can't help welling up a little too. I wish he had agreed to come and join us for his Christmas dinner, as I hate to think of him on his own, but he declined my invitation. Just as I wonder about whether to ask if he might like to come and sit by the fire pit with us all later on, he clears his throat and announces. 'Glynis is coming by soon and we're going to take a nice stroll to work off our turkey dinners with all the trimmings.'

'Well, that is wonderful,' I beam, pleased for him, and relieved to hear he has some company and is seemingly getting on well with Glynis.

'Yes, she's very nice, and the funny thing is Glynis remembers my Dotty. They went to school together… fancy that!' His eyes light up. 'You'll never guess what else we have in common.' He shakes his head in disbelief. 'Her husband was the old fishmonger. The shop closed down donkeys years ago, but I used to sell many a catch to him back in the day. What a small world it is and funny that I didn't make the connection at first.'

After saying goodbye to Mack and delivering the rest of the dinners on our list, we head back home.

Later, having feasted on our own turkey dinner with all the trimmings, plus second and third helpings (for Olly and Oscar) and Christmas pudding with cream and custard and half a tin of Quality Street between us, we are all absolutely stuffed. I manage to haul myself out of the sofa and shuffle over to the kitchen, intending to make a nice cup of tea when I see the tide is far out, revealing Ted's shipwreck in all its majestic glory.

'Come on,' I say, turning to Freya, Oscar, and Olly, 'let's go and wish Dad a Merry Christmas.' And the four of us, plus Henry, walk across the wet sand, the sea air exhilarating as it carries us on. Freya slips her hand into mine, her rosy-red cheeks lifted in a big grin of glee as we get closer. The boys and Henry race to see who can make it to the ship first, leaving me wondering how on earth Olly and Oscar can move at such a pace after all the food they've polished off. It's Henry who wins, and after doing a few spins of joy he hops over the weather-worn wooden side of the wreck and up onto what is left of the stern. With his front paws pushed forward, his nose tilted upwards to sniff the salty sea air, and his curly mane flowing in the breeze he looks majestic, as if he's the captain of the ship on lookout duty.

'Happy Christmas, Daddy!' Freya slips her hand free from mine and pushes it into her pocket instead. After pulling out a piece of paper, she unfolds it to reveal a mince pie and a sprig of holly, complete with red berries, which she pops into the top of the pie.

'What are you doing, sweetheart?' I ask, tucking my curls back into a ponytail, fastening it with a hairband from my wrist, so I can see without a face full of windswept hair.

'Giving Daddy his Christmas present,' Freya says in her matter-of-fact way as she looks up at me, eyes dancing in delight. She looks happy, content, and at peace as she potters over to where Henry is standing and after shooing him away and telling him he mustn't eat Daddy's mince pie, she carefully tucks it underneath a ledge in the ship's hull. Olly, Oscar, and I stand nearby, quietly contemplating together. I put an arm around each of their waists, unable to reach their shoulders these days, and draw them both in for a hug.

Silence follows.

'Dad would have liked Jack.' It's Oscar who says it and at first I'm not entirely sure I heard him properly and so he says it again and then adds, 'do you reckon?' Another silence follows as I wonder if this is Oscar's way of saying he's OK with me having Jack in my life – if I am actually going to, as I'm not so sure now after the way things were left last night. Olly nods. 'I reckon he would. Jack's cool. Way cooler than Dad was.' A dart of panic propels through me. I swallow and then gather myself, as

I don't ever want there to be any kind of comparison between Ted and another man.

'Dad was cool. Dad was amazing. And he always will be.' I squeeze them both in tighter, and smile on seeing Freya sitting in the boat having a little cuddle and chatting, presumably to her daddy.

'Yeah, he was,' both boys say in unison. 'But Dad was terrible at lighting the fire pit!' Olly states, shaking his head in mock despair and laughing affectionately.

'He was pretty good at building sandcastles though,' Oscar counters.

'Yes, he was very good at that,' I chip in, loving how easy this conversation is, and it is everything I wanted Ted's memory to be for the children. Light. Full of fondness and love and happy times that we can chat about together, remembering Ted as a whole person... good at sandcastles, terrible at fire pits. And that's OK. But then Oscar stops me in my tracks when he tentatively says,

'Dad would want you to be happy with Jack, wouldn't he?'

More silence follows as I turn to look at Oscar, who suddenly seems so much older somehow.

'Do you think so?' I ask softly, and find myself holding my breath.

'Of course he would.' It's Olly who speaks this time.

'He wouldn't want you to be unhappy or feel bad about it, would he?'

'I guess not,' I say, thinking back to last night and if my feeling of guilt was because I'm still here living my life, doing new things, meeting new people, and having a good time. I read about it somewhere in a magazine – survivor's guilt. It can be a real thing when a loved one dies and they're missing out on it all. Then, as if reading my mind, Olly adds, 'Yeah, no point feeling guilty. It's not a good vibe.'

'And you should be nice to Jack too,' Oscar pipes up. I turn to look at him, my smile freezing on my face.

'What do you mean?' I ask, but as soon as the words are out, I know exactly what he means – he must have seen my reaction to Jack's advance last night.

'Shoving him.' He shrugs, sliding his hands into his pockets.

'I didn't shove him,' I say, mortified that he's making me sound like a monster.

'Yes you did. I was getting more logs and I saw you shove him and you yelled at him too!' Oscar says, the accusation crystal clear in his voice and his face set back into a familiar scowl. My jaw drops and I blink a few times as I stare at him. 'Sorry, but you did.' He sighs and looks away, his face full of disappointment and it's directed right at me.

'Oscar, I—' But the words get stuck in my throat. Did

I really shove Jack? To be honest, I can't actually remember for sure – it all happened so fast – but if that's Oscar's perception, then... Well, no wonder Jack left in such a hurry! He probably couldn't get away from me fast enough. And now my own son feels let down by me too.

'I like Jack. He was teaching me some guitar chords and he said I could have a go driving his truck, but what's the point now? It's never gonna happen if he's gone too,' Oscar adds, and a slow trickle of realisation filters through me.

'Is that what you think? That Jack has gone for good?' I venture, my voice barely audible. I feel bad because I've been so wrapped up in trying to work out how I feel, that I didn't really stop to think how my children are feeling. Of course I considered how they might feel if I brought Jack into our lives and he then left, but I never for a moment thought about it being me doing the pushing away. And then I realise how precious and what a privilege it is having the responsibility of holding their hearts in my hands too. And what about Jack's heart? Did I consider his feelings? Not really. I just panicked. And I know Jack said it's fine, but he couldn't even look at me earlier today...

'Well, has he?' Oscar asks, bringing my focus back to the conversation.

'Um, I don't know, darling.' Oscar shakes his head, as

I mutter, 'Sorry' and glance at Olly who dips his head, seemingly resolved to this being the case.

We're walking back across the sand in silence when my mobile rings in my pocket. Slowing down as the boys walk on with Freya, I find my phone and see that it's Mum, looking unusually staid in a floaty floral dress that wouldn't look out of place at a WI garden party. Her big hair from last night has gone and is now in a demure side-parted ponytail and she's opted for a natural makeup look today.

'Hi, Mum,' I say, bracing myself as usual, but there's something off about Patty today. She seems subdued, not her bubbly, outrageous self. 'Are you OK?'

'Oh, um... yes. Yes, Bridget, darling, I just wanted to wish you a Merry Christmas,' she says, almost shyly, as she twiddles a gold chain at her neck.

'Thanks, Mum, but we said Merry Christmas earlier on, just after breakfast, all of us on FaceTime, remember?'

'Yes, I know, but, well, I wanted to say sorry for my silly behaviour last night. Would you believe it, I was nervous.' She falls silent and I stop walking.

'Oh, Mum. You don't need to say sorry,' I tell her, feeling my way. It's Christmas Day and I don't want to talk about our differences and potentially end up arguing. That's what happened the last time we fell out – it was a conversation like this and I asked her to be nicer to Ted. But I'm staggered on hearing she felt nervous last night.

'I do, darling,' Mum continues. 'I really want to get it right this time. I should have listened to you, been nicer to Ted.' Ah, so that's why she was flirty with Jack. She was trying to appeal to him in the only way she knows how. 'I don't want us to fall out again and I know I could have been a better mum. I wasn't really cut out for all that—'

'Oh, Mum, please,' I jump in, wondering where on earth this is all coming from, and then she tells me. 'Derek and I had a heart-to-heart last night after the quiz and, well, he said I was a little bit flirty and that led on to a conversation about me calming things down a bit. I don't need to be so… well, "in your face" is what he said, and, well, I guess he's right.'

Silence follows.

My heart goes out to Mum and I take another look at her and see her. Really see her. She looks vulnerable on the screen and I know this can't be easy for her to say.

'Mum, we all say and do stuff wrong,' I start, smarting at the memory of last night when I got it wrong and 'shoved' Jack. 'Do you want to know what I tell Freya and the boys?' She nods. 'We don't do perfect, we do our best! And you always have, I know that. Being a single mum is hard, twice the work – I know that too. Plus, aren't we all just making it up as we go along?' I smile, hoping to lighten the mood and make her feel better because I don't want her to feel bad. Life is way too short for that.

'Bridget, you've always been a wise one. Far wiser than me. I guess that's why I always wanted the very best for you.'

'Ted was the best for me,' I remind her gently. 'He loved me and was kind and caring and he adored the children.' I stop talking, not wanting to go there again.

'Yes, yes of course. I know, and I... oh dear, I'm doing it again. Saying it all wrong.'

'Mum, it's OK. Please, just be yourself, and let me be myself. Then we'll meet somewhere in the middle.'

'Thank you, darling.'

'And, Mum, you didn't need to try so hard with Jack. He was flattered by your "snack" comment.' I laugh.

'Oh, don't remind me,' she groans and pulls a face. 'I know it isn't an excuse, but I think by that point I might have had too many pornstar martini cocktails.' She puts a hand over her face.

'Easily done when you're feeling nervous. Look, let's talk some more later, Mum,' I suggest. 'I'm going to go and find the children now and polish off the rest of the Quality Streets,' I say. And have a think about how I might patch things up with Jack because I do want us to be friends – more perhaps, if he'll give me another chance. I guess I'll have to wait and see. But the conversation with Olly and Oscar has made me realise that it's OK to want to move on. There's no point in feeling guilty. In fact, it's not a good vibe, as my darling son would say.

'OK, Bridget.' She waves and blows a kiss. I'm just about to press the end call button when she adds, 'I'd like that... to talk later.'

'Me too,' I grin and blow her a kiss back. 'And, Mum?'

'Yes?'

'I think I like your colourful kaftans better.' And we both laugh.

I slot the phone inside my pocket and smile, feeling far lighter than I have in a very long time as I walk back across the glistening soft sand towards the beach house. I take a moment to think back on the decision I made to come here in the hope of putting my family back together again... and I'm so glad I did. Mum is my family too and my relationship with her just shifted onto what could be a lovely new path. If I can let go of the past. She seems happier for it. Me too, and the children as well as I look across the sand and see Olly and Oscar strumming their guitars, even if they are clearly still cross with me, pretending not to see when I wave at them like a loon. I smile on seeing Freya, wearing her fluffy reindeer onesie and dancing to their music with Henry, still in his festive sweater, dashing in circles around her.

Inhaling a big lungful of fresh, salty sea air and after shaking back my curls and thinking more about my conversation with Mum and the boys, I put my best foot forward, realising that I've reached a crossroad of sorts… and know in my heart now that I'm not going to be turning left and right and coming back to the same point again and again as I have for the last year or so.

Yes, I'm ready to go forward…

Chapter Nineteen

Walking on, I reach the undulating grass-topped dunes and the path leading along to the beach house. I see Freya clapping her hands together and pointing to something back along the beach where the tide has gone out even further, giving way to a large expanse of wet sand. On looking along the shoreline I see Jack, and OMG... What is going on? He is astride a black stallion galloping across the sand like he's actually in a romance film! My pulse quickens as I take in the scene. The horse's hooves are creating a backdraft spray, a shimmery sheen of sea water as the salty, exhilarating air catches in Jack's coat, making it billow out behind him. I gasp. And promptly squeeze my hands inside my mittens just to be sure this isn't some kind of fantasy dream and he is actually here. But why? He didn't even want to look at me earlier.

I close my eyes momentarily and then open them again as Jack's horse slows to a trot, meeting me as I reach the end of the wooden walkway.

'Jack!' I manage, mesmerised as I stare at him and the horse and the whole straight-out-of-a-period drama scene set out before me. 'You're on a horse.' I state the obvious, still in a daze. 'You can't just turn up on a horse.'

'I just did!' He does the head tilt. 'The truck wouldn't start and I needed to make a delivery so I saddled up Fergus,' he tells me. He says it like of course he did, and so it's just a regular thing to hop on your horse instead and gallop across a shoreline.

'Oh! Right, I see.'

'Bridget, are you OK?' he says, soothing the horse by stroking his mane as Henry comes to have a tentative sniff. Freya hotfoots it across the sand too.

'Er… yes, absolutely fine,' I squeak, loosening my thick woolly scarf a little and wondering how on earth it can suddenly feel so hot out here on the beach in the crisp, winter air. The fire pit isn't even lit yet. 'And, um…' I start, figuring it best to say something now before it becomes even more awkward between us. 'Jack, I'm really sorry about last night. I—'

'Like I said, it's fine,' Jack says. 'Let's talk later. I'm

here to see the boys and Freya.' He smiles, but his words sting as they sink in. He's not here to see me. But what does he need to see the children for?

'Oh,' I hesitate, feeling put out. 'Er, sure, OK.' I nod to cover my disappointment. Before I have a chance to contemplate further, Olly and Oscar come across the sand and Jack pulls a small package out from a pocket in the inside of his jacket and, arm outstretched, hands it down to Olly.

'Thanks, Jack.' He grins, then says, 'Come on, Mum. Let's go and sit in the boat and you can open your present from me, Oscar, and Freya.'

Still flabbergasted and discombobulated, I do as I'm told and follow my sons along the wooden walkway. Jack walks on too and after tethering Fergus to a wooden balustrade over by the deck, he comes back and offers to light the fire pit. The boys nod and thank him and he sets to work while I wonder what on earth is going on. Since when did my children organise a present for me all by themselves and how come Jack is delivering it?

'OK, are you ready?' Oscar asks me, taking the parcel from Olly and handing it to Freya who then gives it to me before clapping her hands together up under her chin in anticipation of me seeing the surprise.

'Thank you.' I carefully unwrap the brown paper and see that there's a little wooden frame inside with tissue paper over the glass to protect it. After carefully lifting the paper away, I see the picture.

And gasp.

'Happy Christmas, Mum,' the three of them chorus.

It's a pencil line sketch of me baking. I've got an apron on and a mixing bowl tucked into the crook of my elbow. I'm smiling and looking happy. Across the top of the picture are the words, *Be happy, B. All you knead is love and baked treats*, with *TC* written in the bottom right hand corner. Ted's initials. Happy tears gather at the corners of my eyes, instantly blurring my vision, but I know I'm not mistaken. I'd know Ted's artwork anywhere. After brushing the tears away, I take another look before pressing the little frame to my chest, leaning across to kiss each of my children, laughing as the boys still wipe their cheeks on the backs of their sleeves.

'I love it! Thank you. Where did you get it?' I ask, quietly. 'I've not seen this sketch before.'

I take another look at Ted's initials and then I see it. Underneath, in the faintest pencil squiggle is a date. But it can't be. I hold my breath as I squint to be sure… and it definitely is. The day before he died. And the memory suddenly comes into sharp focus. I remember the moment like it was only yesterday, that evening, him sitting at the dining room table sketching and not letting me see his art pad. So this is what he was drawing. I read Ted's words again. 'Be happy'. Staring at the words in silence, I ponder on their meaning. They are Ted's wishes for me as he wrote the words and a sense of realisation engulfs me. I've reached the crossroad for myself, but now it's as if Ted is also giving me permission to move on. Of course he would want me to be happy, with or without him, just as I would want for someone I loved and cared about. But it feels like he knew. Yes, it could just be wishful thinking, me seeing things through the filter of grief and love, reading into subliminal messages and wanting them to have meaning. But he wrote these words the night before he died, a message for me to be happy. It's amazing. And sad. And OK. I look again at the picture and the words and what they mean to me, and that's all that matters. Having this picture seems like a bookend to our life together, a goodbye and a new start. And I'm happy with that.

'Mum,' Oscar says, bringing me back to the moment. 'I found it tucked in between some old pictures in the bottom of one of the boxes I unpacked when we moved here.' He grins from ear to ear.

'Jack's friend makes frames!' Freya informs me.

'That's right,' Olly corrects. 'We asked Jack if he knew somewhere we could get the picture framed for you as a Christmas present, and so he asked his friend who runs the gallery by the harbour.'

'But the gallery isn't even open at this time of year,' I mumble, knowing it's a seasonal venture to cater for the tourists in the summer holidays. I'm overwhelmed by the thought that has gone into this present from my kind, wonderful children. Jack has got the fire pit blazing now and so comes over to join us.

'He was happy to open up his workshop and frame the sketch for you,' Jack says. 'I mentioned that it was a very special piece of artwork.'

'Thanks, Jack, I can't tell you how much this means to me,' I say quietly.

'I was pleased to help out,' he says, kicking at the sand but still not meeting my eye.

'And we thought you could hang it on the wall in the kitchen,' Olly suggests.

'I will. And I'm going to treasure it.'

'Good,' Freya says, and for some reason it makes us all laugh as she dashes off to see the horse. The boys go after her with instructions from Jack to make sure they stay calm around Fergus and not to stand near his back legs in case they spook him and he kicks out.

Silence follows as Jack and I stand opposite each other, neither of us knowing what to say, it would seem.

'I'm glad you like it.' It's Jack who speaks first, nodding towards the picture still pressed against my chest.

'I do. It's a very special gift,' I tell him, 'and I should put it safely inside.' I fall silent.

'Sure,' he says, pushing his hands into his coat

pockets and after glancing at him for a moment, during which he still doesn't look directly back at me, I put my head down and go to walk away. I've taken a few steps when I stop, momentarily close my eyes, open them again, and turn back towards him with a sense of it being now or never. *Be happy!* The words are still resonating as I move closer to him.

'Jack, I really am sorry,' I say, my eyes searching his face. I will him to lift his head and look at me. Another silence follows, then I try again. 'Please can we forget about last night and start afresh? Or at least let me explain and see where we go from there.'

'Is that what you really want?' he asks, eventually lifting his eyes to meet mine, and I nod.

'It is, Jack. I know now.'

'OK, so what's changed?' he asks, looking at me curiously, his amber eyes sparking as if searching mine for the truth.

'Well, I... I don't think anything really has changed,' I start, but then to clarify, I add, 'It's more of a realisation. I do like you, Jack. And I'm attracted to you; that is still the same, but... I think I thought by pushing you away I could protect my heart.' My voice fades.

His eyes soften as he steps forward and places a hand on my arm.

'Bridget, please, if this is too soon then we can just be friends. I get it. I do. When Ciara left I closed my heart up for a very long time.' He looks away again. 'I'm not saying it's the same thing, but something Rita said to me not long after things ended with Ciara has kind of stuck with me.' He stops talking and looks straight into my eyes. After ducking down and carefully placing the little wooden picture frame on the sand, I stand back up and tentatively put my hands on Jack's arms, searching his face to be sure, all the while checking within me… and it does… it feels OK this time.

'Tell me, please?' I ask. Jack clears his throat.

'She told me that grief is love with nowhere to go.' We both fall silent as we mutually mull this over. 'You still love Ted. And I still love Ciara. A part of me always will. But I have more love to share… if you'll let me send some your way.'

Neither of us speaks for what feels like an eternity as we stand together on the sand, Jack's arms wrapped around mine, the sound of the sea soothing us as I rest my head against his chest. His hand is stroking my hair and I lift my chin up to his face.

'I'd like that!' I say, and I press my lips to his as he kisses me softly and tenderly before gently returning my head to his chest, enveloping me in a huge, comforting hug, and for the first time in a very long time I feel completely calm.

After taking the picture indoors and bringing out two mugs of steaming mulled wine and the tin of Quality Street, I settle into the boat with Jack on one side and Freya snuggled up asleep underneath her duvet on the other, with the guinea pigs safely tucked up inside the pink grooming parlour that apparently is going to be their new home now. We chat quietly for a while, so as not to wake her, about the merits of the green triangle sweet over the purple one, neither of us able to settle on choosing a favourite. I pick up a gold toffee penny and hand it to Jack.

'Happy Christmas,' I whisper, turning to look at him.

He smiles. 'Happy Christmas, Bridget.' He reaches his gloved hand across and gently pulls my mitten-clad hand into his. After folding his fingers around mine, he lifts my hand up to his lips and plants a kiss that even through the wool manages to make my stomach do an actual flip and butterflies flutter. I steal a look at Jack's broodingly good-looking face and my heart lifts before doing a multitude of little summersaults, making me realise that I do actually like that kind of thing after all.

'I've wanted to kiss you since the first moment I clapped eyes on you in the dunes… with your ho, ho, ho bottom up in the air!' he whispers in my ear.

'You are never going to let me forget that, are you?' I whisper right back.

'Probably not,' he shrugs, giving my hand another quick kiss.

We sit together, cosy and content as we watch the flames dance in the fire pit. Henry is lying on a blanket on the sand, comatose from the heat, and snoring as he sleeps off his special Christmas treat dinner of turkey with all the trimmings, including his favourite sausage wrapped in bacon. A bubble of optimism and hope for what the future may bring fills my thoughts as I look up at the stars twinkling and over to the moon shimmering silver sparkles across the sea, the red, gold, and green lights of the boats bobbing in the harbour beyond, and in this moment I feel so happy to be here.

Soon the boys arrive back. I glance at my watch.

'Just in time!' I tell them. 'Let's Zoom Granny and Granddad in Australia and thank them for your Christmas presents,' I say, gently waking Freya. Jack thoughtfully goes to check on Fergus as Ted's parents appear on the screen. Although I know that Ken and Jan will be happy for me having met someone new, as we had a heart-to-heart some months ago, it's very early days for Jack and me so I'd like to talk to them properly when the time is right. For now, I'm enjoying a cosy Christmas this year with family and old friends. I think of Lorna happy with Liam, and then the conversation I had earlier with Mum. I've invited the Carrington's gang – Georgie, Sam, and Eddie – over for a New Year's Eve beach barbecue. New friends too, with thoughts of Mack and Vicar Joe, Pearl, and Ian.

I wouldn't want it any other way.

Merry Christmas, everyone!

I raise my mug of mulled wine. Here's to comfort and joy and brand-new beginnings in Mulberry-On-Sea... where life is sweeter and nothing bad ever happens, or so it seems.

Make Your Own Louis (Sourdough Starter)

Ingredients

250g strong white bread flour

Method

Day 1

Mix 50g flour with 50g tepid water in a jar or a plastic container. Make sure all the flour is incorporated and leave, semi-uncovered, at room temperature for 24 hrs.

Day 2

Mix 50g flour with 50g tepid water and stir into yesterday's mixture. Make sure all the flour is incorporated and leave, semi-uncovered, at room temperature for another 24 hrs.

Day 3

Repeat Day 2.

Day 4

You should start to see some activity in the mixture now; there should be some bubbles forming and bubbling on top. Mix 50g flour with 50g tepid water and stir into yesterday's mixture. Make sure all the flour is incorporated and leave, semi-uncovered, at room temperature for another 24 hrs.

Day 5

The mixture should be very active now and ready for making your starter. If it's not bubbling, continue to feed it on a daily basis until it does. When it's ready, it should smell like yogurt. You now have a starter, which is the base to the bread. You'll need to look after it and give it a name of course. Keep it in the fridge (it will stay dormant) and 24 hrs before you want to use it, pour half of it off and feed it with 100g flour and 100g water. Leave it at room temperature and it should become active again. The longer the starter has been dormant, the more times it will need to be refreshed – the process of pouring off half the starter and replacing it with new flour and water – to reactivate. If your starter is ready to use, a teaspoonful of the mixture should float in warm water.

Bridget's Top Drawer Potato and Rosemary Sourdough

Ingredients

250ml sourdough starter
250g strong white flour
Chopped rosemary
12ml olive oil
100ml water
10g rock salt
110g baked potato flesh, diced

Method

Mix the sourdough starter with the flour, rosemary, oil,

and water in the bowl of a mixer on medium for five minutes.

Add the salt and mix again for a further two minutes.

Leave to rise until at least doubled in size (overnight is perfect, or a day if you're like Bridget and prefer to bake at night time).

Knock back the dough to burst any big bubbles and to give an even texture.

Gently knead in the diced potato.

Shape, then put into a well-floured banneton and allow to rise again.

Bake in a preheated oven at 220°C on a stone for 30–45 minutes, depending on the shape of the loaf.

Allow to cool and then slice, slather with salted butter and homemade strawberry jam, and enjoy with a mug of Biscoff hot chocolate as you sit on the beach, a balcony, or back garden and gaze up at the stars.

Freya's Favourite Biscoff Hot Chocolate

Ingredients
(makes 1)

Milk of your choice
1–2 heaped tsp Biscoff spread
1 heaped tsp hot chocolate powder
Whipped cream
Crushed Bicoff biscuit

Method

Pour the milk into a mug and stir in the Biscoff spread.

Microwave until warm (approximately one minue).

Stir in hot chocolate powder until dissolved.

Top with whipped cream and crushed biscuit.

Bridget's Special Festive Sausage Rolls

Ingredients
(makes 16)

30g butter
100g button mushrooms, finely chopped
1 tbsp Worcestershire sauce
1 tbsp Tabasco sauce
1 tbsp dried thyme
450g sausage meat
Salt and freshly ground black pepper
450g ready-rolled puff pastry
1 free-range egg, beaten

Method

Preheat the oven to 200°C / 400°F / Gas 6.

Melt the butter in a large frying pan and fry the mushrooms until soft. Transfer to a large bowl.

Add the Worcestershire sauce, Tabasco sauce, thyme, and sausage meat and season well with salt and freshly ground black pepper. Mix until thoroughly combined.

Roll the puff pastry out into a large rectangle, then cut into two long rectangles.

Place a layer of sausage meat mixture down the middle of each pastry rectangle, then brush with beaten egg on one of the long edge.

Fold the other side of the pastry over onto the egg-washed edge. Press down to seal and trim any excess. Cut each pastry roll into 8 sausage rolls.

Place the sausage rolls onto a baking tray and bake for 15–20 minutes, or until the pastry is crisp and golden and the sausage meat is completely cooked through.

Jack's Prawn and Chorizo Beach Barbecue Kebabs

Ingredients
(serves 4)

3 raw chorizo, about 350 g
16 raw large prawns (shrimp), peeled and deveined,
leaving the tails intact
2 tbsp olive oil
2 tbsp lemon juice
½ teaspoon good-quality dried mint
Lemon to serve
8 skewers

Method

Cut the chorizo into 16 chunks, similar in thickness to the prawns.

Put the chorizo in a bowl with the prawns, olive oil, lemon juice, and mint.

Toss the ingredients around to combine.

Set aside at room temperature for 30 minutes or cover and refrigerate for 3–6 hours.

Remove from the fridge 30 minutes before cooking.

Preheat the barbecue grill or hotplate to high.

Put 2 pieces of chorizo and 2 prawns on each of the 8 skewers.

Cook the skewers for 3–4 minutes on each side, or until cooked through.

Serve with the lemon and cherry tomatoes, if desired.

Jack's Harissa Sardines

Ingredients
(serves 6)

12 fresh sardines, cleaned and gutted
Salt and freshly ground black pepper
2 tbsp harissa paste
4 tbsp olive oil, plus extra for serving
Small bunch flat-leaf parsley, roughly chopped
Juice of 2 lemons

Method

Slash the sardines three or four times on both sides,

season with salt and pepper, and then rub thoroughly with the harissa paste.

Drizzle with the olive oil and cook on a hot barbecue for 3–4 minutes each side or under the grill for the same amount of time (you may need a little more or a little less, depending on the size of the sardines).

Serve with the chopped parsley, a drizzle of olive oil, and a squeeze of lemon juice.

Acknowledgments

The lovely little seaside town of Mulberry-On-Sea has a very special place in my heart and so my first thanks is to Kate Bradley, my friend and talented editor of ten years who changed my life when she published my first book in the Carrington's series set there, *Cupcakes at Carrington's*, in 2013. Since then, I've never stopped thinking about Mulberry-On-Sea and the characters – Georgie, Sam and Eddie, and so my next thank you is to the amazing and inspiring Charlotte Ledger for giving me the opportunity to write this Carrington's spin-off series. Thanks too to Sara Roberts, Bethan Morgan, Lydia Mason and all the incredibly hardworking team at One More Chapter, HarperCollins. A special thanks to Rachel Quin for creating the most gorgeously festive book trailer for *A Cosy Christmas at Bridget's Bicycle Bakery* – I'm obsessed with the cute dog and his waggy tail running in the snow!

A very big thank you to my agent, Rowan Lawton, for lifting me and making the future feel bright. Caroline Smailes and Carmel Harrington for being wonderfully kind, patient and generous friends. Thanks a million to my husband, Paul, aka Cheeks, for bringing the festive snacks to my writing desk and calming my drama when the deadlines were looming. An extra special thank you to my darling girl, QT, for giving me joy every day and offering a plethora of potential plot ideas and future book titles. My biggest thanks go to all of you, my wonderful readers. You mean the world to me and make it all worthwhile. Thank you so very much for loving my books as much as I love writing them for you.

Merry Christmas everyone!

Luck & love

Alex x

YOUR NUMBER ONE STOP

ONE MORE CHAPTER

FOR PAGETURNING BOOKS

One More Chapter is an
award-winning global
division of HarperCollins.

Sign up to our newsletter to get our
latest eBook deals and stay up to date
with our weekly Book Club!
<u>Subscribe here.</u>

Meet the team at
<u>www.onemorechapter.com</u>

Follow us!

 <u>@OneMoreChapter_</u>

 <u>@OneMoreChapter</u>

 <u>@onemorechapterhc</u>

Do you write unputdownable fiction?
We love to hear from new voices.
Find out how to submit your novel at
<u>www.onemorechapter.com/submissions</u>